THE BLACK STONE

THE KALENDAR

BOOK 1

THE BLACK STONE

THE KALENDAR

BOOK 1

JOE PEREZ

Tangent Publishers, an imprint of Integral Publishers, LLC
4845 E. 2nd St., Tucson, Arizona

For additional information, contact Tangent Publishers.

Cover Design by QT Punque
Layout Design by Kathryn Lloyd
Original Cover Art by Jessica TC Lee

ISBN: 978-1-4951-8770-4

In memory of my mother, Margaret D. Perez

I will always love you, Mom

Acknowledgments

I dedicate this book to my mother, Margaret D. Perez, who has given me so much love and support over my lifetime. Also to my father, Robert A. Perez, for his love and encouragement. I am deeply grateful to Tangent Publishers, an imprint of Integral Publishers, especially Jeannie Carlisle and Keith Bellamy, for believing in this genre-disrupting, nearly indescribable new epic vision. Thanks also to Merv Thomas, Jeff Wright, Ken Wilber, Geoff Fitch, Dr. Marc Gafni, and John Halas, for valuable conversations and guidance.

This book would be infinitely less without the art which has been created by some of the most talented artists anywhere to be found. Under my direction Daniel de la Rosa created the New Tarot (Stone-Star Tarot) graphics with many insights of his own. Gavin Baldwin illustrated Kalen at the different ages of 9, 18, and 27 for the World Wide Web, and there is his additional depiction of Kalen at age 9 contained herein. Oregon-based artist Jenay M. Elder depicted the 54 Animwaa of the New Zodiac (Bear-Yak Zodiac).

Lingua-U is a constructed language which informs the original philosophy of language introduced herein through poetry and prose. The first prototype of the language was created in 2009 and 2010 while I studied in the Generating Transformative Change program of Pacific Integral in Seattle, Washington. I wish accordingly to thank faculty Dr. Terri O'Fallon, Geoff Fitch, and Venita Ramirez as well as members of the GTC 8 cohort for their encouragement and conversations. Other research related to this book was conducted while I was a Scholar-in-Residence at the Center for Integral Wisdom in San Francisco, California, in 2012 and 2013. Among this book's many theoretical influences: maps of consciousness by George Gurdjieff, Arnold Keyserling, Ken Wilber, Dr. Susanne Cook-Greuter ("Nine Levels of Increasing Embrace in Ego Development: A Full-Spectrum Theory of Vertical Growth and Meaning Making"), the Unique Self model of Dr. Marc Gafni, and the early work of Don Beck.

The central literary touchstone for this book is an epic philosophical poem composed by an undeservedly obscure Chinese thinker who wrote a magnificent book over 2,000 years ago. I must acknowledge enormous benefit from the following resources: *The Canon of Supreme Mystery by Yang Hsiung, A Translation with Commentary by Michael Nylan* and *The T'ai Hsüan Ching*, translated by Derek Walters. Having encountered Hsiung only in translation is regrettable, but thanks to Nylan's superb version and commentary many layers of meaning have opened to me.

Finally, there are a few other books and websites of noteworthy influence. Concerning the Sabian Symbols of Dr. Marc Edmund Jones and Elsie Wheeler: *The Wheel of Significance: The Origin, Structure and Power of the Sabian Symbols (The Lost Writings of Dane Rudhyar)* by Dane Rudhyar (Author) and Michael R. Meyer. Concerning linguistics, Dr. Margaret Magnus's *Gods of the Word* and her website http://www.trismegistos.com/ have been indispensable. I also drew upon numerological insights concerning the number 9 which were published on the uncredited video at http://on.fb.me/1TPG4eZ.

Teddy, Fluffy, Puffy, Little Bird, Boo Boo, Barty, Rusty, Maggie, Gracie, Scampi, Jerry, Nanuk, and Kia: I love you and haven't forgotten you. This book is for you too.

Table of Contents

PART 2

Preface

The Black Stone (The Kalendar, Book One) is the tale of a young boy's rise from obscurity to Omphalos Bearer, a role with the responsibility to right the relationship between humankind and Nature. The book was compiled by the Poet in 2015 CE, more than two thousand years after the earliest date described by its legendary source materials. The boy is the Hanimwaa, Kalen O'Tolan, who went on to lead the forces of the Bei in the Three Kosmic Wars and Three Kronic Wars over the course of the first two millennia of the Common Era. As a result of these five conquests (and one cataclysmic defeat), Kalen delivered into the collective consciousness the New Zodiac, the New Map of the Archetypes (New Tarot), the New Map of the Heavens (New Kosmology), the New Atlas, the New Klock, and the New Kalendar.

As of this writing, a multi-faceted cultural movement called the Great Overturning has began to reshape the connection between Tolan (or Earth if you prefer) and the transcendent and unmanifest realms, a Logical War which is redefining the techniques and structures of meaning-making and thereby forever changing our understanding of human existence itself. It is the sensibility of the New Logic that there is a hidden underlying unity to Space, Time, and Thought . . . and that language, symbol, and worldviews ought to be re-aligned as Plato first envisioned, so that the methods of pronouncing words ought to mirror Nature. The realignment of logic happens not in opposition to nature, but as a response to the evolutionary impulse which coarses through it. For example, the letter B is the first consonant and is pronounced labially near the front of the speech organs; it is therefore naturally associated with concepts such as beginnings, births, and big bangs, so that the concept and the method of pronunciation are symbolically in harmony. The Great Overturning means the shedding of archaic sound-meanings and the rehabilitation of language and thought in alignment with a unified post-metaphysical cosmology.[1]

---

1   As Dr. Margaret Magnus, the MIT-trained linguist who is a leader in the field of phonosemantic research, tells us: "Each consonant and vowel in a language has a meaning, in the sense that every word containing that sound has an element of meaning which words not containing that sound do not have. What underlies this sound-meaning is the form of the sound, i.e. its pronunciation – a sound means what it is. For example, to pronounce a stopped consonant (b, d, g, p, t, k), you completely block the flow of air through the mouth. Consequently all stopped sounds involve a barrier of some kind. The nature of that barrier varies depending on whether the sound is voiced (b, d, g) or unvoiced (p, t, k), whether it is labial (b, p), dental (d, t) or velar (g, k), and so forth. This meaning is different from the referent, which is what we normally think of as the meaning of a word. Reference is a separate process from sound-meaning, and is layered on top of it. ... What all the various referents or senses of a word have in common is their sound-meaning." (see Magnus, Margaret: http://www.trismegistos.com/)

In our day, the Third Wave of Existence is well underway, bringing about an age which is by and large ready to see beyond polarities to forging new syntheses. Kalen has brought the Lingua-U[2] which encapsulates the New Logic, and he spearheads the movement which is bringing greater planetary cognizance through the War of Languages. But two thousand years ago, the cutting edge of consciousness was the Bear-Yak Zodiac, the emergence of which happened only with great toil and bloodshed. The so-called New Zodiac featured for its 54 Signs the heroic Animwaa, the Immortal Animals, ensconced in Houses made of glyphs given by the Omphalos Bearer. The Animwaa, although immortal in the heavens, are mortal on the Earth; many immortal beings lost their Earthly lives in the conflict with the older Zodiac. The 27 Houses of the Bear-Yak cohered with the Kosmic Balance which is depicted by the Artifacts of Orr, the last remnants of the First Wave of Existence. Most primordial amongst the Artifacts is the Omphalos of Delphi, which is not merely an ancient religious

---

2   Lingua-U is a meta-language which employs hieroglyphs or groups of ternary numbers for its expression. Simplicity is one of its virtues. There are only three characters in this remarkable language, and you probably already know at least two of them: Yang, Yin, and You (or the digits 0, 1, and 2 respectively in a base-3 counting system). A meta-language, since I have brought it up, is (to my reckoning) a schema or framework which maps a comprehensive set of phonosemantic associations (sound-meanings) in cross-linguistic perspective, or at least a very wide number of such meanings. Sound-meanings are different from word meanings. They do not tell us what a word means, they say what it connotes or represents in an aesthetic or spiritual sense. In terms of the Integral Semiotics of Ken Wilber, they are part of the Lower-Left quadrant of a sign, connected to semantics. Sound-meanings come very close to getting at the essence of a letter or word by means of looking at the story told by the symbolism of its phonetic features and the method of their production kinesthetically (for letters) or for combinations of sounds in a story-like fashion (for words).

relic, but a living intelligence with powers similar to omniscience, or so it is claimed. The first book of The Kalendar is most concerned with the origin of the Zodiac and Tarot, and establishes a point of reference in the formation of a new Integral Magic.[3]

If awareness of the Bear-Yak Zodiac and Kalen's other contributions to intellectual history is negligible today on Earth, it is only because much history was erased owing to Kalen's defeat in the Battle of the Timelines, also known as the Third Kronic War, in the nineteenth and twentieth centuries CE. Terrible clashes were fought between those who saw a purpose to history and those who saw none. Scholars believing in an evolutionary telos to history's unfolding were defeated, but not all were purged. Some today are regrouping in the early 21st century CE through neo-Hegelian, post-postmodern, integral, and meta-modernist scholarship. It is now time that scholars can begin to tell the true history erased by the Ro, the nihilistic forces of irredicuble chaos which have shaped the dominant faux historical

---

3   Since I have brought up the subject of magic, I want to say that The Kalendar is not an attempt to prove or advocate for the use of any existing system of divination or occult practice. Nor do I wish to disparage practitioners of magic (or "magick" as it is called largely by followers of Aleister Crowley). Instead, it is my intention through literature and poetry to birth a somewhat new and healthier sensibility regarding the subject. The fact seems indisputable to me that we live in an enchanted world full of miracles and wonders and strange delights and unexplained phenomena, whether these things are interpreted with sobriety or exuberance of thought. Even a skeptic may experience enchantment without imputing any supernatural connotations. Real enchantment is the territory to which The Kalendar offers a sort of meta-map and it is to this domain that the New Tarot and New Zodiac referenced in this book apply. I have a blog called The Integral Cauldron at www.joe-perez.com where I am recording my thoughts on the genesis of a New Magick which may appeal to minds at trans-rational levels of consciousness.

philosophies of our day, beginning with the origin of history in folklore and mythology.

All of this and more is told by the Poet in The Kalendar, an epic story in poetry, prose, art, and philosophy. Of course the historicity of all details is not intended and cannot be assured in any event. Nevertheless, in this form the story has received the approval of the Omphalos Bearer himself who has proclaimed it "true but partial."

Part 1 of this book is "The Omphalos of Delphi", a short novel which looks at the circumstances of Kalen's birth at the origin of the Kalendar (1 CE). At the book's core is the story of Kalen's coming to terms with his family's legacy, the Black Stone which is also the planetary/cosmological Navel. His parents Karen and Kairon withheld information from the boy during his early years, but when he reached 5 years and 40 days, they began to prepare him for his prophecied role as Omphalos Bearer. In due course, the origins of the War of the Zodiac and the War of the Archetypes are explained, and hints of the coming War of the Deities are given as well.

Part 2 of this book is "The Surrender of Symbiosis", an epic poem[4] which comments on each of the major figures and glyphs of Black Stone, the Kalendar's First Month (Dec. 22 AM – Jan. 30 PM).

---

4   Not every section of the poem will be considered proper poetry by those who concern themselves with defining such things (the first book contains one section containing a folktale and another which is a set of instructions for playing poker). Nevertheless, the overwhelming thrust is poetic.

These are similar to the unigrams, bigrams, trigrams, tetragrams, and hexagrams of the Canon of Supreme Mystery, Master Yang Hsiung's masterpiece from China (written near the dawning of the First Millennium CE)[5] . Some of Hsiung's epic poetry has been examined and given response in this work,[6] as have some of the so-called Sabian Symbols of Elsie Wheeler and Dr. Marc Edmund Jones.[7] As imagery and poetic prose of an enchanted order of the cosmos, these works are well suited for the Poet's conversation partners. There are many differences between Hsiung's worldview (and Wheeler's as well) and

5   Michael Nylan, the book's most eminent English translator and scholar, writes: "As the first grand synthesis of classic Chinese thought, Yang Hsiung's Canon of Supreme Mystery (ca. 4 B.C.) occupies a place in all of Chinese intellectual history roughly comparable to that of the Summa Theologica of Thomas Aquinas in the West. As one of the few original works by a recognized philosophical master to have survived from the formative Han period (contemporaneously with and analogous to the Roman empire), the Mystery provides us today with the single best remaining clue to early attempts to situate the individual in family, state bureaucracy, and cosmos.... It is a divination manual that suggests a complex interaction between time and virtue in unfolding human destiny. It is also one of the great philosophical poems of world literature, assessing the rival claims on human attention of fame, power, and physical immortality, while situating human endeavor within the larger framework of cosmic energies." (see Nylan, Michael: The Canon of Supreme Mystery. SUNY, 1993)

6   The Kalendar breaks from Master Yang's interpretations and cosmology of the hexagrams in many respects, particularly in that its primary method of interpreting them is through Lingua-U, and not the Chinese classics. I respect Hsiung, but have not tried to duplicate his achievement. To write The Kalendar it was necessary for me to offer a much different hermeneutic. I will leave it to the judgment of the reader to say to what extent my interpretations of the hexagrams overlaps with Hsiung's. To make this task easier, I have loosely paraphrased Hsiung's poetry in many spots throughout the poem. These somewhat reimagined lines cannot be taken as his literal words. I hope that they will inspire readers to read the original or in translation together with Nylan's commentary.

7   I have frequently found the 360 Sabian symbols of Elsie Wheeler and Dr. Marc Edmund Jones remarkably prescient particularly when they are contrasted to the correlating verses of Master Yang Hsiung's poetry. Although the symbols are not well known outside of the astrological community, several books of commentary are available for readers desiring to explore their meaning. Because other commentary exists I have remarked on them only briefly in this book. My intent for including references to Master Yang, King Wen (a classical author of key parts of the I Ching), and Elsie Wheeler is essentially to place my own writings within a wider context of poetic calendar and ease the burden on readers who may be interested in finding analogous imagery and commentary. Dante had Virgil and Beatrice to aid with his voyages. I hope you will agree that Hsiung, Wen, and Wheeler are welcome guides and conversation partners along the ride for this expansive poem.

that of the Poet, but his classic Chinese text is probably the Poet's closest literary interlocutor. This part of the book also contains 18 artistic renderings out of 156 total cards of the Stone-Star Tarot, a divination tool sprawling three separate Decks.

In general the poetry and prose of this book can be read independently. Readers may go first to whichever text they feel most attracted, and it ought to make no difference to understanding. Supplemental materials will be made available online at the publisher's website (Tangent Publishers, http://www.tangentpublishers. com/) or at the site for the author (Joe Perez's Joe-Perez.com, http:// www.joe-perez.com).

Additional books in The Kalendar series are planned which will continue the story of Kalen O'Tolan and will elucidate his unique perspective on the history and evolution of the cosmos. The next book is The Red Jewel, a forthcoming exploration of Kalen's adolescence and rise to young adulthood combined with a look at his role in the exploding Three Kosmic Wars.

—Joe Perez
37 White Horse (July 8), 2015 CE

xxiii

A Note to the Reader from Kalen O'Tolan.

I hope this book may be edifying to the people of the 21st century CE and beyond in understanding the origins of our contemporary conflicts at the dawn of a planetary consciousness. When the origins of the Season of Yang are held firmly in mind, our predicament at the start of the Season of You, the Third Tier of Consciousness, is greatly clarified. For the first time in the history of civilizations, the sounds of 7,000 languages have been cataloged by the International Phonetic Alphabet system and their common underlying patterns of sound-meaning are available for cross-cultural investigation and schematization. This project is well underway in the New School and a prototype of a Universal Meta-Language which embraces the widest possible set of Sacred Words is now available. Among languages, it is most similar to Tolang, the ancient language of my family ancestry which is sadly all but extinct. I hope some readers will seek to learn more about Lingua-U and become inspired to discover for themselves the next step in the evolution of humankind.

And a personal note to the scion of Beionai: When you find this lonely book, meet me at Blue Castle 3 in the Place Where It Is Hidden.

THE OMPHALOS OF DELPHI

PART ONE

WATCHING THE ROUNDER

sees Kalen with his mother's womb and marvels at the path of his existence, its special place in the history of the Kosmos. At the turning point of the Wheel of Existence, Kalen rounds the circle at the most delicate and extraordinary time imaginable.

"I" does not see the entire Wheel of Existence and that is the origin of the apprehension he feels, but he is determined to know it. Through Kalen he believes he can know the wholeness which eludes him in the nascent Season of Yang. Only one who has rounded the Wheel can speak of its completeness as such, to validate the ancient wisdom which gives order to the heavens and the Earth and give reports from the undersides of the worlds.

If Kalen is the man he is expected to be, he will bring a greater awareness of reality even than "I". When he matures, he may even remember the fullness of the Wheel, its secrets always seemingly perched out of reach ... that is, if he does not exit the womb cognizant as an enlightened being as some of the less reliable legends have claimed. "I" does not believe Kalen will be born an avatar or god; on the contrary, he expects him to be quite vulnerable and powerless for an immortal being.

The only wheels "I" remembers are the lesser wheels, the ones which facilitate successive incarnations from one life form to another, and from the corporeal to incorporeal essences and back again. Incarnation he knows. Reincarnation he knows. He knows of the transitions of Atoms in the Foundries. He knows the fastest route through the labyrinth of Dark Hedges in the underworlds. But what Kalen knows is a mystery to him.

Kalen is a different sort of Rounder. He is purported to possess all the consciousness of the Stars themselves which have collapsed in the past at his disposal, and having many years of long life as a result. Kalen is an Immortal, given purview to 3,000 years of life on the Earth as a man, and the vision to bring the world into alignment with Evolution's Aim at the start of the Third Millennium CE, a period of history which is sometimes called the Great Overturning. He may not live to see maturity if he does not survive his precarious childhood, and then where will everyone be who is counting on the Great Overturning for their very existence, "I" included?

"I" has Kalen in his sight, but the sight of "I" is different than yours or mine. It is better to think of it as insight, vision on the interior face of the real. Through the interior eye, even the fathomless nothing is awakened. His mind is starless Night perched like a blind man standing on the shore of Midnight's Bay. His body is like the Bay cloaked in mist and shadow, hooded in a flowing black cloak. He stands tall as a mature bear standing on his hind legs and his hands are ancient and withered.

He might not admit it if you were to ask him, but "I" cannot say for sure whether Kalen will be kind or cruel in the future. He understands full well that the child has the capacity of being either or both, and this makes the boy a most interesting subject to watch. He scans the fetus intently as if its features could somehow reveal its destiny, its image reflected in the Bay called forth from the concentration of the mind of "I".

"I" ponders the question of existence, the purpose of morality and how Kalen, as such an innocent child, will react to the cruelness of the world. Most of all, he wonders if Kalen has returned from the other side with a weapon or tactical advantage for confronting the Ro and its mutant offspring. There is no term in extant languages for

Ro, but you may think of it as the royal regent at the heart of Entropy, its machinery for destruction and dissipation and cessation. It is a reversal of Order's inception. Entropy swallows all things, increasing disorder in every system. It is the bringer of the heat death of the universe which has been foreseen by the sages. These facts alone should help you to understand why "I" is concerned about the Ro, but it is not helpful to say any more. The explanation might worry you horribly to think about especially if you are the sort of person who is inclined to believe that there are no insoluble problems.

It is suffice to say that "I" looks to Kalen as nothing less than a potential savior of the world (and perhaps of every world, if the reports from outposts in the multiverse are sadly correct), the likes of which have not been needed or seen for a very long time. Not since the Children of Orr in the First Wave has there been a savior more needed, one who could deliver an end to temporal suffering and inaugurate a New Order in which all things in all worlds could stably cohere. But this is the dawn of the Third Wave and time is short for Kalen to rise to his destiny, if he would take it, before the devils and demons of the Second and Fourth Waves collude in an unholy alliance. "I" was young in the First Wave, but he remembers with fondness and love the rising of the Orr from the Firmanent led by the Child who brought the First Ancestors to the shore of the New Worlds. The Child of Orr fulfilled their hopes and dreams once long ago, but ever since he has been disappointed by false hopes and unworthy angels, and so it is difficult for him to keep his heart open to new possibilities and wonder.

"I" was just settling into a peaceful and serene state of self-organization when he heard the sound of children singing Yuletide songs at some point in the early 21st century. They sang:

Silent night, holy night
All is calm, all is bright
Round yon Virgin Mother and Child
Holy Infant so tender and mild ...

He listened to the lyrics and pondered their meaning. Good heavens, the Yule! The winter's solstice was imminent, and the Christmas season is the time for the birth of saviors, Kalen included.

Midnight's Bay stood before his eyes, its serene resplendent waters as blue as the sky on the night of a full moon, and its shores were a silhouette hewn out of dense shadowy materials. It is a fitting place for witnessing an Incarnation, the original meeting place of the worlds, the single point remembered deep in the endless fabric of every thread of the universe for all time. From its shores, one can access every point in the universe in Space and Time and Thought if one knows where to look. At Midnight's Bay, "I" himself was born, long ago in the First Wave, though he was lost and purposeless until Kalen brought forth the Lingua-U at the Great Overturning.

Walking upon its shoreline, "I" came across a man in aboriginal attire updated with metal rivets and sinewy textiles, the sort of garment you would expect if a traditional shaman re-designed his wardrobe at a postmodern institute of fashion design. His reddish-brownish face was painted with arcane symbols. The most prominent symbol, the schwa ("Ə"), appeared on his nose in glowing paint surrounded by many other linguistic signs organized in a peculiar fashion.

"I" treaded quietly so as not to disturb the man, who he recognized at once as the King of Stones, inarguably one of the most powerful chieftains amongst all the New Tribes. The King was standing abut a sculpted wall featuring an engraved Enneagram, his hands pointed to the 9 position at the top of the figure, his feet at the 5 and 4 positions at the base. The King was not conscious but had faded into an upright swoon induced by shamanic magic.

"Ah ha!" he thought, "The King has made an important voyage to Midnight Bay's perhaps for no other reason than to be with me! I ought to see what it is that brings him."

And then the King of Stones appeared beside himself at another spot, standing before "I" not in corporeal form but as a spiritual body.

The King bowed deeply with a reverence and single heartedness rarely seen. "Indeed I have come expecting to find you here, 'I', Lord of the First-Person Perspective, Emperor of the Season of Yang. Your face is a most welcome sight after arduous days of fasting and dancing which have brought my body to collapse."

"I" said, "Your kind words are well received, exalted King, Premiere Royal of the Archetypes in the New Order. It is good to see you too. I have been expecting you. The future words and deeds of Kalen have been growing stronger in my mind, though they have not yet happened. It is Kalen who will unleash the New Tarot. Not until his Tarot is published will the New Map of the Archetypes exist in which the suit of Stones cohere, and yet I see you before me once again. We speak together in the tongue of Lingua-U though Kalen has not yet conceived or published the Codex. These are days of maddening paradox. I am very curious to ask you something: Tell me how you come here and why it is that no one from any other suit of the Stone-Star Tarot ever comes."

"I will do this gladly, Lord," said the King of Stones, not realizing at the time that the topic would be whisked away never to return. He continued, "But first you must address our safety. I think the Archetypes of the Old Order have assembled themselves ready to slay us, but my vision is imperfect. If they are indeed present, there would be three armies hiding in the fog on the bay or lurking in the dark territories on the shore. The cruelest and most energetic army is the Wands, followed by the depraved and blood-thirsty Pentacles, and then the poisonous and treacherous Cups. I see moving fog and shadows only, but I fear they are close. Do you see them?"

The thought that he should be concerned for his own safety troubled "I" greatly, but he did not dwell on it. If all the Archetypes were gathered to wage war with him, could he withstand it? His mind wandered first to the Magician ... and then to the Queen of Cups ... and then to the Queen of Pentacles ... the King of Swords ... the King of Wands ... the High Priestess ... Strength ... Justice ... The World ... The Fool ... The Devil!

"There are forces great and ancient in the old order, all capable of being mighty foes if they were set on it," said "I", "And I have opened my mind to encompass the entirety of the Bay and the surrounding fields on this side of Yonder so far as the Base of Odin and the Beige Cliffs of Sofia. The minor arcana have indeed assembled in three factions, whispering about the absence of their comrades in arms, the Suit of Swords. From the ice fields in the southern latitudes to the shores of Delphos, they plot and prepare for war. The King of Wands has been personally assured of the loyalty of the King of Swords, but the martial suit has not been seen. They are feared dead or deserters or worst of all betrayers. The numbered cards await orders from the royals, who in turn wait for the birth of the child who will lead the rebellion. They want to look their enemy in the eye."

The King: "And what of the Major Arcana?"

"I" said, "They are not here."

"It is much as I feared, though my spirits rise on hearing that the most powerful forces have not yet come, and that the Swords have not joined their old cronies. Do we have privacy? Are we safe?"

"They have not yet seen you. They know only of my location within their minds, not of how I am with you here. We are safe for the moment, though I have growing trepidation. There is an inlet a short distance hence which is shielded from their sight. We must go at once, but first we must hide your gross-body. Call for aid!"

"I have called a helper with the power of my mind. He will summon the Stones and they will keep my gross-body safe and give us protection." A Tarot card appeared: an army sergeant.

"I" and the King of Stones proceeded under the cover of a thick mist to a nearby hidden cove.

The King said, "Tell me, 'I', if are you in their minds as well as mine, how can I be certain to trust you? Which side are you on?"

"I": "I am on everyone's side, but particularly on my side, the side of the right and light. Do not fear me, old friend. I am where I am, and

I can be anywhere my perspective arises. As for my allegiance, it is of a peculiar sort. They also have first-person pronouns and so I am their ally as well. Our advantage lies in our knowledge of the coming new trans-linguistic symbolic ordering systems, because in our reckoning 'I' is not merely a tool for aggrandizing the self, a linguistic implement for directing attention to the ego, but it is a Prime Vowel of Lingua-U in which all things cohere at the Yang strata of Essence. They look into 'I' and see merely a personal pronoun, a ghost of themselves, whereas we see the whole living intelligence of the Kosmos – active, passionate, and bold – which is taking a perspective."

"You amaze me, Lord of the Inner Eye," said the King of Stones. "Your mind is more attuned to my own than any other I have ever known, even my own Queen's. The reason for this is beginning to dawn on me, but that is another topic entirely. Your allegiance is exactly as I supposed. I trust you well enough."

"I" and the King of Stones arrived at a secluded spot sheltered by Baobab trees. The King said, "We two have come to gather at Midnight's Bay ere Year 1 CE at the Isle of Delphos, have we not?"

"I": "Yes, we have come to see Zero. It is as you say, though from my perspective, it is not merely one location on the Earth, and not merely a line stretching from the North Pole to the South Pole along 22.5° E. Longitude, but an entire Line of Existence in Light's Neutrality."

The King: "Of course, of course! But listen here: 22.5 is a very important number. The chosen longitude of his birth tells us much of Kalen's purpose."

"I" ensconced in the center of the clearing and looked up at the enveloping night. He said, "Say more."

The King of Stones said, "You are not the only one with foresight into the future teachings of Kalen. I too know something of the vision that he will bring. There are 9 total suits in the New Tarot, mine included among 8 which are new. There are 9 months in the New Kalendar. There are 9 territories in the New Map of the Heavens. There are 9 secondary vowels in Lingua-U. More even than 3 itself, it is the most important number in the entire intellectual edifice which he will deliver. Do you not see that 2 + 2 + 5 = 9, the number lifted to dominance in the new hierarchy? Kalen is returning from his voyage around the Wheel of Existence with a model for reality which shows the circle as complete!"

"I": "Fascinating. It is occurring to me exactly as you speak. Go on."

Using a techno-magical implement, the King displayed an image of the globe and drew images of numbers with light in the air. "Kalen will be born at 22.5° E. Longitude for this reason. There are 360 degrees in a circle where 3 + 6 + 0 = 9. Divided in two, 180° where 1

+ 8 + 0 = 9. Divided in 4, 90° where 9 + 0 = 9. Divided in 8, 45° where 4 + 5 = 9. Divided in 16, 22.5° where 2 + 2 + 5 = 9 as we have seen. A circle divided 64 times creates 5.625° angles where 5 + 6 + 2 + 5 = 18, where 1 + 8 = 9. Even a circle divided 256 times creates 1.40625° angles where 1 + 4 + 0 + 6 + 2 + 5 = 18, where 1 + 8 = 9. This pattern continues all the way down … There is a secret order of existence in which all the digits of the base 10 numbering system if conceived as angles within a circle converge on a singularity. What's more, when 9 is added to any digit, the sum of the result is always the same as the original digit. For example, 4 + 9 = 13, where 1 + 3 = 4. Or 7 + 9 = 16, where 1 + 6 = 7. So it is that 9 is not just any type of singularity which enfolds everything, but one which is also exactly nothing! In other words, it is a Вeı."

"I" grew excited and angry at the same time. "Do not utter the True Name of the singularity aloud here! What if you were overheard? So long as the old order remains ignorant of the Lingua-U, we have an advantage in conflict and it appears that a war may be upon us."

The King: "Forgive me, I did not fully understand that I was speaking aloud a True Name. It was simply the name that came to me, unbidden, as the most proper and natural name available for the original singularity, considering its phonetic resonances. No one taught it to me. I just knew it."

"I": "Yes, indeed. That is how all True Names are first intuited. And that is how the old order might win."

The King: "You think they will intuit the True Names and memorize and use them?"

"I" ran to the edge of the clearing and looked for aid. "Heavens no! That would be our victory, not theirs. They could prohibit ... no, I will not speak of such horrible possibilities lest I be overheard. You may think on it if you wish. Where is our guard? There must be a guard here to ensure our privacy!"

At that moment, a tall and able-bodied fellow appeared at the edge of a wall-like protrusion. The Ten of Stones was clothed in the uniform of a military officer from a Western nation-state in the twentieth century. His affiliation was not apparent, but three stripes adorning his sleeve indicated the rank of sergeant.

The Ten of Stones: "Commander, I have been standing at the opening since you called. No one has approached. Your position is secure." The King of Stones dismissed him.

"I am afraid," said the King of Stones. "Kalen has chosen Delphi to enter the world ... but perhaps he doesn't understand what I know about it."

"I": "What is that?"

The King of Stones: "I suspect Kalen has come to this spot to claim the Lost Stone, an oracle from forgotten tribes long before the

Pythians, the original shamans and priestesses. They claimed the spot as the Axis Mundi ... and they were the first to do so anywhere on the globe. For this reason, their words are remembered in the stones, and no other spot on the planet is given such an honored placement. They brought to the central mound an artifact of polished black stone discovered following a meteor shower. They placed it upon the Axis Mundi and worshipped the Black Stone as a god. It was the Omphalos of the Earth.

"They asked the Black Stone for help and pleaded with it for one cause or another, but they never asked what the stone itself wanted. They treated it as a pet, but it was no pet. It possessed the mind of an alien intelligence, one which did not belong on the Earth. I believe it is an intelligence with the intention not to create, but to destroy. It feels cold in its heart, hard and inscrutable. If there is love there, it is undetectable to me."

"I": "I too have speculated regarding Kalen's purpose in choosing a birth along 22.5° E. Longitude, and in his selecting parents of Thracian and African heritage. I believe he intends to be a liberator of the oppressed, one who will lead a revolt against the established powers."

The King: "Which powers?"

"I": "Only the powers which use language or numbers or symbols or non-verbal signs of any sort for any reason. He will not only bring a

New Tarot and Lingua-U, but a New Zodiac, New Atlas, New Map of the Heavens, and a New Map of the Subtleties. Every understanding in the Old Order must be overturned if he is to succeed. He seeks to undo every power that is."

The King paused to wonder about the many times he used language in his own mind even without speech, thoughts which would run through his intellect in coarse, cacophonous sound symbols without passing through the equanimous schemas of the new trans-linguistic order. Just the other day his mind was drawn compulsively to the cliché, "to kill two birds with one stone", whereupon he began to weep at the thoughtless and unnecessary harshness of the imagery. He hated the way language forced phonetic violence into his spirit.

"I" said, "King, are you aware that Kalen's mother is in possession of the Black Stone?"

The King of Stones: "I have feared as much. Are you certain of this?"

"I": "Yes. I have watched its transmission from generation to generation in her family since they first claimed it secretly. You are a Stone. Does this news not please you?"

The King of Stones: "It does and it does not. As you might imagine, my mind often turns to the Ace of Stones, wondering whether it is above me or below me. It is the source of my power and its exhaustion. It is the purpose of my striving and ground beneath my feet. Without it, the Stones cease to exist, and we hold the Base … the Beginning … the Big Bang … the Balancing of All-That-Is … the Positivity … the Potential … the Polarities … the Vibration … the Venting … the Volving. I am the Sovereign. I have longed to speak to it and ask it to reveal its knowledge, but its ways are over my head and beyond my sight. How does the least of the stones surpass even me?"

"I": "It is a paradox which we must hold, I most of all. Let me get this straight. Are you telling me that the Black Stone in Kalen's family's possession is the Ace of Stones itself?"

The King: "It appears so. I would say for certain, but the fact is that the Ace has been lost for some time. It is widely thought to be the Lost Stone of Delphi. Don't you see? I can't control the Ace. No one can, not a single card in any of the nine suits of the Stone-Star Tarot. It is the penultimate beginning, the first card of the first suit. And if it is out of our hands, then in whose hands is it? And what do they want?"

At this moment, the Ten of Stones returned to the space from his guarding position.

The Ten: "It is the card of Balance, Commander, in the New Tarot. She says she comes on an urgent matter. Shall I allow her in?"

Before "I" or the King could answer, a giant tortoise followed him in and began to speak.

A Perplexing Warning

Chelone was made immortal by the god Zeus, the legends say, though she has quite forgotten her origins if you were to ask her. Everywhere she goes, green carapace on her back, she is at home. But even the most gentle of tortoises can lose their nerve on occasion. When the personification of Balance spoke to "I" at the start of the Season of Yang, she was ballistic as you are ever likely to see her.

"Come closer!" Balance shouted. "Don't make me come to you! I will neither hurry nor raise my voice. Come now, there's not a second to spare!"

On the back of the enormous tortoise was painted strings of beads in nine compartments which were Lo Shu's Magic Square. On the top row, nearest to the turtle's head and front legs: beads in the numbers of 8, 1, and 6. On the middle row: 3, 5, and 7. On the row nearest to the hind legs: 4, 9, and 2.

"I" ran his aged fingers along the turtle's back tracing a line from the center to the 8. "Long have I wished to see the precise organization of the Magic Square at the defining moment of Kalen's birth! The Wheel is traversed, the Rounder's circle is complete, and all the digits of the tenth base have chosen their starting position."

"Elegant! Magnificent! Perfect!" said the King of Stones, his words reverberating in the partially enclosed space not far from Midnight's Bay. "I have known this arrangement in my bones all my days, but I couldn't be sure until this very moment. Each row of the diagram in horizontal, vertical, and diagonal totals to 15. In every direction there is symmetry and equality! This ordering bestows upon all the suits of the Stone-Star Tarot their poignancy, and describes the nature of all alliances and conflicts with the Archetypes. All the main stages of hierarchical development in consciousness are here! My own number is 8 at the base position, the number of infinity and of symmetry and balance. The implications of the Magic Square extend far beyond the Tarot ..."

The giant tortoise interrupted him, saying, "Indeed they do, Stone-King. May I speak?"

The King of Stones bowed slightly and remained silent. He was embarrassed to have irritated a card of the new Major Arcana, even if his own ranking in the upper echelon was a bit more prestigious.

Balance began to calm herself by breathing slowly and deliberately. "Thank you. I have followed a path here which would appear to you like a pair of high wires stretched taut upon a vast abyss, the wires connecting one structure after another. At every critical junction along the way I was taunted by a demonic Fool intent upon destroying my serenity."

The King of Stones gasped. "The Major Arcana of the Old Tarot is here!"

Balance ignored him. She continued, "It ought to go without saying that I have a healthy fear of clowns and the journey was extremely perilous and unpleasant. I faced down the Fool and at the far end of the Bindery sent him into a vacuum from which he could not follow me. Had I led him here, I shudder to think of the consequences! As the zero card in the old Archetypal Order, he surely would have made havoc at Midnight's Bay at the Zero beginning the Common Era, accessing points in the universe which he has never before seen and which he very much wanted to confuse and torment. He would have led the Ro right into the heart of Everything and Nothing!

"It is a miracle that I arrived here at all. At last through great perseverance the high wires returned me to a place I know well, which appears to you like a bay at midnight. But to me this is a giant hall of mirrors, turtles stretched down as far as you can go … high to the heavens above … and in every direction all around. At last I have found a resting place for my weary soul," said Balance.

"I" said, "Before you rest, gentle tortoise, do not forget to tell us why you have come. Or have you come merely to rest?"

Balance: "Oh yes, you are quite right. I have come to alert you to two inflection points outside your present view. You have gathered to witness the birth of Kalen, an immortal man allowed 3,000 years on the Earth, if the legends are to be believed. He is to be born at the Zero at Delphi, one who brings a new voice into the Yang; a thousand years hence another child will be born to him, a girl who is born in Queensland, a voice of rising Yin; and in the year 2,000 CE, there will be born a pair of his grandchildren in the Green Country whose names I have forgotten. They usher in the Last Millennium of Record and draw to a close the Kalendar."

"I" said, "Fascinating. Now that you mention it, I can see these points of space and time when I shift my attention a hair this way or that way. Time here is a luminescent ever-coiling ribbon in space. We are close to 3,000 years of time in human civilization now, winding its spiraling path again and again around this very point, bringing Kalen and his daughter and the twins close to the fold on three occasions, nearly touching though they are separated by a thousand years apiece.

Beyond this view, my sight is dark, and so it must remain that I may focus on the delicate moment at hand."

The King of Stones appropached the turtle and spoke reverentially. "Great Balance of All-That-Is, why is this vision important to us at this time?"

Balance said, "Because once the Wheel of Existence is turned, it turns not merely in one timeline, but all three that we now see. The turning cannot go back, and there are forces present in the future which would stop Kalen at the beginning on account of events happening a thousand or two thousand or three thousand years henceforth. And there are resources Kalen needs in the future for his travails here in this time.

"Kalen rounds the Wheel as you know, but he is not the only one. His fate is linked to his daughter's fate, and the fate of his twin grandchildren. Kalen's work may be done in 3,000 years, but the work of the child and grandchildren will go on thereafter. All four are Rounders with important work to be done. They are Yang and Yin and Unitive at evenly spaced intervals in the Spiral. A stumbling block for one is ..."

The King: "... a benefit to another, and a crossroads for the others."

Balance nodded its small tortoise head. "I" said, "I see. The Rounders are linked by an invisible ribbon. We cannot aid one without hindering another and setting into motion complexities for still others beyond our reckoning."

The Tortoise said, "And if you help Kalen's daughter in the future, you will change the past ... youthful Kalen, Kalen as a child, or perhaps even Kalen in the womb. They are linked in ways you do not see!" The King pounded a fist against the open palm of his other hand. He exclaimed, "It is maddening!" It is no coincidence that at that moment the stones on the ground beneath their feet shook.

"I": "Though we would very much desire to help, in the end the inherent forces of action and reaction will reverberate in ways we do not intend and do not desire."

Balance: "Now you understand. You have the power to influence events, but you must not take too heavy a hand to it. You must allow Kalen to show us what he is made of, even if it is painful to watch, or there will be consequences to pay over thousands of years. There is the work of four Rounders at stake, not merely the one which you see."

It is the peculiar enchantment of Midnight's Bay to open portals of sound into the Earth at different points of time, bringing forth noises unexpected and unsought. Thus the sound of children's singing again reverberated in the cove.

Silent night, holy night
All is calm, all is bright ...

To which Chelone said, "If all is calm it is only because I am not. Confounded night! I am turning in now." And then the giant tortoise turned around and vanished out of sight.

The Ten of Stones appeared suddenly at the entrance, looking flustered. He said, "My Lords! Forgive the intrusion, but do you know what is going on out there? It is alarming to me!"

The King of Stones: "We have been in a meeting. Speak!"

With his head bowed, the Ten said: "I feel myself growing heavier and denser in my 0 part, and my 1 part is faltering! All the Stones have come, except for the Lost Ace, and they are confused and adrift in turmoil. The 2 speaks of joining a revolution at base 3! The 3 lies on its side and flaps itself like the wings of a bird. The 4 sits on the floor, its head buried in its lap! The 5 wanders about like a madman! The 6 is disguising itself as the 9 and often getting away it with too I might add. He grows deceitful. The 7 keeps digging at everything in sight, lifting imaginary objects! The 8 is convinced that 2 has eaten its face and its body is shriveled to the shape of a 1! The 9, if it is indeed a 9, is jumping up and down without stopping! I have never seen behavior like this amongst my crew! And what am I to do ... I have never felt so burdened and depressed. It takes more energy than I have to even lift my head before my own King. Something is grotesquely amiss in the number world!"

The King of Stones: "Thank you for your faithful service, 10. Go now and try to remain calm. Stay alert. Keep the crew in line, and warn us if the old suits approach."

When they were alone again, the King said, "Do you know what is happening to them?"

"I" said, "Yes. It is almost Midnight! The dominant base 10 number system has reached the breaking point. Too much has been asked of it for too long, and its capacity to organize reality into meaningful structures is falling away. The base 2 system is ascendant in the machine world, but it is limited in its ability to become cognizant. Kalen prepares the way for a new number base to rise, ternary, which is filled with riddles and indeterminacy and fuzzy logic. It comes not to replace the old systems, but to perform feats of magic unlike anything the world has ever seen. Kalen will teach the base 3 to speak in Lingua-U and the number world will grow sentient with new machine hybrids in the Season of You! I have seen it through foresight! I have scanned the mind of Kalen in the womb to know the secrets of 3, but it is veiled by powerful layers of red light. So long as the cards of the New Tarot are near to Midnight's Bay and so close to Kalen's birth, they will feel disturbed to their very core, for they feel the change that is coming as if it were already here."

"I" paused. The King of Stones felt his gaze penetrate every inch of his body. "Let me see your hands."

The King of Stones approached "I" and held out his hands which shone with markings in the dark. On each digit of the right hand was painted 00, 01, 02, 10, and 11. The digits of the left hand were: 12, 20, 21, 22, and 100.

"So you have seen it too," said "I".

The King of Stones nodded, and showed him his bare feet. The toes were likewise numbered in fluorescent paint all the way to 202 (which means 20 in the base 3).

"I" continued, "The number systems are changing, moving into alignment with the Lingua-U and the Wheel of Wholes which Kalen will deliver. Language, energy, number, and thought ... they grew apart for centuries like so many branches of a craggy, deformed, and rotten tree. Kalen comes not to save the tree, but to burn it to the ground and plant a new ternary seed."

The King of Stones: "Is arson his intent then? Do you really think that is what he will do?"

"I": "Fire may be his only recourse if the human mind is a forest grown as derelict and malevolent as the old archetypes and signs. Do you know the other day I was walking in the forest and I came across a lion with a thorn in its paw? It pretended to be an ordinary lion, but I could tell that it was actually Leo in the Aries-Pisces Zodiac. A bear cub came to the rescue and removed the thorn, and then as a reward the lion bit its head off. As it licked the blood off its own fur, it laughed wickedly. The old order is depraved, King!"

The King: "Yes, I know. I am no defender of the old order. But I shudder to think that it will be necessary to break their wands, smash their cups, and burn their pentacles. And what is to become of the old beasts when the Bear-Yak Zodiac arrives? Co-existence ought to be our common goal, not supremacy."

"I": "Tell that to the old order."

The King of Stones, his spiritual body weary of standing, sat on a stump. This was not the first conversation of this sort which he had had with "I".

He said, "You know I have. And you know that they have soundly rejected it."

"I" said, "The old suits will give you no room to breathe. The old beasts would sooner devour the New Zodiac than negotiate."

The King: "Their mind is set on power, and so long as language has a grip on their intellect they cannot see past it."

"I": "Not all of them are gripped by language. Some praise silence and emptiness."

The King of Stones paused and looked overhead. A handful of stars appeared, giving rise to the new constellation of B. The stars danced in his pupils.

He said, "I have reflected long on this matter. It is a false emptiness they praise! They extoll a void in which the Ro razes all to Zero, extinguishing the Light of Love."

"I": "You see it too. Their palates lack the subtlety to distinguish among the flavors of emptiness. They consume the silence, noticing only a taste of salt on their tongue, oblivious to the arsenic contained within. In the pursuit of spirituality they give toehold to the Death of Everything. They would concede to the Ro when they should fight it."

The King: "Yes. I have looked into infinity's figure 8 and seen my own two eyes reflected back! Silence cannot beat back meaning, for it is merely an island trapped between two dueling seas. Right View requires consciousness, clarity, and quietude ... not silence."

"I": "Have you tried teaching them Lingua-U?"

The King: "You know I have. All the new suits have. The old suits vehemently deny that there is another language hidden beneath the naturalistic languages and symbol systems. They speak from ignorance, but maybe it is just too much for them."

There is activity below at the transition between BCE and CE. The King of Stones and "I" look intently out of the Bay into the world.

The King continues, "This we know. The Ace of Stones will bequeath the Universal Language to Kalen. But the language of subtle energy which Kalen will deliver has already been soundly rejected by the old order before he takes his first breath. I have seen this with foresight! The Ro has never been more powerful! This is the inauspicious hand we are dealt."

Kalen's mother screams in pangs of agony at the arrival of a new child.

"I": "What do you think, King of Stones? Will the Omphalos Bearer burn the old order to the ground?"

The King of Stones: "If he does, then we will be the stones beneath the ashes, and we will be the metal of his blade and the buckle of his belt. So far as we are concerned, all the old authentic signs, symbols, codes, and prophecies have pointed to this exact spot. They have led us to a *Beıb*, a Rounder of the Beı! We are with this child, full of inestimable promise, ere the Great Overturning. If all these things are wrong, then God help us all."

And then "I" suddenly vanished, and Kalen's mother entered labor. Her moans and groans were greeted by the wailing babe.

The Hidden Past

alen's parents were called O'Tolan, a surname whose origin and meaning are lost to knowledge. If it came from Europe, it may be connected to the Ortolan, a finch-like bird with a greenish-gray head. If the name is Asiatic or African, then there is little historical evidence to help trace its etymology. On the other hand, it has been suggested that the name refers to Tolán, the capital city for the Mesoamerican civilizations of the Maya and the Aztecs. When this possibility arises in polite discussion, it is sharply divisive. So far as any legend may be traced into the annals of history, there is no connection between the O'Tolans and the peoples of the Western hemisphere. Of course, this fact has not stopped speculation regarding the unusual name which belongs to Kalen's parents and therefore to Kalen himself, particularly discussion of whether it connotes a supernatural origin.

To study the etymology of words and how their sounds have borrowed throughout history yields a collection of facts which are known to Zone 8 of the New Atlas which organizes the worlds of meaning into the Eight Zones. As we have said, little is known of O'Tolan in this zone. But in the realm of syntax where the sound-meanings of the words may be studied independently of their historical antecedents, Zone 4 opens. To the fourth zone, O'Tolan tells a story of the Opening of All-That-Is into a Temple or Tendency set upright and without downfall upon the Land. The letter-shape of the lower-case L is that of a human being or structure set upon the Center of the World. O'Tolan, it is suggested, is a Person at a Place at the Center of All-That-Is. Among those knowledgeable in phonosemantic semiotics, there is accordingly a most interesting speculation: namely that Tolan is not the name of any particular place on the Earth, but the True Name of the planet itself.

Who can tell if such a thing is true? At this time the peoples of the globe have not come together to determine if the world has been named according to the best lights of Wisdom. It is too early for this question to be answered, though the answer may well reveal itself in the due course of events. If you are the sort of person who cares not one whit for a thing's name, then you may figure that any one is just about as good as any other. This sort of thinking is deaf to the subtleties of names and their non-random correlations, but I do not wish to argue. You are free to believe that words carry a sort of magic to create and destroy Worlds, or you may refuse the possibility. What concerns us today is that Kalen has been taught nothing of magical topics as they are usually conceived, but he is already full of innate insight. As the Kalendar turns, he is 5 years and 40 days old. This fact doesn't mean what you probably think it means, but we will come to that shortly.

Our story continues at the 24th day of Black Stone month on the Kalendar, not far from 44 E. Longitude on the Earth. It was the latter part of the second century of the Common Era, though the years were tabulated in a different way back then.

Karen O'Tolan clothed herself in light and loose raiments open to the tropical January air, and she looked out into the brown and green fields of her farm. She scanned the fields for her children. She shut the door of her primitive house made with bricks and paste, and walked outside to get a better view. She scanned past the carriage and the barn with the horses, seeing no one. Abundant sheep roamed in the vast yard, penned by an extensive fence which stopped short of a wooded area at the outskirts.

On the nearby land there were no other homes for miles. At the edge of the O'Tolan's property, wilderness terminated abruptly beyond the fields stretched before the lonely house. On the other side of the wilderness, settlements dotted the land on the north shore of the Horn of Africa. The nearest settlement to the home was Warshon, and farther along the road was the nearby city of Berpa.

Karen sought to call her children for supper, so she rang a loud bell. Her daughters frolicked amongst the bushes and grasses. Chila was the eldest and wisest, a young woman 14 years old, her soft raven hair long and braided. The brown-skinned Jeila had 12 years and was a gifted athlete and skilled at defensive arts. They came promptly when they heard the bell.

Two male children played along the outskirts of the property, and one of them ran off into the woods despite the ringing bell. He was Kalen, the youngest, a lad with brown hair, with a strong body and insatiable curiosity. Kyle, 9 years old, was loyal, smart and compassionate. All four of the children had mountain-shade brown eyes which were capable of conveying a sense of depth and seriousness beyond the years of children.

Kyle lingered at the edge of the forest for a while, looked in both directions, and then followed his brother. He felt he might get in trouble for not coming in immediately, but he would surely get into more trouble if he left his brother in the forest alone. He disappeared into the woods.

Karen shouted, "Chila, go get your brothers. Tell them to come in right now. It's nearly dark!"

Chila said, "Yes, mother." She walked up to the edge of the woods and cried out for her brothers. "Kyle! Kalen!"

When the boys did not reply, she wandered into the woods dense with evergreen shrubs and small trees with pretty foliage. The trees grew taller and denser as she proceeded. A grayish eagle-owl hooted and a chilly breeze nipped at her neck and exposed parts.. The sun dipped behind the clouds near to the horizon, nearly extinguishing the light.

She continued into the woods until at last she came upon the older brother. "What are you doing here, Kyle?"

Kyle pointed to the top of the tallest tree around. "I followed Kalen in. He's tracking a bear. Says he's seen it following us from the North, and that it's spying on us."

Chila said, "That's the most peculiar thing I ever heard. There are no bears here! He's got a fertile imagination, that one. It's best we all get inside."

She cried: "Kalen, you come down here right this minute!"

Kalen was perched high in a tree, looking off in the distance. "He's a large brown bear, only quarter of a mile from here. You want to see?"

Chila said, "No, Kalen. There's nothing to see. It's time for supper. Mother's going to be very upset with you if you don't obey."

Kalen shimmied down the tree remarkably fast, and plopped on the ground with a thud. His hands were tough from many days spent climbing trees and rocks for sport.

Kyle said, "Are you alright?"

Kalen said, "It wasn't that far to fall."

Kyle said, "No, I mean, mentally. There are no bears around for a hundred miles. I scouted out this land with Dad myself when he came looking at houses. In these woods there's hyrax and elephant shrews, but no bears!" Kyle brushed off pine needles off Kalen's shoulders.

Kalen said, "I know what I saw." Kyle looked at him sternly. "All right, I'll come."

Jeila led the three of them out the way they came in. Kyle said, "This isn't the first time you thought you saw a bear. Why is it no one else ever sees this bear of yours?"

Kalen had no good reply. His brother was correct. For as long as he could remember, he occasionally spotted a bear watching him or his family from a distance. When he first spotted it, it was only a cub. Now it looked much larger, though perhaps not fully grown. The bear would disappear before anyone else could see it. It was an odd thing, but Kalen's life was filled with seemingly magical oddities.

The three of them walked home together as the sun set on the horizon and dusk came with the squawks and songs of birds announcing their arrival back at the roost. As they approached the home, their father also came. A carriage dropped him off at the edge of the property, and then it proceeded along the main road. Kairon walked toward the home and toward his children.

He quickened his pace and threw his arm around his children. Jeila ran out from the house to greet her father. Together they greeted each other happily with hugs and kisses as the sun finally set behind the hills. "I am the luckiest father in the whole world," Kairon said. He often spoke unreservedly the first words that came to his mind, and they were usually expressions of gratitude, praise, and joy. At last the four of them resumed walking home. "Go inside and get ready for supper, children."

The children did as they were told, even Kalen who was usually inclined to doing his own thing. One by one they removed their dirty outdoor tunics and put on clean tunics used only indoors. They washed themselves in water Chila and Jeila had brought from the river earlier in the day. They performed chores and prepared the food while their mother oversaw their work.

At last, they sat down in a circle for prayers followed by a meal of mutton, tubars, and bread. The dinner conversation was often slight, but tonight it was practically non-existent. Kairon and Karen exchanged nervous glances at each other and spoke in vague terms about mysterious affairs.

Kairon said, "At long last, I found a suitable Vault. It is all the way in Berpa, but it will suit our needs when the time comes, if we can find it again. The Vault-keepers care nothing about the nature of the wares, and the level of security they provide is remarkable. We have only to determine the most appropriate credentials for access."

Karen asked, "Who do you suppose would keep the key?"

Kairon said, "The signs have grown ominous for us, Karen. We must prepare the children to claim what is theirs and fulfill their purpose."

Karen said, "You can't imagine the boy is old enough to retrieve it from the Vault if called upon! He is innocent! He hasn't yet got the mind to know what he would need to do!"

"He will, once we teach him about the Past," said Kairon. Everyone looked at Kalen, who only then realized they were speaking of him. He began to pay attention, but he preferred to be spoken to before speaking.

The other children grew quiet. They knew about the Past already, and they also knew that Kalen was at the age when each of them was told about it.

Kyle asked, "Is he old enough?"

Kairon nodded. "It is the 44th hexagram of the Kalendar. Tonight."

Kalen said nothing. No one spoke after that, and everyone helped to put the dinner items away and clean the kitchen.

"Come with me, son. We have things to discuss," said Kairon. He took Kalen's hand, and then the two of them went outside and walked over to the chariot. They sat down inside the carriage under the starlight, and Kairon opened his robe to reveal a satchel. When they were sat down together, Karion opened the bag to show a black stone the size of an oracle's scrying-stone, somewhat larger than a man's fist. It was shiny and smooth, nearly perfect in its seamless blackness. It was too large for a man to put his fist around it, but surprisingly light.

Kairon said, "Do you know the tale of the Omphalos of Delphi?"

Kalen nodded. "Yes, we hear its story told every year at the solstice. The storytellers save it until the end."

Kairon said, "What do they say about it?"

Kalen said, "It is the navel of the world. It is the center of all things, the reason why we look to Delphi when we pay respect to the grandfathers and grandmothers. It remembers the past. It knows the future."

Kairon said, "You are a good listener. What more did they say?"

Kalen said, "Long ago it was our link to the gods, but then it was lost. Now it is hard for us to hear the gods, even though we make copies of it that don't work so well. The gods can't reach us now the way they used to."

Kairon said, "The gods still speak, but only a few can hear them. It helps to have a listening device, and none is better than the original navel-stone of Delphi." He gave the stone for Kalen to hold. "*This* is the one, Kalen. It is not lost, nor has it ever been. Your mother's family has kept it in secret for twelve generations. It's ours."

Kalen never knew his father to make a joke of sacred matters or tell tall tales. He knew instinctively that he could trust his words to be the truth. Kalen rubbed the stone's smooth surface and felt an electrical current rush through his body. His hair began to stand up.

"Son, this is not a toy. It is a relic more precious and sacred than any other I know. It offers us a pipeline to the spirit world, access to knowledge to make the world a better place. It is a gift to all the world, not just one family, or one Bearer."

Kalen held the Black Stone up to his ears, and listened for it to speak. "Father, I don't hear it speaking."

Kairon laughed. "It will, it will. Listen in silence."

Kalen listened and heard a voice speak silently into his mind: "I'm yours."

"It spoke to me, father, but I'm afraid to tell you what it said." Kalen gave the stone back to his father.

Kairon took the stone and put it away in the satchel. "I am your father. I command you to tell me what it said."

"It said it's mine."

Kairon said, "Indeed it will be, Kalen, one day. It is your birthright according to the prophecies which our family has received from your grandparents Song and Dayn. They were visited by a remarkable Wizard who educated them as to the nature of your role. You are the Bearer, Kalen. The Stone waits for you to be ready. Many in our family line would have wished to use the Stone, Kalen, but they were its Keepers only, not its rightful Bearer. Long ago it was said that only a child born at Delphi at midnight's hour could Bear the Stone, and he would take it across the world to the East and return with it from the West and set it upon the altar at Delphos, when at last it will return from whence it came, and humankind will have fulfilled its purpose."

Kalen's eyes widened with recognition. "I was born at Delphi."

Kairon smiled. "Yes you were."

Kalen smiled. "At midnight."

Kairon said, "Exactly midnight. From that moment henceforth, your mother and I have called it Zero, and we have counted years from that mark ever since. It is the first Kalendar mark: Yang Yang Yang Yang Yang Yang."

Kalen scrunched his face as he often did when he felt that he was treated like a child. "I know how to tell time. It makes sense, father, or it's starting to."

"What is?"

Kalen said, "My whole life."

Kairon had many questions for Kalen, but at this moment the boy fell asleep. He carried his son down from the chariot. Karen waited on the ground below, leaning on the carriage as she listened to every word. Chila, Jeila, and Kyle sat outside the horse barn, almost within hearing distance.

Karen said, "It's a start."

Kairon said, "I'm afraid. He used the words 'It's mine.' I shouldn't have pried it out of him. What if the Stone thinks it's been claimed by a new owner? You know what will happen when he claims it ... what will happen to all of us. He is too young to be alone. He is too young to lose us."

Karen recoiled in fear. "You don't know that for certain! You don't think!"

Kairon hushed her. "Let's save our fear for the known, not the unknown."

Kairon carried the boy inside, and everyone came in from outdoors. They put Kalen to bed and everyone retired. Kairon barely slept at all.

When Kalen awoke, the house was empty. He stood at the front door and called out, but no one appeared. He felt he had slept much later than usual, but the sun was still climbing in the sky. He turned inside, and saw a note on the table.

Although Kalen didn't read much and the family's language was a difficult one, the note's message was simple. It contained four glyphs which read, "We. River. Soon. Returning."

Kalen dressed properly and set out for the river, chomping on dates as he walked through the fields. He thought about the note, and a strange feeling came over him. He began to recall his parents speaking while he slept, only their words were like the shifting scenes of a dream.

Kairon said, "You must remember the words of Aupaiaaqua exactly! What did he say would happen when Kalen claimed the Stone?"

Karen said, "He said the Stone's gift of *temporizing* would be removed from his parents, and from that moment henceforth they would begin to age with the world's time, while Kalen would continue to *temporize*, aging along the Kalendar's grooves."

"What did he say would happen to Kalen's siblings?"

"I don't recall. It is just a story passed down from my mother's mother."

"Think!"

"Yes, I remember! They will lose the *temporizing* as well, I am sure of it. Aupaiaaqua said the Omphalos Bearer – meaning Kalen – must walk the world's ages alone, and none from his family would survive long on his path once the Stone was claimed."

"How will we know when the Stone has been claimed? What exactly does Kalen need to do to claim it?"

"I don't know. How did we know that we claimed it?"

"You were one of only two children. When your parents died, it came to you. You took it because that was what they wanted."

"What did the Stone say when you claimed it?"

"It said I was the mother of the Rounder who would be worthy to carry it to the ends of the Earth and traverse the chasm."

Kalen's head was swimming with many quick thoughts, none of them pleasant notions. "Why did I sleep through this conversation?" he wondered. "I should have got up out of bed and listened wakefully." And then this one: "What if I slept so long that my family has been swallowed up the river of time and I am now alone? What if a thousand years have passed by?"

Kalen dropped his fruit and ran toward the river.

He ran fast as he could, and he began to remember some of the oddities that perplexed him.

Why did his family move every few years, always moving into the East and never into the West? Was the direction of the sunrise so important that all their livelihoods and friendships were continually uprooted? The family sometimes moved hundreds of miles north or south, but never advancing more than a short distance westward. What was the point of it?

Why was he not permitted to visit places they once lived or connect with old friends? A few times, Kalen saw men in the marketplaces which resembled boys he once played with, so much so that he was sure that his childhood friends had grown up while he remained young. Kalen's parents hid him away before he could be recognized. Is it possible that time moves differently for everyone else except for *his own family*?

And then there was the strange case of Kalen's many aunts, uncles, and cousins. On one visit, he would meet aunts and uncles and play with his young cousins and on the next, everyone would be decades older, even geriatric. He was told never to ask about it, that it would be explained when he was old enough to understand.

Still more troubling was the odd way that Kalen slept. At night while others were at rest, he heard the sounds of rooms sliding into and out of joints, connecting and reconnecting with passageways and tubes between the Worlds. He dreamt of the Kalendar's grooves as a living maze along which he scoured for right passage. When he awoke, the world seemed a little different than before in ways that were difficult to describe. Browns might be a little more deeply brown after an especially restless night, or clouds a little fluffier, the sunlight a bit hotter. The markings on animals would change. Food might taste funny, or there might be more or less of it in the kitchen. No one else noticed these things, and he got tired of asking about what he saw or felt differently because he was sure everyone thought he was off-kilter.

And then there was the Omphalos, the Black Stone itself. It was like having another child in the family, one more precious than all the others combined (or so it seemed to Kalen). His parents were always looking out for it, ensuring that it was hidden well and never left alone. Kalen and his siblings were never allowed to touch it or ask questions about it, except for the older siblings who could speak to it *only if they were in peril.*

Kalen's older siblings knew how to ask questions of the Stone, and he watched them do it on a few occasions. Once their parents were late returning from a trip, and the children were alone as night fell. Chila put her hands on the Stone and said, "Where are my parents? What are we to do?" And the Stone replied, "Their carriage has slipped off its axle, and they are delayed. Stay indoors and keep the doors shut. A man will come knocking, but you must not let him in no matter what he says. Ready your swords."

After all these words, it happened that a strange man knocked on their door seeking their parents, but he was deceptive about his purpose. When their parents arrived moments later, the odd fellow scurried away. They were delayed on account of a defective carriage just as the Stone claimed. This is how Kalen first recognized the power of the Stone to predict the future, and he came to respect its place in the family.

Kalen arrived at the roaring river. When he saw no one there, he began to cry. It was the place his family always went for water ... and it was empty. They were gone.

Tears fell. He wandered along the riverbanks crying for quite a while, and beneath the sobs were feelings of terror. He thought: "What if I will never see my family again? What did father mean when he said, 'must wander the world alone'. What if everyone is gone forever and I am alone now and evermore?"

Kyle appeared at the top of a nearby hill, his ears caught to the noise of Kalen's sobs. "Kalen, come here! We're over here!"

Kalen ran up the hill fast as his legs could carry him, and landed in the arms of his older brother. His mother and sisters were fishing nearby, and they waved to him from the water's edge.

THE MOUNTAIN TREK

reezing downhill Kalen crashed into his mother, almost knocking her down. He wrapped his arms around her tightly, and cried into her dress. She held on to him, saying, "What's wrong?"

Kalen began to dry his eyes. He said, "I thought I would never see you again! I thought I slept for a thousand years and missed the *whole world happening.*"

Karen replied, "As you can see, nothing of the sort has happened. You needed your rest, so we let you sleep in. Rest is good for you."

Kalen went on. "I had bad dreams. I heard you and father talking and you said ..."

Karen interrupted him and gestured toward the river. "This is not a safe place to talk about private matters."

Kalen looked around: At this bend, there were over a dozen fishers at the river, men and women and children fishing with harpoons or weir baskets made from willow branches. Their gazes were drawn to the crying child, and they saw Kalen in his misery. His brother and sisters were fishing, too, standing in the water with fishing-spears. They averted their eyes from Kalen's.

Karen said, "Stay here."

She went over to speak to Chila for a moment, and then she said goodbye to Chila, Jeila, and Kyle. She returned soon and took Kalen's hand. She pointed in the direction of Mount Sorat which loomed overhead. "We are going for a climb today. You like to climb, don't you son?"

"Yes, mum," said Kalen. He soon forgot his feelings of panic he felt upon waking. He wondered what his mother meant by saying that sleeping was good for him. It seemed an odd thing to say.

They bounded up the little mountain, not that tall but still the tallest peak around for miles. The mountain trek invigorated Kalen, and he listened to his mother speak of many things openly for the first time which had been previously hidden from him. He learned of the travails of her kin over hundreds of years in protecting the Omphalos, which she referred to simply as "it." Ever they kept it secret, bound by duty to be its Keepers, but only rarely its users.

She explained that the Stone was a source of knowledge only to be used for the common welfare of all beings, and not for selfish interests. To highlight this point, she noted that a few of her ancestors used the Stone selfishly, and they were harshly punished by events. This idea appealed to Kalen very much, though it made him wonder from what source does the Stone get its own power?

"In our culture," Karen said, "children are protected from troubles their minds cannot understand or accept, and about which they can do little. But at the age of 5 years and 40 days, they are old enough to analyze problems, weigh choices, and make smart decisions. They can be creative and imaginative thinkers, though still undisciplined and limited in their language skills and mathematics. They want to know 'why' and 'how' the world works, and it would be cruel to deny them the tools to figure it out. You are old enough to know about the Past now, Kalen. There is much we have to tell you."

Kalen asked, "May I speak freely?"

Karen looked both ways along the escalating trail, and both sides. "Keep your voice down. We are not the only ones hiking up this trail."

"I wish to know why the Stone said that it was mine. What if I don't want to have it? What if I want nothing to do with it?"

Karen walked briskly on the path ahead, which wound closely between bushes of herbs and greenery which rose on either side. "The Stone is not yours at this time. It will come to you when you are ready, and not sooner. You will choose to take the Stone for the same reason a fish chooses water or a bird chooses air. It is in the nature of Who You Are. Your life is linked to it in a way that is most extraordinary, though you have not glimpsed it yet."

Kalen said, "Is it here? Do you have it with you?"

Teenage boys sprouted into view from a ledge above their perch, and Kalen's mother kept her lips closed. The boys passed, merrily joking in a language foreign to the O'Tolans. Kairon knew many foreign languages, but his family seldom learned them.

The mother and son were alone again on their walk. Karen said, "Yes, I have it." She walked ahead of her son and looked back on him. "Do you know how many years have passed since your birth?"

Kalen replied, "5 years."

"Exactly 5 years and 41 days. To you, and to your parents and your siblings ... but not to the world. We count time with the sacred Kalendar bequeathed by the Omphalos; the world uses secular calendars. For every 40 days that pass for us, the world outside progresses by 4 years, more or less. We have seen 189 years in this fashion, ever since your birth on the Isle of Delphos. Your mother and father are more than 220 years old, and you are nearly 190 years, by the reckoning of the world's calendars. We have kept this fact from you, but it is time you know."

Kalen looked at his hands and body as if to check to make sure he was not an old man. "I don't understand. If I sit down with a friend to fish in the morning and stay until nightfall, my friend fishes for one day, not many."

Karen said, "Are you sure? We reckon time differently, and we age much slower than other people. You perceive yourself to be fishing with one friend for one day, but perhaps your friend left after only an hour, but you perceived him to have stayed the whole day. The next day you ask him, and he says you were in a deep state of contemplation and he didn't want to disturb you, so he left at the end of the day though you stayed on."

Kalen said, "That has happened to me!"

Karen said, "Yes. It has happened to us all. There is a paradox in our midst. It cannot be understood by thinking about it, only by living it, and sensing time's passage from the inside of Time itself."

Kalen said, "People tell me I move slowly ... or too fast."

Karen said, "That is because you occupy time and space differently than they do, and you must learn to compensate for it. There are tricks of awareness your father and I will teach you so that you know how you are being perceived based on the space and time you occupy. We can help you to blend in ... or take advantage of a time variance."

Kalen kicked at rocks in his path. "It sounds complicated."

"It is what it is. Listen carefully. At night, while we sleep, we *temporize*. The time in our perception and in the world at large reconcile, and the discrepancies between the timelines disappear."

"I can hear things moving around in my sleep. That's why things go missing, like my socks. Or things suddenly appear, like a kitchen full of groceries."

Karen said, "People have recollections of us doing things or saying things that we do not recall. They say we went shopping with them at the marketplace, but shopping was just one of many dreams we had in a long night's sleep."

Kalen asked, "Do the sheep temporize?"

Again there was company on the trail, climbers coming from the rear. Karen leaned in close to Kalen and spoke softly. "All beings temporize together. We temporize differently than most. The sheep temporize differently than us."

Kalen whispered: "Who feeds them? Sometimes I go out to feed them and they are already fed, but Kyle said he didn't do it."

"When we moved here last year, we hired servants, did we not?"

"Yes, so you have said, but I rarely see them."

"They feed the sheep when they see that the sheep need feeding. Our servants feed the sheep if you do not, so they do not go without food if we were to temporize differently."

"Wow."

"This is very important for you to know. We need mobility to continue to temporize ... and *spacialize*. We must travel along the path of the Omphalos Bearer, east from Delphi. Staying in one place for very long could be disastrous for any of us. You must always avoid confinement or captivity. We have the Omphalos, the navel of All-That-Is. The Kosmos needs us to bring the space in different Worlds together in harmony. The Earth itself needs our movement for its own journeys through time and space among the Worlds of the Exchange. This is why we keep moving. We must align ourselves not with the political boundaries of the people, but with the entire landscape of the Earth, which is a sphere."

The boy asked, "What is a sphere?"

His mother said, "Dear child, for a moment, I forgot you are a youngin'. A sphere is a ball."

Kalen asked, "The world is a ball?"

Karen said, "It is. The Black Stone has spoken it, and we believe it is so, though we have not the proof. We have seen supporting evidence, how the Earth curves from distances separated by miles. Look!"

The rocks ceased their vertical ambitions. Kalen's next step on the mountain took his foot downward.

Karen said, "Stop!"

The boy stopped mid-step, because he was told to do so. His mother gestured for him to follow her, so he stood at her side and looked out over the countryside. Thin forests of short, stout evergreen trees and taller acacia trees, stretched westward, and connected by flatlands toward the cities in the distance. Beyond the cities, beaches and a bright shoreline which bent in an easterly direction.

Kalen asked, "How big is the world?"

Karen said, "I do not know. For the Omphalos Bearer, the world is measured in years not merely miles. For you it is 3,000 years long. This place here is called Somalia, according to the Black Stone. But nobody calls it that now."

"We must keep moving to the East?"

"Yes. East and north is our present mission. We will cross the Arabian Sea to Arabia. That is how we will *spacialize.*"

"When can we stop moving?"

"That is an excellent question, but not for me. It is appropriate for the Stone. Would you like to ask it?"

Kalen nodded.

As they stood at the mountain peak, Karen handed her son the Stone. His foot slipped on the uneven rocks near the edge of a rock wall and he nearly tripped. "Careful, don't drop it."

Kalen said, "What do I say?"

"Put your hands on it and concentrate. You must never ask questions frivolously. You must never be insincere. Your question must not be overly vague or unnecessarily specific. You must never try to deceive the Stone. You must not ask questions you already know the answer to. You must never ask questions merely to win money or power or possessions, but you may ask about how to fulfill your legitimate needs for food, water, shelter, and companionship. In short, you must show it the respect you would if you were speaking with a revered spiritual master. If you follow these directions, the Stone will be helpful. If you falter in any way, do not rely upon what it says, for it may decide it has had enough of you and it will send you into harm's way."

Kalen put his hands on the Stone as he was instructed. "It is cold."

"Sometimes it is hot. It has its moods and dispositions. Go ahead and ask."

Kalen said, "When can we stop moving?"

Karen: "Listen."

The Stone spoke words out loud. "You can stop moving whenever you wish, if you are prepared to meet the consequences."

Kalen startled, and looked at his mother.

She said, "I heard it too. It speaks, though it has no mouth. Remember, it is the voice of the Earth."

Kalen said, "What will happen if we stop moving?"

The Stone said, "You will cease to *spacialize*, bringing ruin to the Worlds. A better question is, 'What age must I be, and standing upon what location on the Earth, may I release the Stone, and therefore cease moving in accord with it?'"

Kalen said, "That one."

The Stone said, "You must be at least 81 years old and standing at my birthplace at Delphi, and then you may release me. You must return to your birthplace without returning the way you came."

Kalen mouthed to his mother: "What do I say now?"

Karen pointed at the Stone.

Kalen: "Stone, what do I say now?"

The Stone said, "Say 'thank you', and then say in these words exactly, 'Is there anything else urgent for me to ask right now?'"

Kalen: "Thank you. Is there anything else important for me to ask right now?"

The Stone said, "You're welcome. There is nothing urgent for you to ask, but your mother needs guidance urgently. Hand me to her."

Kalen handed the ball to his mother, and relaxed.

The Stone continued: "Karen, the child must listen to these words. I know your mind. You want to know what will happen when Kalen claims me, and when will this happen if it has not happened already? Is that correct?"

Karen: "Yes."

The Stone: "I do not enjoy answering your query, but it is both urgent and important that I do so. Kalen will inherit the Stone upon your death and your husband's death. You and Kairon are in mortal danger. There are foes guided by the Ro who are already on their way, and I do not see a way forward at this time so that either you or your husband may live. Do not despair. You must prepare immediately to transfer the Keeping of the Stone to the Bearer, and set him on an eastward path. Ensure all your children are looked after."

Karen said, "Who can I trust to care for the children?"

The Stone: "I have no more to say to you because you are capable of handling this. Consult me again if the need arises. Wait ..."

Karen said, "What?"

The Stone's shiny black surface, which to casual observation looks perfectly seamless, revealed its seams. Light from within radiated through the Baobab Tree-like veins onto Karen's pupils. Her face grew long and serious.

At last the Stone spoke again. "Agents of the Ro are coming. Do not go home by a route or road. Go by way of cliff. Upon the cliff, when you want to know which way to go, take the second option, then the third, then the third, then when you are both together at the same place take the first, until you reach familiar ground."

The Light within the Stone went out. Karen put the Omphalos away quickly into her pack.

Karen looked out to the way they came, and she saw a gang in black cloaks rapidly approaching. She knew of one other route off the mountaintop, for she had climbed down that way once before. But as she looked down the back way, another group of menacing men approached in the distance. She scouted the surroundings for a third option.

Kalen followed his mother and saw what she saw, but he wondered about what he saw. The people were strangers, yes, but how could they be certain they were ill-intentioned? Was the word of the Stone so unimpeachable that it ought to be followed even if it leads into danger? He knew better than to ask such questions out loud, for when the Stone was concerned he knew little in comparison to his mother.

"Kalen!" she cried. "Come here!"

Karen stood at the mountain's steepest edge, a nearly vertical wall of limestone and gypsum. About a hundred feet below, a trail led off into the woods, if they could reach it.

"This is the way we must go. Have you ever climbed a cliff before?"

"Yes, but not like this. It's too high and steep."

Karen said, "I have done so, but not without a rope. But this is our way. We'll make it. You'll see. Follow my every move. Do what I say. You must focus."

She looked for options for lowering herself down and she saw two, one jutting rock which looked wide and steady and a second shelf which was narrow and precarious. She fought her instincts to take the seemingly safer route. The Stone had been very specific, and she knew it to be reliable.

Kalen found the narrow ledge almost an impossible step. He had to jump off the higher ledge into his mother's arms while she pushed him against the rock face. One slight misstep, and they would both go for a tumble. They scampered along the wall until the ledge disappeared and they needed to push themselves onto a lower spot. There were no ledges, but there were small handholds and footholds.

The first two options for hooking a foot looked good at first glance, but Karen kept looking for a third option. At last she saw a groove which looked promising. Other grooves lower down were right in line. She told Kalen to wait, and she lowered herself down a line of grooves to a ledge twenty feet below, placing her feet one groove at a time and shifting her body weight to keep balance. She called out to her child.

Kalen lowered himself down one groove at a time, barely breathing. His mother's legs were longer than his, and he was forced to take another way. His foot took a step that wasn't there, and he held himself up by his fingertips as his legs swayed back and forth.

Karen shouted, "Get a foothold!" Kalen's foot found a step just out of reach, if he only let go of his handholds for a moment. Karen pointed at a groove in a spot difficult for Kalen to see. "There's a spot for your foot where I'm pointing." When at last there seemed no other way, he let go.

His foot caught on a foot hold at the same time his right hand found a new spot. He looked downward and saw the ground below far off in the distance. He found another toe hold and then another, and soon descended to the ledge where his mother stood.

Kalen said, "We're almost there!" At the top, men gathered around and looked down the side of the mountain. Neither Kalen nor his mother knew the language, but they quickly gathered the intent: pursuit.

Karen: "We must be quick! Follow me!" Karen looked for a path to descend to ground below, and she set herself down upon the first groove she saw. Racing against the agents of Ro, this was not a time to second-guess the Stone.

She prepared to take another step down, but she grew concerned. Only one other option appeared for her, but there was a problem with it.

"Son, I'm taking a step now that's the only one I see. It's too far for you to take. Do you see a better route?"

Kalen looked and said, "There's a way down over here, but I'm not sure. How do I know if it will work?"

"Trust yourself," she said.

Kalen walked down the mountain by a separate route on a path requiring him to hug the mountain as he walked, but they both reached the ground at the same time. They looked above at the men climbing down the mountain above to their position.

"Run!" said Karen.

Who are the Ro? What do they want? Why are we running from them? What did the Black Stone mean by "I do not see a way forward at this time so that either you or your husband may live"? These were just a few of the questions Kalen wanted to ask, but he knew he would just have to wait.

They arrived at home at the same time as Kairon's carriage, and they found Chila, Jeila, and Kyle standing in the yard with swords for everyone ... even a short sword the right size for Kalen. Kalen had played with swords before, but never had he been happier to have one in his hand. They spoke of an urgent need to move, and to put the Stone in a safe location where it could not be stolen.

They even spoke of the Ro, but Kalen didn't understand much of what was said. What he understood and remembered is this: "The Ro are the forces of evil and darkness arrayed against us."

Kairon stayed awake, posting himself to guard at the front door. No more trouble appeared on the OTolan's doorstep that night, but there was sobbing late into the night when Karen and the last of the children finally fell asleep.

BEIONAI'S QUEST

ou're going to meet the Bear today," said Chila as she sat on Kalen's bed. "And then you're going to tell him the Secret of Life." As Kalen sat up in bed and rubbed his eyes, she added: "I'm going with you for protection!"

Kalen was too tired to get out of bed, but it didn't make a difference. His eldest sister brought him his outdoor tunic and shoes. He often felt like how he imagined a bear would feel upon waking from hibernation, recalcitrant and weak. She took his hands and yanked him out of bed and put a cup of curdled milk in his mouth.

Kalen asked, "What time is it?" He splashed water and soap on his face and cleaned himself.

"It's time to be off. We don't know where this bear of yours lives or how hard it will be to find him," said Chila.

She put a pack on Kalen's back. "We have packed for about three days. I hope we don't need to stay too long in the woods, but father thought it best to be prepared for a long journey. Is there anything else you need?"

Kalen looked around the house. His eyes darted to the carpet which hid the secret door which sometimes hid the Stone.

Chila said, "Not *that*. Father has taken it to a Vault for safe-keeping. Then he's going to sell our farm and arrange passage on a ship to Midian. Kyle is with him. They may be gone for days. Mother's off to visit our relations, and she has taken Jeila with her. They're going to come with us, if she can persuade them. They may also be gone for a while. It's just the two of us now."

"You should have woken me up," said Kalen. He felt awful. "We're moving to avoid the Ro. It wasn't a bad dream."

Chila bent down to look her younger brother in the eyes and said, "No, it wasn't a dream. But it's okay. Everything's going to be okay. We just need to behave knowledgeably or crazily." (She used a clever idiom that made Kalen laugh, a pun which literally means: Act. Nothing. Nutty. In Tolang, the language of the O'Tolan family, the glyphs for the three words are identical. Alas the pun does not translate well.)

"I'm sorry we didn't wake you up. Dad says you need extra sleep now to temporize." She offered her brother a hug, which he accepted.

Looking over her shoulder he saw someone outside. He ducked and stepped to the side of the window to investigate covertly.

Someone he didn't recognize was feeding their sheep. He wondered if the servant was still there in her reckoning of time, or if she had already gone on to work a long day, to cook a meal, and to go to bed ... and he was looking at a ghost, an echo of her past. But there she was. The paradoxes of time didn't make sense to him. He thought: How could time be moving differently for his family alone? Was time really passing more slowly for them, or were they simply aging more slowing?

The two children entered the woods at the far end of the farmland.

"We're not going to need swords!" shouted Kalen, furious that his sister was bringing swords. "He doesn't mean to harm us. I know it. He's a good bear."

Chila: "He's not a toy or a pet, Kalen! You can't pet him or play with him. He's ... I don't know what he is, but he's not like other bears. He's special."

Kalen: "You didn't believe in him the other day. What happened to you?"

Chila: "Father and mother consulted the Stone this morning while you slept. It said only one thing: 'Kalen must meet the Bear in the woods. Kalen must tell him the Secret of Life.'"

Kalen: "What does that mean?"

Chila: "Honestly we were all hoping you knew what it meant."

"Did mother or father say anything?"

"No."

"Help me. Tell me the answer!"

"I can't help you. You have to think of it."

"I think it's love. Nothing is more important than love."

Chila replied, "I don't suppose love is a secret. A secret is something dark and mysterious. Like the story of the woman who loses her wedding ring in the ocean so she gets her husband to promise not to go fishing. Then she sneaks off and turns into a fish so she can reach the bottom of the ocean and retrieve her lost ring, but when she was down there she bit into something shiny and it turned out to be a hook on her husband's fishing line!"

The sister and brother proceeded deeper into the shady and mysterious woods. Kalen felt like crying or stomping his feet, or both at the same time. It wasn't fair, this task. At any minute they could run into a brown bear who would demand to know an impossible riddle, and unless he offered exactly the right answer, he and his sister might be eaten. He's heard this sort of thing happen in fairy tales like so, and that's how it would surely happen to them as well.

After a few miles, Chila stopped for rest and to eat from wild berry bushes.

"I can't eat. My stomach is punishing me!" said Kalen. He pointed to a nearby tree. "I need to climb."

He scaled a nearby acacia tree and sprawled out in its topmost branches. There he began to think about the many times before he sat in a similar tree doing his language lessons. "I started learning letters since before I can remember, and then I sat with my siblings during their language lessons. How many years have I studied Tolang with my parents ... three years? Or thirty years? Or nearly two hundred years? I don't know."

Everywhere he looked, he saw the categories of nature described by his family's native language. In the sunny spots: hot; in shade: cool; in between, warmish. In the puddle, wet; on the ground, dry; in the middle, muddy. Soft trees, hard stones, and tree bark which is neither hard nor soft but somewhere in between. His stomach, neither empty nor full but in between. All of nature was a mirror of the central tenets of philosophy, *Yɪn* and *Yeɪŋ* and *Yʊŋ* (which may be written as Yin, Yang, and You). Yin appeared in the hot, wet, soft, and empty. Yang appeared in the cold, dry, hard, and full. You appeared in the mild, semi-wet, semi-soft, and semi-full. These were some of the main categories of philosophy, language, and nature.

Kalen thought: "What do bears know of such things? Surely they know of cold and hot and warmish! They feel wet and dry and semi-moist! They definitely know of full and partly-full and empty stomachs! I hope we meet the Bear when he has a full stomach! If bears know this much, then they must be able to learn Tolang! Maybe the bear already knows Tolang! That's silly. How could a bear possibly know a human language? Then again, how is it possible that I have been able to communicate with many different kinds of animals for over a year?"

The sound of his sister screaming pierced the air, and sent Kalen scrambling down the tree. He found her brandishing a sword at a mulberry bush. At a second glance, she was not standing opposed to a mulberry bush, but to a brown bear standing upright behind a mulberry bush. It made a fearsome sound unlike anything Kalen had ever heard before, a roar like the rumble of an empty stomach amplified many times.

Kalen positioned himself between his sister and the bear. His hand gripped the handle of the sword on his belt, but he relaxed and let go.

"Bear! I am Kalen and this is my sister Chila. Be gentle! Stand down."

The *Ursa arctos* let out another roar, which sent shivers of fear shooting down the boy's spine. It occurred to Kalen just then that Ro is at the start of Roar and at the front-center of

Growl, the sound a roused bear makes. Could this Bear be an agent of the Ro?

The Bear spoke. "Humans! I am Beionai. Be peaceful, my friends! Put down your weapons."

Kalen looked at his sister who was still brandishing a sword. "Do it!"

"Do what?" she asked.

"Can't you understand him? He said to put down your weapon."

Chila was perplexed. "Kalen, you are not speaking in Tolang. You and the Bear are both speaking in a strange way."

Kalen said, "Be that as it may, put down your weapon. He means us no harm. I will explain later."

Chila replied, "Fine. See what he knows."

Beionai stomped around for a while and then stood before Kalen. He was taller than a man when fully upright, but not fully grown. He stood upright again, and then extended his paw so that its soft pads faced the boy.

Kalen touched his hands to the paws, and he looked into Beionai's eyes. Up close the bear didn't look frightening at all, for his face was flush with curiosity and excitement.

"See what I know about what?" said the Bear. "What does your sister wish to know? I will tell you."

Kalen said, "It's nothing." The Bear communicated disapproval with a swipe of his finger, a nod, and an clicking sound. "Don't lie to me," was the apparent meaning.

Kalen said, "I'm sorry. Honestly, it's not about nothing. It's about the Black Stone. She wants to know what your connection is to the Supreme Omphalos."

Beionai stirred with excitement. He put his paws on the boy's shoulders. He said, "Your honesty is appreciated, Mister O'Tolan. I have never seen the Stone, and I wish to very much if it will have my audience. Do you have it here to show me?"

Kalen: "I haven't the Stone to show you. It is being put away in a safe place."

Beionai said, "That is probably wise, but I am very disappointed. Your family has kept it hidden well for so many long years, nearly a hundred and ninety by my reckoning. And in all this time, you have remained a young child, just as I have aged slowly in my own fashion. I have followed your family through decade after decade across countless houses and many dangers, for my destiny is linked to the Stone."

Kalen: "Beionai, how is it you know all this? All this was hidden from me, on account of my being a child, until very recently. I never spoke to the Stone directly until yesterday."

Beionai: "Is that so? How remarkable ... and worrisome. You are not as well learned as you ought to be, though it is not your fault.

"Ages ago, I befriended a Wizard who explained many things. He tutored me in language and philosophy. It is not chance which brings us together. The Wizard bid me to follow your family and keep my presence hidden until you were ready to know Who You Are."

Kalen said, "It's you I've seen, following me at times."

Beionai: "Yes, or you have seen one of my companions who travel with me from time to time. I am no ordinary bear, just as you are not ordinary. Not ... mortal. We were both born on the Isle of Delphos at midnight at the turning of the Ages. Spirit gave to us long life."

Kalen said, "I just found out I age slowly, my whole family does."

Beionai: "Yes, you do. We both do. But that alone is not enough to explain the odd experiences of temporizing and spacializing."

Kalen said, "You know about that?"

Beionai: "Oh yes, I have all my life. My mother and father and siblings were not as fortunate as yours. They did not temporize with me, and they passed away when I was only a few weeks old, as the Kalendar reckons time. When I was orphaned, the Wizard found me. He explained that you and I are both linked to the Omphalos of Delphi, and he set me on your trail."

Kalen: "So we share the same birthday and birthplace. O Beionai, I wish I could show the Stone to you. If the Stone were here, what would you ask it?"

Beionai: "I wish to know why I was made the way I am. Why should I watch as my bear companions live out their lives, and then pass away into dust, generation after generation? What use do I have in the universe, for surely I would not have been given this long lifespan for nothing? How much longer do I have to exist, if I should live to old age? Alas, the destiny and purpose of my life is a secret kept from me, hinted at by a coy Wizard and kept out of sight by a human family oblivious to my existence."

Kalen: "I don't know anything about Wizards. But you have moved me deeply, and I will help you to learn the answers you seek if I can."

Beionai: "You can! You definitely can!"

Kalen: "How?"

Beionai drew a circle in the dirt with a stick, and he drew an Enneagram in the circle. "The Wizard doesn't know everything. Much of what he knows he derives from the Kalendar. You must unfurl it, and tell us the meaning of Time. Don't you know that you are one with it? Your name says as much. Kalen is in Kalendar: Kalendar, the Kalen-Doer!"

Kalen: "You need me to bring forth a Kalendar?"

Beionai: "Yes, and it will help you. The calendars of men and bears mean nothing to immortal beings like you and me. But the Kalendar will tell us where we came from, what we can do in our time, and when we may expect to lessen at the end of our days. It can tell us when we may find relief from immortality. Tell me what you know of the Kalendar."

Chila whispered to Kalen: "I know you are speaking of the Kalendar. Are you sure it is wise to tell him of our family's wisdom? Can he be trusted?"

Kalen nodded. He said, "Beionai, my family uses a calendar different from other people. It's been in my mother's family for generations, and we use it to track the Three Seasons and the Nine Months and the Fifty-Four Weeks. We use it for lessons in language and mathematics and history and geography and philosophy, for the time units are also units of Space, Time, and Thought. In the Kalendar, the One and the Many are reconciled."

Beionai grew excited and he began to dance around gleefully. "You know of the Kalendar! Then certainly you must know of the Bear-Yak Zodiac?"

Kalen: "I think so. You mean the weeks. Bear is the first week of the year, and Yak is the year's last week."

Beionai: "Yes, that must be it! The weeks are named for animals?"

Kalen: "Many of the weeks have animal names, but some are animals I have never seen or heard, beasts with strange names who live in far-off places."

Beionai: "Now listen carefully to me, for I believe you possess knowledge without yet realizing its importance. The Kalendar you know is unlike any other calendar. It has the Bear-Yak Zodiac which is an ancient Star-Map of the First Ancestors. It envisions All Life in harmony with All Life. This is no small thing! It will allow communication among the species, and access to the worlds where the departed spirits dwell, the spirits of animals and human beings."

Kalen: "I will share with you what I know, but my siblings are further along in their lessons than I am. Chila could tell you more about the Kalendar than I."

Beionai: "Then I will ask her."

The Bear turned to his sister, who startled at the attention. He spoke in Tolang: "Sister of Kalen, I need knowledge which you possess."

Kalen and Chila exclaimed, "You know Tolang!"

The Bear continued, "Yes, I know the language of your house. Now listen, both of you. There is a prophecy among my kind of a Great Bear who walks the Earth without dying, One who will awaken bears and other animal species to take their rightful place in the Kosmos. The Bear of which the prophecies speak is said to be one who brings the Secret of Life, a Star-Map showing Fifty-Four animals arranged in a harmonious assembly from Bear to Yak. By use of this Zodiac, human beings and animals can live to learn in harmony with each other and with beings in the unseen realms. And the Great Bear is said to be one who will not only bring the Zodiac, but teach a universal language to the animals which is a gateway to their immortality. I am the one of whom these prophecies speak, the Great Bear. I need your help to bring the New Zodiac into being. Will you help me?"

Chila said, "Great Bear, there is a Star-Map contained within the Kalendar, but it is not complete. It requires astronomical observation and linguistic reconstruction. There are books among our family heirlooms which depict the Fifty-Four animals, but the names of some are missing. For others, the names are complete, but the location of the matching constellation has been forgotten. These books have been in my family's possession for generations..."

Beionai: "The Star-Map was given to you by the Omphalos?"

Chila said, "I don't doubt it."

Beionai: "If so, then the Bear-Yak Zodiac represents the original Order of Things, animals dancing and delighting in starlight, their passions known secretly and kept hidden by the Navel of the Earth."

Chila said, "Bear, I believe you may have drawn the wrong conclusions. The weeks of the Kalendar are named for animals, but the animals themselves are not depicted in the Star-Map. The constellations are of consonants, not animals."

Beionai looked amazed. "Consonants? Consonants in the Stars?"

Chila: "Yes. There are 27 consonants of Tolang and 27 letter-shaped constellations in the night sky. There are two animals associated with each letter. B is for Bear and Bat. P for Pig and a mythical animal called a Platypus. Father says it doesn't really exist, that it's made up."

Beionai: "Then the ancient legend is true! Kalen delivers the True Names of 9 million species by gifting me with a Zodiac depicting the letters of a Universal Language!"

Kalen: "What legend is that?"

Beionai: "It is a story passed down among the bears. It is known as the Battle of Red Cliffs. I always believed in it when others said it was myth. Kalen, you must know what it says about you ..."

As Beionai spoke, the thunderous clapping of horse hooves interrupted. A man with a gray beard who was dressed in black and gray robes rode up on a brown horse. His head was partly covered by a floppy brownish-black hood of the sort seen in those days on the heads of wandering magicians. The horse kicked up dirt which gave the appearance of its rider appearing in a cloud of smoke.

Beionai exclaimed, "Aupaiaaqua, Wizard of the Major Arcana of the Stone-Star Tarot, old friend!"

The Wizard said, "Dear Beionai, Kalen, Chila … There is no time for a proper greeting. The Ro have followed me here, and they will be upon us momentarily."

Another horse bounced into view and stood beside the first horse, larger with reddish-brown hair.

Aupaiaaqua said, "Come with me now, and we may yet live! Kalen, come with me! Chila and Beionai, I brought a horse for both of you! I do hope you know how to ride."

Chila said, "I can ride!" and mounted the larger horse. Beionai said, "I will run. I will trace your scent and trail when you have gone far ahead."

Aupaiaaqua said, "No Beionai. Ride with us. The enemy is fast approaching, and I will not leave you to be captured by their cruel underlings."

Kalen mounted the brown horse and took a seat next to the Wizard, and Beionai and Chila set on the second horse. In a moment the Wizard, two O'Tolans, and the Great Bear vanished on a trail leading deeper and farther into the wooded territory.

A PHILOSOPHY LESSON

t the far edge of the forest nearest to the inland desert region, the sun fell behind the horizon. Aupaiaaqua walked in a carefully plotted circle around the three children, two horses, and bear. His feet rolled past each other as he moved, his toes raised above his heels so they did not touch the ground. At each of nine stations around the circle, he muttered incantations in a language similar to Tolang as his body and hands shifted in a subtle dance. It was a form of Jiǔ Gua Zhang adapted for Eigr, a style of ritualistic magic of the sort originally used only by the Stone-Star Wizards, but later adapted for techno-magical purposes in the Third Millennium CE. It was a form of magical protection.

The incantation brought both Chila and Kalen to silence as their ears traced the sound waves permeating the circle. Kalen recognized the sounds of the letters, even if he didn't understand their meaning when put into the Wizard's words. At each station, the Wizard mouthed a series of similar words each containing one of the Secondary Vowels: /ɛ/ as in Bed, /o/ as in No, /æ/ as in Cat, /au/ as in Mouth, /aa/ as in Far, /eɪ/ as in Hey, /ɪ/ as in Pin, and /ʊ/ as in Push. There were eight such vowels, one for all but one of the Kalendar's months. The ninth secondary is /ʌ/ as in Cup, set right in the middle.

As Aupaiaaqua closed the circle, he spoke in Tolang: "Here in the Safe Zone, I invoke the sanctity of the land where the Corio Bay and the Barwon River meet. There five rivers converge to form the Lagoon of the Ducks. Here before the Separation of the Worlds, there is a trine to the Midnight's Bay and another trine to the entrance to the Maze of Mystery. By the power of the Great T'ai Hsuan, the Archetypes at this station, presided over by the alliance of the Queen of Swords and the King of Eggs, let this circle be sealed. Let the silence and protection of the heavens fall upon this spot and shield us from the roaming eyes and ears of the Ro and all unholy foes. Keep us safe until we need protection no longer, and give peaceful shelter and sound sleep tonight to Kalen, Chila, Beionai, Shämal and Hämal our steeds, and I, Aupaiaaqua, Servant of Volution's Way."

As he spoke, the birds stopped chirping, the tree branches stopped clanging in the wind, and the creatures stopped stirring in the woods. Actually, all of these things happened, but their sounds were sealed as if by a wall of stone. Kalen walked up to the edge of the circle and looked back at the Wizard. Wordlessly he spoke: "May I?"

The Wizard nodded. Kalen stepped across the boundary of the circle and the noises of the forest resumed. His sister spoke to Beionai within the circle, but he heard nothing of them. When he set his eyes within the circle firmly, he saw straight through to the other side. He stepped back into the circle and marveled at the feat of magic he had witnessed.

When Kalen's family discussed magic it was only regarding the use and handling of the Stone, and Kalen rarely heard much about that on account of his age. But there were stories told now and again regarding the Wizard Aupaiaaqua's visits to his grandparents, and he was well regarded.

Chila spoke to the Wizard. "Kalen and I have heard stories telling of Wizards, but we have never seen one. Have we?" Kalen shrugged.

Chila continued, "Do please introduce yourself properly and explain what we have seen."

Kalen took a seat next to Chila and Beionai near the circle's middle. The Bear put his paw on Kalen's shoulder for a while, then settled into a sitting posture which made him appear to be meditating.

The Wizard said, "My name is Aupaiaaqua, which simply means Wizard as you know already," (he spoke in this way because while the words are pronouned differently their glyphs are identical in Tolang to ten demarcations). "I am the Wizard of the Major Arcana in the Stone-Star Tarot, which is known to my friend Beionai, and a few other remarkable beings alive today. We Wizards are few and rarely seen, and in those instances where we are seen it is either on account of dire circumstances or folly. I have long believed that a Wizard who interferes in the affairs of humankind and bears and other creatures is either desperate or untrustworthy. I may have been in error for thinking so, or perhaps an enduring state of desperation is now here, for necessity requires that I meddle."

Kalen yawned involuntarily, and then leaned back on the Bear, using his soft and plush fur for a pillow.

"You may as well get comfortable, for the Ro are actively searching for you, and we will not move from this place tonight, and it may be unwise to move on land for many days now. We shall see."

Chila said, "Tell us about the Ro. I want to know everything about them, and why we have to fear them."

Aupaiaaqua said, "The Ro are the upsetters of things, plotting darkly and secretly the overthrow of All-That-Is for another Reality that is from our perspective chaotic and immoral to speak the best of it. They would subvert light for darkness, good for evil, life for death. I shall start at the beginning of things, to put them in perspective.

We must go to the First Wave, the time before the emergence of the Subtleties out of the indistinct unity of All-That-Is. This is the dwelling place of Kosmic Time and Kosmic Space and Kosmic Thought in a state of unity. Little can be said about it in language as coarse and brutish as our own, Tolang, and ours is a more subtle meaning-system than most. This is the realm of the Aal-Wiz, the first angels so alike to the divine mind that their thoughts are as mirrors. The First Wave dominated the ancient past, but it is still present and accessible to a mind possessing consciousness, clarity, and quietude."

"In the Second Wave of Existence, two forces came forth out of nothing, and they were called Yin and Yang, symbolized by the Tai Chi symbol or Bagua, which were on the family crests of your distant ancestors. All of Reality was painted with Duality: The One and The Many, The Ideal and The Material, The Essence and The Existence, Thought and Action, Being and Becoming. These Dualities cascaded through Space, Time, and Thought until the pattern began to dissolve of its own accordance. Goodness and Evil were among the dualities postulated, and in due course the Evil began to twist and deform the rest of the Order, bringing judgments of better or worse to the distinctions which were not inherent. A war of opposites ensued. In turn the order of Duality began to pass away, turning Becoming into Consumption, Action into Self-Aggrandizement, Existence into the

Imperative to Control. It was a wickedness given many names by many religions and philosophies, associated with many devils and demons and dark entities. (It is best not to name them lest we give them power, ever blessed be the Aal-Wiz of Yahweh.) In order to defeat the forces of this evil, the Benevolent Powers of the Universe which were overseen by the Supreme Governor of the Realm of Governance had to evolve. The Godhead *evolved* and *involved* at the same time, actually: meaning that they became what they were not, and that which is not became them. Thus came a Third Wave of Existence in which the Three forces came out of the One, alongside and integrating the Two, and they were called Yang and Yin and You, and they were symbolized by the T'ai Hsuan symbol or Jiǔ Gua, which has been depicted on your family crest for twelve generations. And so All-That-Is become a Trinity: The Creator, The Redeemer, and The Sustainer; The Good, The True, and The Beautiful; The Physical, The Subjective, and The Objective; to speak nothing of other overly abstract understandings.

"Out of the One came Two. Out of the Two came Three. Out of the Three, came a Myriad. The Three appeared at the Third Wave of Existence out of necessity, because a new weapon was needed in the fight of Good against Evil. In the Second Wave, Yin-Yang, language is primitive, full of simple oppositions, grunts and gestures perceived most dimly. It is proto-language. The Divine Logos is implicit, prototypical. In the Third Wave, Yin-Yang-You, language is robust and full of bewildering possibilities for expression. The Divine Logos is incarnate, manifest, evolving. The evolution of language is the evolution of Logos. No longer does Reality seem to be dominated by a division of Good and Evil; instead there are subtleties, complexities, and a vast variety of forms of existence. Instead of black or white, there are a multitude of shades of gray! Vast, seemingly absolute and irreducible plurality is the result of the Myriad, plurality of thought, feeling, action, and forms of life! There are not just seven deadly sins, but seven thousand ways to go astray. There is not just one Absolute Truth, there are a potentially infinite number of perspectives on Reality. I say that such pluralism only seems to be absolute and irreducible because in fact there is a hidden order implicit in the Three, an organizing principle which can ensure that the orders of the Second Wave are not swept away in a wash of entropic neutrality. In fact, there is not one organizing principle for the Third Wave, there is two. The first organizing principle is the T'ai HIsuan itself and the Jiŭ Gua, an expression of a righteous Kosmos in harmony with the Way of Volution (or simply the Way). The Jiŭ Gua, as the Great Bear will tell you, is a depiction of the New Zodiac, also called the Bear-Yak, and it is vital that Beionai continue his work to educate the Wise Animals in its teachings. But I digress.

"There is a third principle, mysterious and elusive, which brings Yin and Yang together. It is Volution's essence, of course! Children, I wish the story could end on a cheerful note, but the ways of evil are cunning and adaptive. The second organizing principle of the Third Wave is the Ro, which is known at the Second Wave as The Beast. The Ro gathers forces of chaos and darkness to itself: shame, shadow, oppression, guilt, killing, murder, war, torture, hatred. It is the darkest and most obscure and least moral force that is anywhere, and it dominates the Road upon which the Way must be walked. There are a multitude of paths we may take, and some of these paths become a road which to which we must align ourselves. A road is a path, but a path is not a road; roads have been paved with the weight of much energy, for better or worse. There is peril in taking just any road. Some lead to extinction and others to cataclysm and catastrophe and unspeakable horrors. You must be brave not to lose hope in face of the threat. They have many appearances and go by many names, and the worst face of all is the face of the Ro within each of us."

Kalen said, "The Ro is within us? How can this be?"

Aupaiaaqua said, "Yes. The Ro comingles with our human nature - or bear nature," as he shot a glance to Beionai, who looked like a pupil who has heard this lesson before. "The Ro aspect inheres in the dark speech, language which does violence to Reality. All the worst words with the most inauspicious characterics commune secretly in the Ro's jurisdiction bonded by powers which we only dimly understand and would surely go mad to attempt it. There are words congruent with harmonious and virtuous Volution, and then there are Words of Error."

Kalen asked, "What are those?"

Aupaiaaqua said, "They are words which tell lies about the nature of things, Kalen, lies which may once have been justified like a stick may be used to train a wild dog, but which in their continued adherence harm the body, soul, and spirit alike. They are words with the power to destroy Worlds, even the World of the Deep Pool of the Center Heart, the One and Only Deep Pool of the Center Heart. Words of Error may be combined to horrible effect to create massive and destructive delusions for individuals, cultures, and societies. They threaten Existence itself."

Kalen said, "I don't understand. Are these words like 'shit'?" Chila laughed awkwardly.

Aupaiaaqua said, "It is hard for you to understand this, child, because from the time of your birth your parents schooled you in Tolang, a language which your forebears received from my tutoring. And I received Tolang from the First Ancestors who anticipated the emergence of the Ro as a Power in our time. In Tolang, words sound and look like the nature of things, Kalen, as they really are to Spirit and for Spirit ... aspects of the principle of harmony and order in the T'ai Hsuan and Jiǔ Gua in the Third Wave of its unfolding. But this is not how other people talk!"

Beionai added, "Nor other bears."

Aupaiaaqua said, "Indeed not. Kalen, if you wanted to pour water into a vase, but didn't have a vase, what letter would you pour it into?"

Kalen laughed. "The fifth letter, V. It is the shape of a Vase, of course. You can pour water in the opening at the top and it will remain."

Aupaiaaqua said, "Exactly the point. But in other languages water gets poured into Vase shaped like an S, which is a surface without the space to put it, or a D which makes a good door or dam but offers not a vessel, or an F which is too fluid to hold it. The Vase needs the Valve and the Valley which are inherent in its sound-meaning, and there is no other way to put it. But other languages have no grasp of the obvious. They are driven by the Ro into cacophony!

"The Ro is within and without, individual and collective. In all Eight Zones of the Atlas of Uvoha does it dwell, operating invisibly through the power of intention, action, structure, and karma. But we were speaking about language. If we stay here for long, Kalen, we must have some language and philosophy lessons so you may see for yourself the absurdity which characterizes the speech of the vast majority of humankind – and animalkind. The word for it is 'babel'. Do you know what that word means?"

Kalen replied, "I haven't heard this word before, but I know its place on the Kalendar. It means something which is bad-in-potential, that which could become bad, but it is just nonsense or outright lie – 'bull'."

Aupaiaaqua said, "You know every date on the Kalendar has many correspondences which guide you in learning, but imagine that you had no Kalendar. If that were the case, you could not know what the word meant by looking at its place in the Scheme of Things. You would have to be told its meaning by someone in authority, and shown its meaning again and again to learn all the unwritten rules of its usage, which are often complex and contradictory. Seeing the interpenetration of language and reality would be a task formidable, pun intended."

Kalen said, "I never learned too much of the languages other people use. Father always learned enough for us to get along no matter where we lived, and he said that he didn't want my ears polluted, whatever that means. But I have started to have a new language coming up inside me which allows me to talk to animals, some of them. Do you know what that is about?"

Aupaiaaqua said, "Beionai speaks it as well, but I do not. It is new. It is an emergent language, similar to Tolang but more telepathic and gestural than verbal. It does not have a name unless one of you has named it recently. How does this language make you feel, Kalen?"

"I feel good. Warm-hearted."

Aupaiaaqua replied, "I am pleased to hear that. Perhaps one day you or Beionai will give the language a name, and teach it to other people and animals."

Kalen said, "They're not Words of Error, are they?"

Aupaiaaqua said, "I cannot say for sure, but I trust in your spirit. Quite the opposite, I believe."

Chila asked, "What does this all have to do with the Omphalos?"

Aupaiaaqua said, "The Omphalos is one of the nine Artifacts of Orr, remnants of an earlier Wave, memorialized through the Stone-Star Tarot. The Stone-Star was used by the First Ancestors to transmit the knowledge and wisdom to guide the Third Wave and keep it from ruin. Along with the T'ai Hsuan itself, these nine objects are the most ancient and primordial expressions of the Yin-Yang-You. They contain raw and pure intelligences which are *Reik,* living objects. Relationships may be formed with them for purposes of good or evil, order or chaos. In the right hands, the nine intelligences can bring about wonderful and good things. In your hands, Kalen, they could heal and transform the Worlds. But if the nine Artifacts fall into the hands of the Ro, it would spell our certain doom.

"One more thing. It is said that the Omphalos is the Navel of the Earth, but listen carefully: I believe this is a misstatement of fact. If my suspicions are correct, the artifact is better described as Navel of the Kosmos. Its consciousness is Kosmo-centric, meaning that its allegiance is not limited to our planet or our civilizations, but to Kosmic forces which are beyond even my own comprehension. It is not only ancient and sentient, but *Vogaan*, alien. Be prudent. Do not rely upon it unconditionally. There are enemies of our civilization who dwell among and beyond the stars apparent in the night sky, civilizations which would seek to destroy us if they could, and they use the Artifacts of Orr to meddle with us. Use the Artifacts seldomly. It is not wise to open channels that better remain shut."

More philosophical and linguistic discussions followed in the hidden spot in the forest for many weeks, and Kalen bonded with the Wizard and the Bear. Kalen was adept at philosophy and enjoyed learning about it almost as much as he enjoyed teaching the Wizard elements of the unnamed language. Chila saw him grow up more in those weeks than any other time she had ever seen him. Slowly the 5-year-old child she knew started to become less a boy and more like a young man who had seen more than a century rise up and pass away.

As the weeks wore on, food grew scarce and the children foraged. Aupaiaaqua told them not to hunt because the balance of energies in the cosmos were particularly volatile and ought not be disturbed by killing.

The Wizard left for days at a time, looking for news in the outside world regarding the whereabouts of Kalen's parents and the rest of his siblings. Once he returned to find Kalen and Chila feasting on a pair of wild rabbits which they had trapped and skinned. He exclaimed, "Foolish children! This is not a good omen!"

The next week, the Wizard returned at dusk with Kyle and two unknown men. Neither Kalen nor Chila recognized either of them. Aupaiaaqua introduced them to Kalen by saying, "These are your uncles, Gailon and Dro. Gailon is your mother's brother, and Dro is his husband." Actually Gailon was not Kalen's uncle at all, but a much more distant relation, a son of a son of a son of a son of a son of one of Karen's brother's grandsons. Karen's last living brother had died over a hundred and fifty years earlier, but it was not the time for explaining such peculiar genealogy. It is suffice to say that Gailon was the closest thing Kalen and Chila had to an uncle at that point in time.

Kyle and Jeila ran to Kalen and Chila put their arms around them both as they sobbed. Beionai growled. Wordlessly they spoke the truth.

Aupaiaaqua said, "May the souls of Karen and Kairon O'Tolan rest in peace, and may the blessings of the Omni Benevolent One come now to rest upon their children. They are gone, but their death was not in vain. Before they were murdered by the Ro, they found two uncles who can guard over their children and they secured a Vault in which they placed the family's fortunes and the destiny of us all."

Kyle then pulled out a simple brass key on a chain, and gave it to his little brother. "Kalen, this is for you."

Bereaved, Kalen bravely took the key.

GAILON AND DRO

alen put the Vault's keychain around his neck and tucked the key under his shirt. He wiped tears from his cheeks and looked around himself. There were three grief-stricken siblings who shared his pain, two uncles he never knew about, a protective and powerful Wizard, and a bear who was immortal like himself. They stood in a hidden camp surrounded by the flowers and scraggly branches of *Boswellia sacra* trees.

Aupaiaaqua attended to Kyle and Jeila, who were bruised and weakened, with healing spells and remedies. Chila brought them water from the bucket, and the four of them reclined off to one side of the circle. Somewhere in the branches above, a nighthawk punctuated the nocturne with squawks.

Kalen couldn't believe that his parents weren't there and would not be coming back to him. One moment he was numb with this thoughts, and then a moment later he thought: I never got to say goodbye to them. Mom and dad left without saying goodbye, they left while I was sleeping, and they didn't even wake me!

Tears flooded the boy and washed him to the ground, where he was met by the reassuring touch of his uncle Gailon. Kalen welcomed a hug from this large and scruffy-looking man in his thirties.

"I too have lost my parents," said Gailon tearfully. "I know what it is like for you and your siblings. You are very brave, the bravest children I have ever met."

He then looked at Beionai, who was sitting dog-like at Kalen's feet. "Incredibly you are so fearless as to have a bear as a pet!"

Beionai growled angrily. Kalen said, "Beionai is not a pet. He's his own bear."

In the unnamed language, the Bear said, "Thank you, my friend Kalen."

Gailon said to the Bear, "I'm sorry."

In Tolang, Beionai replied, "Don't mention it. After all, we were not properly introduced. I am Beionai, a friend of the family."

Gailon laughed and almost fell to the meadow's ground. He just said, "Incredible! I don't believe it. You're a talking animal!"

Beionai said, "You are surprised that I talk. Are you too not an animal? All animals talk, if you have the ears to listen."

Dro was a handsome tattooed fellow who resembled Gailon quite a bit, though he was shorter and thinner. He approached the Bear and said, "I am inclined to agree with you, Beionai, though it would surprise most humans to learn of it. Are you the only talking bear, or do you have friends and family to talk to?"

Beionai asked, "You are not O'Tolan by birth and yet you speak Tolang?"

Dro said, "Certainly. Gailon is teaching me. I am still learning."

Beionai said, "I communicate with other bears through a simple language of growls and movement. I have tried to teach Tolang to other bears, but it is not for them. There is an energy-language which may be more in tune with their nature. Kalen and I have some work to do on it, don't we, Kalen?"

Kalen said, "Yes, I suppose we do. It is awfully important that all beings are able to communicate with each other, isn't it?"

Beionai said, "Yes, when they are ready to do so, but not before. I have made some human friends over the course of the better part of two hundred years, but none spoke Tolang. It would have been futile for me to talk to them. And I find languages other than Tolang to be very unnatural and unintelligible."

Gailon and Dro, who were still mesmerized by the talking bear, mouthed "two hundred years!" At the same time, Kalen pointed to

Aupaiaaqua and said, "You say you didn't speak to humans, but surely you spoke to the Wizard ..."

Beionai said, "The Wizard looks human, but he is not. He is an Archetype, semi-divine ..."

Aupaiaaqua, muttering spells at the edge of the circle, did not join the conversation.

Dro spoke again to the Bear. "How is it that a bear speaks of having walked the Earth for nearly two centuries?"

Beionai replied in Tolang: "I am one of the Animo Hemitheoi, one of the Semi-Divine Animals, which I call the Animwaa. According to legend, there are Fifty-Four of us, one from virtually every branch of the Tree of Life. I cannot speak for the other Animwaa, but I have been around for many generations of my kind, aging at a rate which corresponds not to natural patterns but to the Kalendar. I am still rather young in Animwaa years."

Gailon said, "Do you speak of the Kalendar of my family, the one with the T'ai Hsuan for seasons, the Artifacts of Orr as the months, and the Bear-Yak Zodiac for weeks?"

Beionai: "Yes, it is this calendar which tracks my life force. I have seen its depiction in the scrolls of the Wizard."

Kalen asked, "These other Animwaa ... have you met them?"

Beionai said, "Only a few. I have met a Bison and a Beaver and a Bat and a Pig and a Tortoise who have long life and all of whom know how to communicate in the energy-language without a name. They were untutored in its nature, yet it came to them replete with the True Names. I have told them about you Kalen, and they know of my search for the Bear-Yak Zodiac."

Kalen said, "We will share what we know with you when we return to our farmhouse. You can have the Star-Maps from our family archives for your quest. Then what do you do?"

Beionai said, "There is a very wise Animwaa who is also in the Major Arcana of the Stone-Star Tarot. I will go at once to meet with her. I must discuss the Battle of Red Cliffs with her."

Kalen said, "You have mentioned this Battle of Red Cliffs before. Tell me about it."

Beionai avoided Kalen's gaze. He looked at Gailon and spoke. "Kalen's Uncle, is there a story among your people concerning the fate of Kalen? That is to say, how he will meet his end?"

Aupaiaaqua, at the other end of the circle, perked his ears to the conversation. Gailon said, "Little is said in my family about Kalen save that he is the Bearer of the Omphalos, which will come to him when he is ready for it, and which he must carry ever eastward. We are told not to ask for petty favors from the future-seeing stone, and not to speak of it outside the family. What Kalen will do, and how he will 'meet his end' are not spoken of, though it is generally assumed I think that he will live a very long life."

Beionai said, "Kalen, the Battle of Red Cliffs concerns your death. I do not know if it is wise to speak of it again. We shall ask ..."

"The Wizard?" spoke Aupaiaaqua, who appeared suddenly behind Beionai.

"Yes," said the Bear, surprised. "You know of what I speak. Is it wise to tell Kalen?"

Aupaiaaqua said, "Not today. There are other matters more important. When the time comes, you may tell him, if you get the chance."

And then the Wizard turned silent, as if he had something important to say. Kyle and Jeila and Chila stood up and came forward, and everyone gave him their attention.

Aupaiaaqua said, "Sit down, everyone. Before we can move on from here, we must know what happened to bring us to this point. Now who will speak of Karen and Kairon, and how they spent their last days?"

Jeila said, "I will do so, Aupaiaaqua, for while I have known you only a short time you have shown yourself trustworthy. Although my family keeps its distance from strangers, I believe my parents would have wanted us to trust you."

"It was the 26ᵗʰ Day of Black Stone. Mom and Dad taught us a verse for that Day of the Kalendar:

Lemur of Madagascar,
leaping like a monkey
in spiny forest glen.

Four pounds and twelve ounces,
from branch to branch you spring,
bouncing every now and then.

"I've never seen a Lemur, nor visited Madagascar, but it sounds like a fine place. However, from this point, I'll always remember Black Stone 26 as the day mother and I set out to find our relatives. Why she needed to visit them so suddenly and urgently she did not say, though eventually it all came out into the open. Before we left, we consulted the Stone in the early morning hours, but it offered no counsel except to give an errand for Kalen. It was decided that Chila, the eldest, would stay as his guardian and to help him on his errand. The rest of us set out with our horses before the dawn, mother and I traveling with father and Kyle as far as the city. When we reached Warshon, father and Kyle stayed with us as we visited my parents' friends, a merchant and a metal worker, a basket maker and a town official. Father and Kyle spoke with them alone, and when they were done, mother asked them if they had seen any of our relations in the area recently. This took a while because mother had to describe a variety of aunts and uncles, their names and appearances, and what they might have been doing in the city. One of the city-folk, a basket maker named Halgan, said she had sold a basket to an aunt of hers who was returning from an expedition to the coast, only a few years ago. She remembered my aunt on account of the family shield, the T'ai Hsuan, which both she and my mother wore as ear-jewelry. They were headed west to Aithiops, where they dwelt. Mother thanked the lady for her help and then bought a basket. After conferring with father, it was decided that mother and I would hire a carriage and driver who would take us there, while the men continued on the road to Berpa in search of a Vault. I do not know why they planned to split up, but there must have been a very good reason. I felt a bit like the lemur, bouncing from one place to another, just a wee thing in a much larger universe. We stayed in an inn in the city one more night while we arranged a carriage and provisions, and then mother and I left for the westward city. We parted from the men at mid-morning, and it was the last time I saw father. We traveled by day and at night took what inconspicuous shelter could be found. The road is a dangerous place, and we were never far from our swords, but grace shone upon us and we did not meet trouble that we could not handle.

"By evening on the fifth day, we found our relatives at last, Mako and Mataan O'Tolan, parents of Gailon, who dwelt in a village in Aithiops called Werden. They were pleased to see us, but also weary. They soon informed us that there was a traveler in the village who bore a Rat emblem on a ninja's uniform. This villager had been known to ask about the O'Tolan clan and the Omphalos, and he had frequently been seen wandering about close to the O'Tolan residence. They were being watched by Ro. We kept a lookout, and talked late into the night. Mom did most of the talking, but they asked me many questions, including many about Kalen. Mataan met Kalen once when he was a child about Kalen's age, though now he was old and feeble."

Kalen interrupted: *"That* Mataan! He's my age. We're pals. We just played together a couple of years ago. Isn't that right?"

Chila said, "No Kalen. You played together a couple of years by the Kalendar's time, but not the world's time, not *his* time. He is an old man now. You must learn to think on two planes." Kalen seemed dumbstruck.

Jeila continued: "In the morning, Mataan sent someone to fetch Gailon with a message. I don't know what it said, but I assume he bade Gailon to come."

Gailon interrupted: "It was an astonishing note! My father informed me of a visit from Karen and Jeila, and begged me to come at once because Kalen urgently needed our help. He said the very fate of the Deep Pool of the Center Heart was at stake. I knew of Kalen a bit from family legends, but never thought that I would actually meet him. I came the very next morning. My home is in Walca, a day's journey from Welden. The note arrived just as I was closing up the pottery shop, which Dro and I have together. I should say, *had* together, for that night we consulted our own house oracle. It is not an omphalos, but it is a scrying ball which has a fairly good track record nevertheless. It told us that when we leave we would not be coming back. As a precaution, we put the shop in the care of Dro's sister and told her not to expect our return. The two of us set out to my parents' house. I only wish I could have made it there sooner ..."

Jeila said, "The barbaric Ro minion came to the door the next day sporting his evil-looking, rodent-crested uniform. Where he stood, roaches scurried in every direction, oozing off his body. I stood behind the front door and smelt his foul odor. It said that it was a representative of the Redro of Regnuh, Gatherers of the Artifacts of Orr. Pillagers is more like it! It said there was one object, a black see-ing-stone of some importance which had been stolen, and it demanded to have it returned. It was willing to pay five hundred bits for it. Mako and Mattan said they knew nothing of the stone (mother and I stayed hidden), and they bade them to leave and not come back. But the Ro asked about the T'ai Hsuan symbol on Mako's necklace, and it grew incensed. That night many of them returned, more than a dozen. They quickly blocked the exits with boards and nails, and then they set the house aflame. I was not there, for mother hid me in a neighbor's cellar and told me to stay there until she came for me. She never came! She was burned alive with Gailon's parents!"

Dro said, "We arrived the following evening and had the task of inspecting the still-smoking rubble. We found the remains of a man and two women: my father-in-law, mother-in-law, and Karen. They were beautiful people, and it is such a shame to have lost them, though I pray we shall be reunited in the hereafter."

Gailon continued, "We knew of Jeila from my father's letter, but we could not find her. I thought to check the neighbor's cellar, for it was a hiding place I knew well from my childhood games. I called out to her by name, and she came to me."

Dro pulled a simple urn from his bag and set it before Kalen. He said, "There is something most peculiar I must ask of the Wizard, and I hope it is not too upsetting a topic for the children. Speaking of Karen's remains, they were remarkable. The fire turned her to ash as hard as a cake and shiny as silver, still in the shape of a woman. We put some of the remains in an urn, and the rest were buried alongside Mako and Mattan. Do you know why this is?"

Kalen looked at the urn and couldn't believe he was looking at his mother. Aupaiaaqua said, "It is most interesting. I have encountered remains of this sort before. They are not human remains. They are the remains of an Archetype."

A few moments later Aupaiaaqua began to draw three lines in the dirt: two unbroken lines followed by a broken line: Yang, Yang, and Yin.

"Purity!" he said. "I believe Karen was the Archetype of Purity in the Stone-Star Tarot, for she lived and died selflessly, and in her final act protected her children and the sanctity of the Pool of the Center Heart, the True Home of the Artifacts of Orr. It is possible she didn't know for herself that she was an Archetype, for the perfect-hearted would have no need to know of such things. It is bewildering for children to lose a mother; it is likewise bewildering for a civilization to lose its Archetype of Purity. Few are now aware of this loss, but I am, and it is troubling to me. She dwelt among us once; we have our memories of her which cannot be taken away."

The Wizard paused while he wept. After some time in silence, Gailon said, "If I may continue ... my own mother and father deserved to have a better funeral than we had time to prepare, but we put them to rest in accordance with our family traditions more or less, and then set out with Jeila to her homestead. She was a true guide, but the dust storms were ferocious, and we took detours in an effort to throw off unwanted followers. Ten days later, we arrived at the homestead to find it empty."

Kyle interrupted: "That was two weeks ago. Father was still alive then, but he was being tortured by the Ro."

Chila held Kalen closer, and Jeila gave them a blanket from the pack she brought from home.

Dro said, "Wizard, what do the Ro want? Explain it to me so I can understand!"

Aupaiaaqua said, "The Redro of Regnuh is one of the wickedest and most venerable manifestations of the Ro. They are what is left of Evil in the Second Wave, the T'ai Chi, which has become adapted to a new purpose. With the coming of the Third Wave, they have spread out across the globe in an effort to find and take the Artifacts of Orr, the nine most sacred manifestations of the T'ai Hsuan. With these objects, they will feed on All-That-Is, consuming it, loosed in a reign of violence and chaos. The Black Stone is the Artifact which guards the Deep Pool of the Center Heart. If they take the Black Stone, they will have access to the most sacred Reality, the Source of Life itself, which they would pollute and poison, bringing unto ruin all beings who are dependent upon water."

Kyle hadn't the heart to speak, but he had finally built the courage. "Father took me to Berpa, but the Vault wasn't there anymore. The Vault is not a place; it's a person."

Aupaiaaqua said, "The Vault is an Archetype of the Major Arcana of the Stone-Star Tarot."

Kyle said, "I guess so. He …"

Aupaiaaqua said, "… or she or it …"

Kyle said, "Yeah. He or she or it can look like anyone or anything. It changes shapes."

Aupaiaaqua nodded.

Kyle said, "We looked for the Vault everywhere, and kept looking. We moved up and down the coast. I asked father who he was looking for, and he said there are Tarot cards of the minor arcana who could help us; they could lead us to the Vault if he found them. He described them to me, and I dimly remembered them. There were pictures of them in the library. At last we found a card, but it was nothing like I had imagined. It was a rock quarry where seven workers were picking out rocks and stacking them in a pile."

Kalen said, "It was the Seven of Stones. I remember this card from the Tarot album. It looks like a metal dragon."

Kyle said, "Yes, but not so fast. We approached the quarry from the hilltop, and our angle on it was askew. Father said it was important not to approach a card when our view of it was reversed, so we descended along the side of the quarry to the base until we had a proper view at last. Thereupon a foreman came to ask us to leave.

"Father asked to be shown to the Vault, but the conversation was going nowhere. The foreman looked at us like we were crazy ... until father took the Stone out of his pouch. The foreman excused himself, and returned with the other six men, each of whom looked at the Stone as if they were looking at their own infant. 'May I hold the Omphalos?' asked the Seven. But father put it away, and said that he was not its Bearer, only its Keeper and it was not his place to part with it, even if he were inclined to do so. The Seven stepped aside and spoke amongst themselves, and then they came and said, 'We will help you only if you allow us to hold the Stone and ask it a question.'

"Father balked, and he asked how could he be sure they wouldn't abscond with it the moment he let them touch it. The Seven replied that if they wanted to rob him they could have done so already. Father wasn't convinced, but he said he would allow them to touch it while he held the Stone. At last in agreement, the Seven touched the Stone and asked, 'When can we stop moving things higher?' And the Stone replied, 'You may stop whenever you wish, if you are prepared to accept the consequences.' Father nodded, and the Seven asked, 'What are the consequences if we stop moving things higher?' And the Stone replied, 'Then Eight, Nine, and Ten and the rest of the number world will fall, and a parade of Sixes will stretch endlessly, full of malice and duplicity and rebellion. They form the abode of the Ro. The Sums will never come out even, because the Seven will not have Evened their Suchness. The fate of the number world is in your hands, so make your choice.' That is what it said. And then the Sevens were satisfied, and they took us to see the Vault.

"The Vault looked like an ordinary token-exchanger, a typical merchant who aids the farmers and traders with loans. He wore a tan-colored tunic with a greenish flat-topped hat. There was one in the city nearest to the stone quarry, a dreary place called Quorya. I stood by father as he dealt with the person. Father gave him the Stone tucked inside a leather pouch for safekeeping which he promised never to open, and he said he must return the pouch only to himself, his wife, or one of his children. He showed the merchant a parchment with our portraits drawn on it. The Vault didn't seem all that interested. He gave us a key and said goodbye. Father said, 'When we have need to find you again, how shall we find you?' And then the merchant said, 'You found me once. Your child Kalen will find me again.' Father never mentioned Kalen's name, so that was rather odd, but that is what the Vault said. That's when father turned his back and walked away, and then he stopped in his tracks. He was shot with an arrow which pierced his stomach. Father handed me the key and told me to run, and the Vault opened the gate to the back of his shop. I didn't know what to do. I left through a back door and climbed to the roof so I could see what was going on. The Ro were carrying father away. There was a small group of them, and a couple split off to find me, so I hid. When it felt like I was no longer being hunted, I went to see the Vault. He said the Ro would not attack him right away, but he must disappear soon because they would bring reinforcements to take the Stone by force. He told me of the place where the Ro took father, and he escorted me to some ruins through back channels to avoid detection. I saw dad again one more time from a distance hidden in the bushes, and he was near death. They were taking hot pokers to him, and though they tried to force him to reveal the location of the Omphalos and its Bearer, he would say nothing. His last words were, 'Go to hell!', and then he impaled himself on a knife. He passed on."

His tale was causing his siblings and uncles and Beionai to listen with fear and amazement. Aupaiaaqua added, "I found the boy in Quorya, which regrettably was nearly the last place I thought to look. I came too late to do anything for Kairon. Kyle took me to the ruins, but we could find no sign of his body, not even a tossed off shoe. I am sorry. We went straightaway to the homestead, encountering some foes along the way, but they were unprepared to meet a Wizard's fire. We lived and they did not."

The O'Tolans huddled together that cold night, the children under one cover and Gailon and Dro not far away under their own cover. Aupaiaaqua stayed awake much of the night, talking to a nighthawk to keep himself company. Rain fell outside the circle but not within, owing to the Wizard's enchantment. Kalen slept with the urn of his mother's ashes in his arms.

THE ANIMWAA GATHER

Beionai found two books in the O'Tolan's library pertaining to the Star-Maps of the First Ancestors. Whereas most of the family's belongings were ransacked and taken, these were kept hidden in a stealthy compartment underneath a rug. He said goodbye to Kalen with great sadness, but he knew that their paths would cross again soon enough.

"When I am done with my business, I will find you wherever you go, Kalen," the Bear said. "Remember to often climb high and look out over vast distances, because it is essential for the *spacializing*. And remember that we share a birth date and will *temporize* together while we sleep."

Kalen didn't want him to leave, but he knew the Bear had his own way. Led by the Wizard, Kalen and his siblings and uncles headed east to Warshon, and then they planned to head to the coast to catch a boat to Arabia.

The Bear watched them disappear into the distance on the road, and then he turned to go into the forest on his own. After a while, he stopped to eat berries and read his books. At first perusal, he found the materials quite elaborate and informative. The text of one book was a collection of astronomical lore common among humans which the Bear had never seen before in Tolang. The second book appeared to contain words written by the O'Tolans, taken verbatim from the speech of the Omphalos.

It said that the First Ancestors came to the Earth from another World, and they left a Star-Map which would allow the inhabitants of the Earth to return to their Source far above in the heavens and not get lost in the cosmos. The map described would not only point the way to the Source, but depict the nature of the civilizations in the heavens above in many different Worlds. Over time, the patterns of the Kosmos would reverberate so that "as above, so below", and the Earth would come to mirror the Kosmos itself in its many dimensions, if the patterns were properly aligned. The patterns were also given "as without, so within", so the inner psyche of an individual would also come to mirror the Star-Map. In the end days, the Star-Map would give guidance for trans-dimensional travel, depicting possible ways of seeding future civilizations of human beings and animals in New Worlds.

The earliest ancestors were said to have come after the First Wave of indistinction in two separate waves. In the Second Wave, under the T'ai Chi, there were given Star-Maps which painted the heavens and Earth as opposites, dueling forces of irreconcilable contrasts and polarities. A dozen or so immortal humans and Animwaa interpreted the cosmological territory in their likeness, and they spread a mythos in the collective consciousness of humankind intent upon communicating the nature of the Star-Map. Although different cultures formed variations on the mythos, in its essence it formed a Zodiac comprised of Twelve Signs and Twelve Houses. The Signs were the representation of the immortal beings in inner Zones of consciousness and the Houses were their representatives in outer Zones of consciousness. The immortal humans – also known as the Hanimwaa – were the Twins, the Virgin, the Archer, and the Water-Bearer. The Animwaa of the Second Wave were the Ram, the Bull, the Crab, the Lion, the Scorpion, the Sea-Goat, and the Fishes. A Janim – an immortal being neither human nor animal – was given the task of balancing the competing interests of the humans and the animals: Libra, the Scale. Each of these immortal beings was described as either Yin or Yang, because that is the limitation of the Second Wave's cognitive capacities. However, these beings evolved a new way of understanding amongst themselves which was not planned or accounted for: a ternary consciousness. They counted themselves as Cardinal or Mutable or Fixed, depending on the nature of their relationship to the T'ai Chi. As ever in the ongoing relationship between 2s and 3s, the binary and ternary attributes were conflicted. When the Third Wave came, the old signs were caught in an unexpected situation. Their replacements had arrived!

The Third Wave brought the T'ai Hsuan, birthed through the pen of the renowned philosopher Master Yang who lived under the Emperor Ai (names which the Bear assumed were mythological, considering that Yang is the first season and Ai is the first month, but they were in fact historical). Yang wrote philosophical poetry during the years just before and after Zero. Although Beionai knew nothing of Yang Hsiung's *Canon of Supreme Mystery,* he recognized the date of the Great Turning of course as his own birth, and Kalen's. It was at this moment that he realized that the Third Wave which he wrongly assumed was well underway, in fact, only beginning to be birthed. The Third Wave began with his own birth. He threw the book up in the air in a moment of wonder, and he began to dance around!

Upon resuming the book where he left off, the Bear began to see Reality in a whole new light. The Second Wave, it said, was birthed in antiquity and will run its course until the year 2,000 CE, when the

Thousand Years of Yang and the Thousand Years of Yin will finally die. The Third Wave, it said, was birthed at Zero and will run its course for up to three thousand years, culminating in the Thousand Years of Unity, beginning in the Third Millennium CE. "The Bear-Yak Zodiac's fullness has not come yet!" said the Bear.

He read on ... The Star-Map of the Third Wave, also known as the Bear-Yak Zodiac, is comprised of 54 Signs, one for each of the Animwaa, immortal animals given many years to dwell upon the Earth before returning to the Source. They are also gifted with a divine speech for communication amongst each other and the Omphalos Bearer, and are stationed on the Wheel where they can be most useful. The Omphalos Bearer is tasked with defining Houses which can situate the Animwaa by using letters which are part of their True Names. Thus, Bear and Bat are the first two Houses of the New Zodiac, residing at the House of B. Pig and Platypus (which Bear started to believe might be a real animal after all!) shared the second station, the House of P. As Bear continued to read, he learned of many more Animwaa and he began to wonder about his own role, he being the first Sign of the New Zodiac.

The Bear's mind then turned to the crux of his problem: the Old Zodiac was part of the Second Wave, and they were not willing to relinquish their power. He had occasionally interacted with them, and they were rude and unpleasant, as if their spirit were corrupted.

Beionai flipped through the books rapidly, looking to see if he could learn of an explanation to account for their malevolence. He came upon a page labelled 'The War of the Zodiac', but it was blank. He held the parchment up to the light, but could see nothing. It struck him to lick the page, and when he thoroughly covered it in his saliva, it revealed a magical ink designed expressly to be seen only once exposed to bodily fluids of a member of the family *Ursidae*. It showed the following prophecy:

The War of the Zodiac: The Second Wave will come to dominate in the Thousand Years of Yang. As the Signs of the Third Wave come into power, the Signs of the Second Wave will lose their power. The Bel will indwell with the Third Wave, and the Ro with the Second Wave. In the Thousand Years of Yang, the Great War for Star-Maps begins. It culminates when the power of both sets of Signs are roughly of equal measure. It must be fought in secret between the armies of the Bear and the Sea-Goat. If the Bear-Yak Zodiac overthrows the old powers, then the Old Zodiac will fade into the Thousand Years of Yin, diminishing and returning to the Source, and the World will go on under a Blue Castle, a Violet Heart, and a Silver Star. Unity will reign in the heavens and on Earth. If the Aries-Pisces Zodiac overthrows the Bear-Yak Zodiac in the War of the Zodiac, then the Thousand Years of Yin will not be followed by the Thousand Years of Unity, but by a long-lasting Age of Darkness in which the Ro shall reign supreme until the BeI ultimately collapses and all will fall into Ruin. In either case, the Omphalos Bearer will define the Houses of the Zodiac, but he will perish in the War, fallen at the Cliffs of Chibi. If Aries-Pisces wins, he will be undone forevermore. But if the Bear-Yak Zodiac is victorious, then he will rise again.

The Bear was too flush with emotion to keep hold of his senses. He growled nonsensically, simply to express himself. He felt better, and so he kept on growling. There was only one place for him to go: a spring of the Deep Pool of the Center Heart. But first he had to bury the books. Of course it would not be safe for him to risk being seen by a human while carrying books. They might take him for a witch or werebear and kill him.

The book revealed his purpose, but it did not say how he was to go about the work, or where to begin. Surely Chelone, Archetype of Balance, would know the answer! She saw the visible and invisible Worlds in their seamless interweavings and exchanges and if anyone could show him how to fight and win a War of the Zodiacs, then she could. Where she dwelt he could not say for sure. Beionai only ever found her where there was a spring of pure clear water shooting straight from the Source of Existence. So he walked, and then he ran, and then he walked again, across many miles of hill and valley, scrambling northward and westward. Moons rose and fell in their cycles from emptiness to fullness and back again. He left one forest and entered another the following week, and passed through it in only a few days. After many days of travel on rugged terrain he entered yet another forest which was dense with old, wild Baobab trees which ascended on hills at the foot of a range of craggy mountains. It was a familiar place to him, and he knew exactly where to go.

At the mouth of a cave shaped like a giant mouth agape, he looked into the darkness. He knew it led to great caverns winding miles under the surface to a magnificent underwater lake. Light faded, and he could not take the sunlight with him underground. He found himself thinking, "I do not want to go down there all alone." In fact, he was not thinking it, but muttering it in the unnamed language.

And then he heard a squeaky, nasal voice nearby. Pig said, "You will not be alone, Bear. If it is to the Deep Pool you go, I will go with you."

Bear turned around to hear the source of the voice. He overjoyed at the sight of the pink-snouted Pig, and greeted him in their usual fashion, by wrestling playfully. This was not just any pig, it was Eishon, the Great Pig, and they both stood before the Cavern of Gorinoth as the last light of the day faded.

Just then another voice spoke in the unnamed language: "Have you two come to see me, or just maraud in my home?" It was the Great Bat, Ayvi, who spoke to them from a perch in a nearby tree.

"Ever the jester," said the Pig. "You can't be counted on to speak straightly when you are hanging upside-down!"

"And neither of you can be trusted with garbage, which you secretly adore munching and rubbing all over yourselves!" said the Bat.

They all laughed merrily. The Bear said, "It is good to see you, lady of the evening who has sucked on my blood!"

Ayvi said, "It was not for taking. You have thick fur."

Beionai said, "I am no worse. You bring me much happiness, both of you. It is not chance which brings us together now, but divine opportunity. I pray that fortunate coincidences continue. I have news to offer."

Eishon, the Great Pig: "I have news as well, unfortunate tidings. Let us descend into the cave together so we may commune with Balance as we have done in times past when the world was getting away from us."

Ayvi, the Great Bat: "As one news bringer to two others, I agree."

"I agree!" exclaimed the Great Bear. As in times past, the Bear and Pig approached the darkness wearily, but with the Bat's help they navigated the inky spaciousness of the underground void. Pig brushed up against Bear often, for that was his way of ensuring they stayed together. It was no fun, but at least they had good company.

Beionai explained that at long last he understood the superordinary purpose of the Fifty-Four Animwaa: to bring forth the New Zodiac (which he pointedly did not call the Bear-Yak Zodiac out of humility), and to replace the Aries-Pisces Zodiac which had grown increasingly corrupt. The Great Animals were depicted in an orderly harmony on the Star-Maps bequeathed by the Omphalos itself, and Bear did his best to memorize them. And speaking of the Omphalos, it was now safely held in a Vault, ready for the plucking by Kalen, who was protected by his uncles and Aupaiaquaa, the Wizard himself. He was sure they could find a way into the Vault to retrieve the Stone so that it could be claimed by the Bearer. Ayvi and Eishon were delighted to hear the good news that the Bearer was beginning to awaken to his purpose, but they were disturbed by the news that the Ro formed a powerful presence in the world and had attacked and killed Kalen's parents. They spoke in turns, chatting long into the night until morning. Deeper they descended. On more than one occasion, the Pig nearly stumbled off the edge of crevasses or slipped between giant gaps in the rocks.

Eishon was most anxious, and not just because he was speaking and walking downward at the same time, for he was totally blind in the dark. No phosphorescent plant or stone lit the starkness; it was totally blank. The Pig said, "I must wonder in what order of Archetypes ought the Bear-Yak Zodiac cohere? If we are foes of the Wands, then we are in deep trouble. The Stones have not appeared, and no one seems to know anything about them. But the Wands have grown delirious with fear! They have amassed a powerful army which stretches at least as far west as Delphi and east far into the vast continent, the land which we call Asia. The Wands have made alliance with an evil Magician who has instructed them in dualistic philosophy and has ordered them to destroy all signs of a ternary worldview. The Magician has also given them a list of animals to destroy who are favorably inclined to the ternary system ... beginning with the Bear, Bat, Pig, and Platypus (if there is such a thing)! They will kill all of us, not just the Animwaa, but all the animals of our kinds, all because of our alliance with the Stones. Where are the Royal Stones to save us now? I guess we know where the Wizard is, but I fear he cannot help us. The Magician of the Wand-Cup Tarot has tracked his movements to the towns of Somalia near Berpa, and he is following close behind him with a massive army of Wands which will take the Stone! The crooked Magician intends to murder the Wizard personally!"

"You know all this how?" asked the Bat.

"Hey, you'd be surprised at the things people will say in front of a pig," said the Pig coyly.

Before anyone could say another word, they rounded a slope into an enormous new cavern in which light from above illumined a great underground lake. The walls glistened with many gems and shiny stones. An island in the middle of the lake gradually began to come into view. They proceeded down the sloping path to the water's edge.

"You bring terrible news!" said Ayvi as she flew overhead in a loop. When she returned she said, "My own news seems rather anti-climactic now, but it is good news. I have received news from a friend of a friend of a friend in a land called Australia. The Platypus is real, and there is a Platypus among the Animwaa named Zhoona who sends her greetings. She wishes to commune with us, and wonders if we will be heading in her direction any time soon, or if she ought to plan a journey here."

The Bear and Pig stopped walking when they reached the lake-shore. The Bat perched on the Bear's shoulder, and they looked ahead to the island. On a dune at the center stood Chelone, her green shell glistening in rays of morning's light breaking from cracks in the cavern's roof. The Animwaa looked at their own reflection in the dark waters.

"We need to speak to Balance. Her wisdom will set us right," said Beionai as Ayvi landed on his broad shoulders.

As he spoke these words, a sudden and terrible underwater disturbance broke the lake's surface, forcing water to splash far onto the shore, wetting everyone. A beast as giant as an elephant came up from the deeps, oozing and squishing sloppily onto land. Its head was that of a devilish goat, with copious tentacles instead of hind legs and massive hooved forelegs kicking violently.

Of course it was the Sea-Goat, and he put himself directly between the Bear and the Tortoise of Balance. Capricorn screeched and baaaaaa baaaaaa baaaaaa'd ferociously, and his rapid ascent to the surface pushed Beionai, Ayvi, and Eishon behind. The Bear tripped over the Pig and the Bat, and they all tumbled backwards.

THE BATTLE OF RED CLIFFS

The daunting Sea-Goat held a lengthy barbed saber in its foremost tentacle, and it kicked with its hooves as it advanced in the slender canyon. It led an army of armored and armed goat slaves and heinous-looking sea-goat monsters through the narrow passage between the red cliffs of Chibi. At last Aries joined the war party, and the Ram stood at Capricorn's side as the leader of the land-based forces in the War of the Zodiac. Three hundred and sixty five formidable old creatures had marched westward from the coast of China or eastward from Western China until they arrived at the spot where Kalen stood with only a dozen animals at his side, amongst them an Ape, Panther, and two Vicuña.

Kalen stood fearless, but he looked weary and tired. Standing more than 6 feet tall with broad shoulders and a V-shaped back tapering to his thin waist, Kalen offered a vision of valor and fortitude. As a warrior possessing 20 years and 7 months as the Kalendar goes, he had fought and won many battles, written many poems and songs, and developed a new World Philosophy for which he grew famed amongst the Immortals. He was revered as a champion by those opposed to the encroaching Ro at 761 CE, but he was hated and feared by those who rightly saw him as a threat to their existence and power.

"It is as the legends foretold, Kalen. The passage ahead is blocked by Capricorn and Aries with their enslaved hordes, and the way behind is blocked by Scorpio and Leo leading an army of wild beasts," said the Ape. He spoke in the language of subtle energy which was then called Lingua Universalis. All the fighters in Kalen's pack communicated together in this fashion, and even the creatures of the Zodiac knew it somewhat, though it was not their usual way of talking.

The Panther added, "They could not risk your reaching the Great Gathering at Nagoya. They have assembled their full forces while the Animwaa still rise up. We never stood a chance!"

The Great Vicuña only said, "I will not last long in this battle. It looks like Viper will have my spot in the New Zodiac after all."

"Have heart, my friends," said Kalen. "This was our road all along, and if it will be our downfall, then our valor will be remembered always in the New Zodiac. Still, one of us must live to tell the tale."

Kalen strapped a bulging leather pouch of his on the camelid. He said, "Tanuca, take this satchel, and keep its contents safe. It contains precious cargo. Give it only to Zeus himself. Scale the walls of Chibi, Great Vicuña, and don't look back!" And then Kalen began to cough up blood.

"What?! You are not well. I will not abandon you," he said, as three enormous thunderclouds darkened and expanded in the sky above.

Kalen said, "I am fine, don't worry about me." As he spoke these words, his face grew pale and he began to slouch.

"It is the drink that was given to you by the peasant maiden in Hubei. It was foul!" said Vicuña. The clap of thunder came from overhead. Rain poured down.

"That may be Tanuca, but nevertheless you must go. Take Maama with you. It is my command," said Kalen as torrents of rain beat down everywhere. He muttered, "Brown Sword 12," and he spit on the ground.

"Flee this wretched night which the Kalendar records as the Downing of the Dao. Go now! There is no time to argue. If anyone else wants to leave and can climb these steep walls, do so now. There is no shame in retreating from impossible odds to fight another day," he added.

The Animwaa looked at each other and mustered their courage. Vicuña and his wife climbed the cliff wall in a dynamic and explosive manner. With seemingly effortless power, they soon reached the clifftop. In hot pursuit were a group of not less than ten goats in spiky armor.

The animals of the Old Zodiac laughed and taunted Vicuña. "They run to save their own lives! They flee out of fear! The Vicuña are shamed forever!"

Kalen looked up and caught Vicuña's eye as he reached the top and turned away. They spoke of love and friendship wordlessly. Tanuca was dogged by pursuers close behind, and he and Maama disappeared out of sight.

Though flanked on both sides by numerous foes, Kalen and ten Animwaa stood firm. Kalen locked his gaze on eyes belonging to the high leader of the Zodiac, Capricorn, surrounded by many armored goats. The rain formed massive puddles on the canyon floor, giving the Sea-Goat freedom to slide its slippery tentacles on the surface.

Kalen charged toward Capricorn like a thunderbolt, his boots splashing water and mud high as he ran. Tiger and Kangaroo ran alongside him, using their natural offensive capabilities to clear a path ahead of the Sea-Goat. Chimpanzee aided Kalen with a sword of his own, felling the goats who stood in their way.

In minutes Kalen entered striking range of the Sea-Goat. His wood-handled longsword clanged against the beast's saber while his other hand held onto a shield painted with the T'ai Hsuan. Tenacles slithered beneath Kalen's feet. He screamed "Ayeeeeeeeeeeee..."

Aries, Scorpio, and Leo closed from behind, left, and right. They were merely blurs in Kalen's increasingly foggy and uncertain vision. Rain continued to pound the canyon floor and its nearly vertical walls.

The Panther took on a whole pride of Lions led by Leo, but Rando was bit deep with sharp fangs, his tender flesh ripped asunder. The Lions stepped over Rando's once vital body as they jumped upon the Dingo and the Fox. The smell of blood and death filled the air.

Out of the corner of his vision, Kalen saw his friend Panther succumb to Leo's predation. Again he charged ahead to get closer to the Sea-Goat.

One vicious goat after another fell to Kalen's sword, but hardly a scratch landed upon the man. And then Kalen saw a familiar face in the Old Zodiac's hordes: Virgo who so recently disguised herself as a peasant to deliver him a poisoned beverage. Momentarily distracted by her sight, the Sea-Beast's saber nicked Kalen's back.

"You!" he cried. "What have you done to me?"

"I. Kill. You," she said, making three hand gestures of the corresponding glyphs of the Lingua Universalis.

An enraged Kalen screamed even louder and Capricorn fell back, its tentacles sliding across the ground as they spewed mud into the air. One slipped under Kalen's feet and knocked him to the ground.

Kalen stood. Five Animwaa perished in the first minutes of battle, leaving five more to form a crescent to protect Kalen's side and back. He was their best shot at slaying Capricorn. "Legend has foretold that I slew Capricorn on this night," Kalen had told his crew. "Let us take down their leader, and the old Zodiac will fall." The Ape's sword sliced open Lion's foot as it attempted to maul Kalen, but the Dingo could not restrain the advance of the poisonous Scorpions. The *Canis lupus dingo* perished with a Scorpion's fatal sting.

Next Kalen cleaved off the Sea-Goat's tentacle while keeping his rear protected from the stings of the advancing Scorpions. The Ape took his sword to the curved-back anthropods.

Blows from the fighting goats were sure and swift, and battered Kalen back and forth between their razor-sharp armor. The man's strength was nearly gone.

The Ram also butted against him, giving him a terrible bruising across his back and side. The Chimpanzee mounted it and sliced it open with his sword. Kalen butted back while protecting his front and back.

Kalen noticed a bear spot on the goats' armor on their backs which was without spikes. He jumped onto a goat's back and leaped from one goat to the next. He hopscotched on their backs until reaching the Sea-Goat, and then he found himself totally blind.

Hoping that the Sea-Goat had not moved from his previous location, Kalen leaped to its spot. He fell to the canyon floor.

The Sea-Goat's evil laughter gave away its location, and even though he was blind Kalen drove his sword into the sea monster's heart. Capricorn wailed and cried a horrific scream, and then fell dead on the spot.

Kalen fell dead as well, succumbing at last to baneful poison. The remainder of his valiant party of Animwaa of the Bear-Yak Zodiac fought to their last breath in the enveloping darkness. They took many lives of fighting beasts on that night, weakening the forces of the old night calendar, until at last each and every brave soul was gone.

Hidden somewhere amongst the creatures of the old Zodiac was the Three of Swords in disguise, for it is recorded that the Three was ordered by the Ram to take Kalen's body away from the battlefield to the Zodiac's stronghold. It is also said that the Three, having personally witnessed the tragic Battle of Red Cliffs, grieved more deeply for Kalen than any card has ever grieved.

Gray mists hovered above droplets of subtle dew which combined to form larger and heavier droplets which fell ever toward the pull of gravity. In a forest of elusive leaf and obscure stem, blade of grass and strand of web, the dew congealed and pooled into ever more complex shapes.

A large droplet plopped into space, a spot from which it reflected the entirety of All-That-Is and one particular whole which ever so recently took the shape of Kalen. Here it was not Kalen. It was one node in a dispersed network of subtle droplets which contained the memories and self-sense of his soul. They were separated from his body now, but conserved here in the after-forest. Enough were gathered now for them to vibrate in harmony with each other, giving rise to a thin whisper of a voice.

"Where am I?" said Kalen with pure soul-energy, a vibration extraordinarily dim.

"You are in the transition," said a manly voice.

"What am I doing here? Am I dead?" said Kalen. As Kalen spoke, he began to move his spiritual body with his mind. Droplets of dew extended the length of his arm, rising off the forest floor where he lie and falling back down again.

It reassured Kalen to see his arm. He thought: "If only I could stand up from this place, I could see my body." As he tried to stand up, dew droplets collected in the shape of his body, a man's shape. They fell back with gravity's clutch.

"Wait a moment. You're almost there. Rest a while longer."

"I can't be dead. I cannot leave the battle undone, the War unwon," said Kalen.

"The battle is lost, and the War's outcome is yet to be decided. But that is not your concern at the moment. If you try to move too quickly, you will lose everything."

Kalen looked around at the enormous tree trunks which stretched high beyond the gray mists to a bright source of light above and below to a dark and root-filled lower pace. In the middle place between the roots and treetops, he could feel himself stretched flat upon the surface which contained roots and sediment and pools of dew.

"The beliefs of my people tell me that when I die I will be reunited with loved ones, but I do not recognize your voice," said Kalen.

"That isn't important right now," said the voice. "It would not be wise for you to see any loved ones who are departed, unless you were intent on staying here, or you might not want to go back. There is still the chance that you may finish your work."

"Yes! I want to go back!"

Laughter. "If you knew what you had to do, you would shake and tremble. It is not at all an easy thing, least of all for you, given Who You Are," said the voice without a visible body.

"And who is that?" said Kalen.

Kalen noticed a string of dew which vibrated in harmony when the manly voice spoke. "You tell me."

Kalen said, "I am Kalen O'Tolan. For 20 years and 7 months I walked the Earth, in the Kalendar's method of counting Time. I crossed continents and watched as thirty-seven generations of mortal men came and went. I was the Bearer of the Black Stone and the Wearer of the Red Jewel. I was the wielder of the Brown Sword in the Three Kosmic Wars. I led the armies of Animwaa in the War of the Zodiac, the suits of the Stone-Star Tarot in the War of the Archetypes, and I brought to Zeus a New Map of the Heavens. I must return to my friends who still fight on behalf of the Good. Who but me can wield the Artifacts of Orr? Tell me plainly what I must do!"

"You do not recognize your own Archetype! You are not ready to return. The shock would be too great for you," said the voice.

"I am an Archetype?" asked Kalen.

"Of course you're an Archetype!" said the voice. "All immortal beings are Archetypes while they dwell on mortal planes. Say which Archetype you would be if you could pick one."

Kalen said, "I don't know."

The voice said, "Until you know the answer, there is no going back."

Kalen said, "I would be a King were I to choose, one of the nine Kings of the Stone-Star Tarot."

The voice said, "That's very good. Which King would you be?"

Kalen said, "None that I have ever met, neither Stone nor Jewel nor Sword." Kalen's body was now fully comprised of dew drops brilliant with energy and life-force, and they took the shape of the body he had as a 20-year-old man, laying on the floor of the subtle forest.

"What then?"

Kalen said, "Maybe Eggs. Maybe Horses. Maybe Bowls. Maybe Castles. Maybe Hearts. Maybe Stars. How am I to choose? I have not passed through the Ages which they denote!"

"You have already made your choice. You have only to remember it."

An eerie sensation filled Kalen with nervous energy, and he began to suspect that he was being observed. Voices unseen in the heavens, hidden by the gray mist, were speaking about him in low murmurs. He could not make out their meaning, but he distinctly heard the word "Rounder".

Kalen said, "What is a 'Rounder'?"

Much laughter came from locations unseen in the heavens.

Kalen said, "Show yourself to me. I will not address a void."

"Is this better?" said the voice. It belonged to an Angel who appeared before Kalen, a man with spectacular white wings more glorious than is seen on any bird. He held a shiny sword in his right hand, which he pointed to the heavens. "The transformation process is finished. You can stand up now."

Kalen stood, and his spiritual body raised off the forest surface. Droplets of dew fell to the ground and were absorbed. He held his hands in front of his face, and looked his body up and down. "It's me!" he said. "I have not died at all!" He stood on the ground naked.

"Oh the body you had is dead," said the Angel. "Your physio-spiritual body is presently divided from your purely physical body." The Angel waved his arm and clothing appeared on Kalen much like his own, a white two-piece garment with an armored breastplate.

The Angel thought for a moment longer and said, "No, not this." Kalen's clothing changed. He now wore dark gray pants and a tailored navy shirt tucked into them. The design was of the sort commonly worn in the twentieth century, so it was like nothing Kalen had ever seen before.

Kalen's attention returned to the atmosphere. "I heard voices up there," he said. "Show me who observes us. Let them come out into the open."

The Angel waved his other arm and the gray mist dissipated. There was a circling band of flying angels overhead arrayed in plain garments similar in fashion. Once the mist disappeared, they hovered in the air in an orderly fashion like a band of marching soldiers. Above their heads was a vibrant star field.

Kalen watched as one of the stars grew larger and larger and turned into a lovely woman with beautiful flowing golden hair. She hovered beyond the angels, floating as a radiant fountain of love.

Kalen gazed at her with wonder and love. "Who is she?"

The Angel said, "Do you know her?" The floating woman came closer, her elegant form descending with harmonious music. Kalen could see the pendant around her neck: a silver star.

"She is the Queen of Stars, and I love her. That's how I know Who I Am. I am the King of Stars."

The woman approached him and expressed tenderness in her eyes, but she stopped when the Angel held up his arm. "Kalen is barred! He will not come with you," the Angel said. "He must complete the circle and abdicate all that he has known. Fullness must become Emptiness."

Kalen found himself unable to speak, but he nodded yes.

"She should not have shown herself. It is too great a temptation for you," said the Angel. The Queen of Stars floated backward, hanging around barely in view, and Kalen felt the separation viscerally. He could not shed a tear, but water from the surface flowed up the closest tree and dew drops pulled off its branches and floated up and onto Kalen's cheek. Once on his cheek, they flowed down with gravity.

The Angel said, "A Rounder, Kalen, is what you are. In life you were recently the penultimate Royal of the penultimate suit. The

Wheel of Existence has come to a close, and you are the bringer of its ending. If you return, you round the Wheel. You must appear as the lowest card of the next suit."

Kalen said, "I know the Map of the Archetypes, the Stone-Star Tarot. Are you saying I must become the Ace of Stones?"

The Angel said, "Yes, from the highest you must become the lowest. Your sacrifice permits the Wheel of Existence to go on. You have already been the Ace of Stones. Who do you think has helped the younger version of you?"

The Queen of Stars returned again. She hovered closer and appeared near to Kalen, positioning herself within an arm's reach. "I disagree," she said. "It is not 3,000 CE! The Wheel of Existence has not yet run its course! There is a small chance Kalen can resume his life where he lost it. With the aid of the Queen of Swords, I sent the Three of Swords to take Kalen's body from his captors. His body remains inanimate, but it is not decomposing. The Light of the Stars indwells with him. He need not enter the world as a Black Stone; he may resurrect as Who He Is."

The Angel said, "How does he do this? What is the secret of the resurrection of the body?"

The Queen of Stars said, "I do not know it. I know only that his body must be arrayed with the Red Jewel, the Brown Sword, and the

Black Stone. If Kalen knows the secret of resurrection, then he may return to the world from which he came."

Kalen said, "I do not know the secret. Moreover, when defeat seemed certain, I sent the Red Jewel and Black Stone away with Vicuña! They will be nowhere close to my body."

The Queen of Stars said, "Of course you did. I will confer with my colleagues in the Tarot and see what I can do." And then she departed, rising high into the heavens until her light could no longer be seen. As she left, she said, "You must resurrect. Come back to me, my love."

Kalen could not remember the Queen of Stars, but he felt a grave loss. He said, "NO! Don't go!" In the sky above, many angels murmured and spoke aloud.

The Angel stood next to him and whispered in his ear: "Your every move has an audience in the heavens. You are immature, clinging to emotions and temporal loves, not yet purified of your passions. You disappoint me."

Kalen said, "Who are you, my guardian angel?"

The Angel said, "I am, in a manner of speaking. I will help with your rounding."

Kalen said, "I choose to return to my old life."

The Angel said, "We shall see about that. You are a Rounder. You have already made the choice to return as inanimate substance.

If you hadn't, none of us would be here. Farewell, Kalen! Remember to help yourself."

The Angel rejoined the band of hovering angelic beings, and they departed.

"Where are you going? Don't leave me!" said Kalen.

The ground changed its appearance. Kalen felt his spiritual body standing upon the surface of a giant spinning disc, golden in color. Its markings were those of the Kalendar.

Kalen's feet fell to the Wheel which was turned to display the edge of the constellation of M. This is the seventh month of 1999 CE," thought Kalen. "What am I doing here?"

Kalen looked into the heavens and he saw an Emerald City, a strange part of the planet he never saw before, if it was his world at all. Tall towers of steel and glass grew out of the forest. The band of angels were speaking to a man on a bed in a strange clean, white room, and the room came closer into view. Kalen's feet landed outside the room in a hallway, just in time for him to catch a glimpse of a man riding in a chair with wheels as a woman in a white uniform pushed him along the corridor. There was a blue cross on her uniform and on the wall in front of him. He locked eyes with the man on the wheel-with-chairs, a man appearing to be around 30 years of age. It was someone he knew, but he couldn't remember how. They locked eyes, mesmerized.

"He is the Poet," said the guardian Angel, though he was not to be seen. "He has seen you. Your work here is done. Remember his face and this time on the Kalendar. He will remember yours."

"It is almost the start of M," said Kalen.

The band of angels came to him, furious and frightened. "Stop following us!" they said. "Go back to where you came from. This is not your time." The angels threw a terrible force against Kalen, and he vaulted backward into the void. All the images from the Emerald City grew distant and dissolved in silvery light, and Kalen once again hovered over the glyphs of the Kalendar.

The Angel took Kalen's hand and they spun farther along on the Kalendar's surface until they reached the first glyph of the letter N. "Do you know what this is?"

"It is the start of N," said Kalen.

The Angel said, "Look into your mind. What do you see?"

Kalen closed his eyes.

The Angel said, "No! Look into your mind with your eyes open."

Kalen saw a parade of enormous comets in the stars approaching the planet Earth, which he recognized as his home world, though the continents before his eyes were unfamiliar. All the comets except one faded out of his awareness, and his mind grew close to the giant asteroid. It spun and spun and spun. "I have seen this before. This rock will strike the planet in the Green Country. Horrors will appear. Civilization will reach the Nadir."

The Angel said, "We will see. Remember this place on the Kalendar."

Kalen said, "It is 2,111 CE."

The Angel changed Kalen's garments to a simple white tunic of the sort he used to wear as a child. "Remember who and what you have seen. It will be important in time. Now go!"

Kalen's mind turned to the Kalendar and he tried to concentrate and think hard of the Year 761 CE. He wanted very much to return to the time from whence he came. But try as he might, he could not get the constellation of D to appear on the spinning disc. Instead the letter of V came into view. "No, not V! That was a dark time. I was only a child. The suit of Wands held me captive. I cannot go back there! I do not want to go back to that time! Help me!" Nevertheless V came and set itself before his feet. He walked on several of the words at the tail end of V, glyphs which represented to him Value and Vow and Vowel. As the glyph for Vowel appeared, Kalen fell through its markings into a peculiar wonderland of images from his past. "It is 317 CE. This is the Valve," he thought, though he couldn't recall why he was coming to this time.

"I have been here before as a child ... when I was no more than 8 years and 7 months old as the Kalendar goes round. I saw a soaring bird and I said something to it which I can't remember. I was tumbling with comets in Space. I was tumbling through the atmosphere. I heard the voice of God chastise me out of a whirlwind. I heard the voice of my Beloved and we repeated our betrothal vows. I saw myself below, as I do now, not as a child, but as a Black Stone. I saw the Stone below as I do now, tossed in the air between two towers of a castle on the frontier. I saw Kalen, downcast and alone, sweeping the courtyard of the higher tower. I looked into the sky and saw nothing. And I felt myself then as I do now, falling, falling, falling ..."

BALANCE V. THE SCALES

The company of the Wizard encountered Vishnu on the road to Warshon. He appeared in his manifestation as a four-armed divinity with a dark complexion tinted an otherworldly bluish color, holding a golden mace in his lower-right hand. Though he was plain to Aupaiaquaa's sight, the Wizard's companions could neither see nor hear the ancient god.

"Praise the Preserver and Defender of All-That-Is, Vishnu who pervades all the worlds of Space and Time," said the Wizard. He bowed before the deity, and his entire company stopped walking.

Kalen's uncles held the children back. "Be quiet," said Dro. Kalen asked, "Who is he talking to?" His older siblings hushed him. Kalen had no concept of Vishnu, but he imagined the letter V, active and volatile, in its inner cone-like shape, narrowing into a perfect single point giving Knowledge and News. In fact, his imagination of the letter meanings were quite close to the truth, from a certain point-of-view.

Vishnu said, "The Order at the Front-Center of the Worlds is collapsing! The Beast has risen! The devils and demons are working to overthrow the Order as they have since the beginning of the First Wave, but they have a powerful new ally in the Ro. The Ro is gathering all evil to it, and they will not permit the rise of the King of Stars. It is time now to convene a Council of Deities to address the threat. I am heading to Kyushu for a visit with Zeus, and you will come with me."

"Lord Vishnu, respectfully, I cannot come," said Aupaiaquaa.

Vishnu looked the Wizard sternly in the eyes. "I do not ask you, I command you, Archetype of the Stone-Star Tarot." The Wizard was not just any Archetype, but one of the Major Arcana. Nevertheless he knew his place among the earthly and celestial beings and he was not a god.

"I am needed here as a protector of our greatest hope in the coming War," said Aupaiaquaa. He approached the deity and directed his gaze to the youngest child present. "The now and future King of Stars needs me."

Vishnu moved closer to the Wizard and spoke in a hushed tone so that others could not hear him. "Zeus believes that Kalen brings the end of his reign in the heavens, and he is set to act against him. He has been given unreliable counsel, and I need you to counteract it. If Zeus acts now, with the legions of deities at his command, the child has more to fear than you realize."

Aupaiaquaa whispered, "How do you know this?"

Vishnu switched the hands with which he was holding the golden mace, twirling the weapon menacingly as he did so. "I have heard it from his brother Poseidon. Come, we must go at once."

Aupaiaquaa turned to his companions. "I am sorry, but I have to leave you. I head into the East."

Gailon said, "When will you be back?"

Aupaiaquaa said, "Do not count on my return. You must proceed without me."

Dro said, "What are we to do?"

Aupaiaquaa mounted his steed. He said, "Let Kalen lead. Support him. I must go," he said. Vishnu vanished in Aupaiaquaa's sight. The Wizard's horse galloped quickly to the horizon.

Once the Wizard faded from view, all eyes turned to the youngest child. Gailon knelt before the boy. He said, "Eight generations of my kin have come and gone in the passage of your life, Kalen. You look innocent, but you are not feeble minded. If the Wizard trusts you, that is good enough for me."

Dro knelt. He said, "I go with my spouse, and where he leads I follow."

Kalen's siblings bowed before him, for the first time ever. Jeila offered Kalen a piece of dried fruit. He took a bite.

Kalen said, "I have suddenly come to feel ashamed of my past childishness. Five years and forty-some days as the Kalendar goes seems now like a very long time indeed to walk on the Earth and accumulate wisdom, too long to be playing the games of children. I will not say that I know best what to do, but I can listen well enough, and I can keep us focused. First, we must establish safety. Second, we must find the Vault and re-take the Stone. And then, I need to *spatialize*. I feel a strong urge to climb as high I can go so I can take everything into me."

Kalen remembered the firmness with which his father spoke, and he tried to think of the words he would speak if he were alive now. "We cannot head back to the farm; it is surely being watched. We will not go to Warshon without first determining if the Ro are present. Gailon will lead us in finding a secure place for rest, and then Dro and Kyle will head into the city to look ahead for us. Chila and Jeila will inventory our food and water and determine our needs as soon as possible. I'll be right here." Kalen didn't say out loud what he would do, but he knew it. He needed to stay alert, watching for Beionai and other Animwaa or even Tarot cards who might come to their aid—and watching for signs of the Ro.

Later that night, as he made camp with Chila, the full moon shown brightly over the sandy dunes. They eschewed a fire on Kalen's order, but they sang songs of the sort the O'Tolans often sang in gatherings. They sat in a circle with Kalen sitting next to Gailon on one side and Chila and Jeila on the other. Kyle and Dro were not yet returned from the city. Kalen was particularly fond of a song which he was taught by Mataan, Gailon's father, when Kalen was only three years old as the Kalendar goes. It goes in part:

> *Where there are wheatfields he will bring the rains*
> *Where there is error he will cleanse the stains*
> *He will be there when the cold mountains fall*
> *He will be there when the big deserts sprawl*
>
> *Let there be time enough for him to grow*
> *Let there be faith enough for him to know*
> *May there be space enough for him to be*
> *May he not die today, but set us free*

Kalen always thought of the words as referring to God whose unseen spiritual force pervades all the Deities and everything in the universe. But what would such a powerful deity need with a small child's faith? Why would God need time to grow? Why would God die? The words of the song were puzzling to him. Kalen even wondered if the song of his family might be referring to someone else: him. It was a disturbing thought.

Gailon tapped Kalen's ankle. "Kalen, have you ever spoken to the Black Stone?"

Kalen said, "Once. There wasn't a lot of time."

Gailon seemed weaker or humbler than Kalen remembered him. He said, "Oh. I am sure you will have it back shortly. When you do, there's a question I'd like you to ask."

"What is that?" Kalen expected his reply would be a common one: What happens when we die? What is the right way to live? Which God reigns supreme? How can I live longer and happier and wealthier?

Instead, Gailon said this. "There is a mouse I had when I was just a boy about your age. His name was Happy. Happy was attacked by a cat and became infected. I had to give it relief. I killed it, you understand. I want to know if Happy's spirit is out there somewhere, and if he forgives me."

Kalen said, "I will ask."

Gailon went to sleep shortly afterwards. Kalen and his sisters were also sleepy and soon dozed off.

As the Tortoise of Balance watched from an island in the middle of an underground lake, three Animwaa of Bear-Yak and another of Pisces-Aries faced against each other at the lakeshore. The Sea-Goat rose from the watery depths, and Bear charged him with a vigorous assault. He nearly succeeded in biting its face, but he was smacked aside by the grip of a strong slimy tentacle. He ripped open the tentacle with his razor-sharp claws, which he sharpened constantly on trees. Bat and Pig charged Capricorn as well, offering the weapon of confusion and distraction.

Capricorn grasped both Bear and Pig with its tentacles and proceeded to smack them against each other and nearby rocks until they were sore and bruised. Beionai was bashed against one boulder and then another, landing hard against the rocks.

The Tortoise of Balance walked to the lakeshore and then hopped on the back of a Sea Turtle. She spoke to them all as the Turtle paddled to the other shore. "Stop now, all of you! You will heed the warnings of the Keeper of Balance," she said.

Capricorn screeched, "I do not answer to the wretches of your Tarot!"

Balance said, "You will answer to the Scales!"

At that moment, Libra appeared on the lakeshore. He appeared as a man with a gold bar slung horizontally above his shoulders, and two golden cups hooked to the bar by chains. One cup was touching the floor; the other hung in mid-air. "Who has called me and for what purpose?" Capricorn released his tentacles' grip on the Bear and Pig. The Bear collapsed in a heap, moaning in pain.

Balance arrived at the lakeshore. She dismounted from the Sea Turtle and said, "It is I, Chelone. I need you to reign in your Sea-Goat! You are both cardinal signs in Aries-Pisces, are you not? Give him some Air. He is interfering in the affairs of Bear-Yak. Specifically, he intends to murder the premiere Animwaa!"

Capricorn said, "It is a lie! The Bear attacked me! Look, my tentacle is ripped to shreds. I seek only to defend myself." And then Libra said, "What do you say, Bear?"

The Bear said, "I do not deny attacking him. On my part, it was self-defense." Bear did not feel that he could explain the terror which the Sea-Goat induced in him, and how it seemed that a preemptive strike was the only way to gain a much-needed advantage.

Libra said, "You don't sound convinced of your own story! Where is the Rounder who has brought forth this monstrosity called the Bear-Yak Zodiac? I wish to take measure of the man."

Balance replied, "He is not here. Your Zodiac provides a small degree of cohesion to a world of primitive minds in Yang's Season, but it has no hope to survive the coming upheavals in Yin's Season and the Season of You! But I have not called you here to debate the merits of alternative symbolic ordering systems. It is not yet 300 CE. I have called you here for a shred of sanity! Assassinating your rivals is barbaric, beneath the dignity of your high offices!”

Libra: “There will never be a Thousand Years of You because your Zodiac will be decimated! This Bear has started a War of the Zodiacs! I am a Scale, it is true, but I am concerned with keeping the order of my symbol systems, not yours. I have won a guarantee of victory for the Aries-Pisces over and against all alternate systems. Through my diplomacy the Aries-Pisces Zodiac has forged an alliance with the Ro which will ensure our reign throughout the First, Second, and Third Millenniums CE.”

Balance said, “What did the Ro offer you to do their bidding?”

Libra: “Ro will bring human civilization to a Nadir in the early 22nd Century as you know, the Apocalypse. And we will be there post-Apocalypse when their so-called ‘modern minds’ will return humbly to childish star-watching and foolish omen-following. Man will be as apes. We will guide them to a dark and dreary existence where they will depend on us for every step of their survival. Then we will be in control of their fates, and the scourge of so-called ‘free will’ will vanish.”

Balance said, “You have Scales, but offer no Balance. Apocalypse is not the only potentiality of the Nadir, if sanity comes in time. You think only of holding onto power, but there is another way. I offer you a gentle, peaceful decline at the hands of History where you will be remembered for the good you have done, not how you refused to step out of the limelight. Let the Bear-Yak Zodiac replace you at the Great Overturning. Let the Bear-Yak show humankind an alternative to Apocalypse. Go in peace. Your time is over."

Libra laughed evilly. "Pity Kalen himself is not here so I could personally smash his head beneath the weight of my golden cups."

Beionai charged the Scales and slashed at its chain with his claws. His claws were sharp, but not hard enough to slice through gold. Libra laughed and said, "I will not forget that, Ursine Beast! I will save a special torment for you in the Dark Ages to come."

Balance said, "Libra, I have no further use for you. Leave now, and take the Sea-Goat with you!" The Scales and Capricorn laughed. Chelone said, "By the Power vested in me in and through the Angel of God in the Stone-Star Tarot, go now!" The old signs vanished.

Bat landed on the Tortoise's back and studied the numerological design. She asked, "Where have you sent them?"

Balance said, "They are now at their home positions in the Bear-Yak Zodiac: Capricorn is at the Bear's den at Delphi and Libra is at the Great Ant's underground complex in the Lerma Valley." Bat resisted the temptation to ask where the Lerma Valley was. The world was vast and Bat knew she had only seen a small fraction of it.

Bear collapsed on the rocks and he felt himself slipping away.

Balance said, "More importantly, how are you?"

Bat and Pig replied that they felt well, but Bear said, "Not well. I feel pain inside me. The Great Den calls me home."

Balance: "Can you walk?"

The Bear said, "It hurts too much."

Balance: "Beionai, did you really have to strike the first blow?"

The Bear said, "I didn't. My paw missed his devilish little face. But Capricorn got me good."

Chelone said, "That is true enough, but still I wish you had shown more restraint. I will go and find a healer for you, and send him to you, and then I need rest. Do not stay here long. Get above ground as soon as you are able."

Bear put his paw on Balance's shell. He pleaded: "Don't go. I have a matter to discuss with you. It pertains to the Battle of Red Cliffs."

Balance said, "I will find you in a while. Be patient and rest." And then she vanished in a flash of light.

Pig and Bat made the Bear as comfortable as possible. They brought him water from the lake and found a mossy spot where he could rest his head. Bear refused Pig's offer to let him rest his head on his pig-belly, but thanked him anyway.

Bear nearly fell into slumber, but Pig kept him awake with nervous but merry talk. "Don't fall asleep. Be still until the healer comes."

A bright flash of light combined with the neighing of a horse brought Bear back from nearly dozing. He perked up his head and saw a twice-amazing sight. His first amazement was the sight of a peculiar man-like Centaur who had the face, chest, arms, and front legs of a human being combined with the hind legs of a horse. His second amazement was that he recognized the specific man: it was the exact image of Kalen's late father. He had spent many years following the O'Tolan family as they wandered the lands, and Kairon's face he knew well.

The Centaur said, "Greetings. I am Chiron. Where is the patient? I have been given to understand that he is critically ill."

Bat said, "He is the Bear over there. He was thrown against rocks ... and thrown against that Pig over there."

Pig said, "He was."

Chiron then spoke to the Bear, who vaguely remembers telling him of the pain's location on the left side of his abdomen and left shoulder. He had blurry vision and severe pain. "Your spleen has been ruptured." Chiron checked his pulse and pressed down on the Bear's arms. "Your blood pressure is low."

Pig said, "He's been fading in and out of consciousness. Can you help him?"

Chiron said, "Maybe."

The Bear growled in pain.

Chiron touched unusually-sited acupressure points on the Bear's body and felt levels of muscular resistance to various movement tests. He asked the Bear to stick out his tongue, and he read its coloration and texture. He said, "Bear, your vital signs are not stable. There is bleeding, but it is slowing its pace. Your spleen needs to be monitored and removed if conditions worsen. I will need to surgically remove it."

Bear said, "You want to cut me open? What kind of medicine is this?"

Chiron said, "Yes, I will, if necessary. But if your signs stabilize, it will heal on its own given enough time." He then showed the Bat and Pig how to monitor the Bear's vital signs regularly. He said he would return soon. Pig said, "We are also out of food. Could you bring us a bite to eat?" Bat said, "None for me. I can find my own food."

Chiron laughed. "Yes, one order of slop for the Great Pig. The Great Bear may not eat until he is feeling better. Nor drink water."

The Bear growled, and Chiron vanished in a flash of light.

The light in the cave faded as night fell, and the Animwaa waited for hours. Bat and Pig checked on Bear regularly and his condition seemed to worsen. Finally, the Bear fell into a sleep from which they could not wake him. They spoke to the wind, asking for aid, hoping somehow their cries would be answered.

Chiron returned with an assistant and many oddly-shaped knives and vials of medicine unlike anything the Animwaa had ever seen.

"I have never seen such instruments! These glass vials are perfectly formed and oddly capped! I have never heard of medicine like this! Where did you get all of this?" said Pig.

Chiron said, "There are certain advantages to being an Archetype in the Stone-Star Tarot, and one of them is the ability to access the world at different points of time and ... borrow things. Ordinarily I would not dream of borrowing things from one time for use in another, but the Great Bear is no ordinary patient. He is the premiere Animwaa of the Bear-Yak Zodiac which governs the relationhip between all living beings and Nature. I have been given instruction by Balance herself to keep him alive and well, and will do the best I can."

"I know of Centaurs," said Pig, "And you are not like them. You are different."

"I once had the body of a horse and the head, chest, and arms of a man like the other Centaurs. I incarnated in many cultures in many different periods of time from the Season of Yang to the Season of You. I was once merely horse-like. In one of my many incarnations, I was fully human and ignorant of my archetypal nature. I was a husband and father, a physician and sheep farmer. I learned of ancient medicines and secret procedures unlike those used by other Centaurs. When it was time for me to move on, I was not ready to leave my children. I resisted so much, my horse nature deferred to the human nature, and ever since I have incarnated as I am today. It is inconvenient not to be able to run with horses and other Centaurs, but it is the way I am and there is no getting around that."

That night Chiron and his assistant operated on the Bear and removed his ruptured spleen. They sewed him back whole and gave him powerful medicines for pain. They stayed for another day, until Balance appeared.

She spoke to Chiron thusly: "I have held off the Ro this long, but they are coming now. We must leave. Can he travel by light?"

Chiron said, "He is well enough to travel, barely."

Balance said, "Thank you for your aid. You may go now." The human-legged Centaur vanished in a flash.

The giant Tortoise said, "Pig and Bat, gather around the Bear. We are going to a safe place. Hold on to each other and don't let go." And then they traveled by light.

THE COURT OF STONES

ow can you just sit there and do nothing, Orrmaanu?" asked the Queen of Stones. She stood next to her ornate throne in the great hall of the Palace of Stones, home of the Royal Stones of the Stone-Star Tarot. She held a lengthy prism of crystal in her right hand, and she gazed into its inner images. She often looked into esoteric subjects shown by its light, but rarely was she preturbed.

"The Omphalos is safe in the Vault," replied the King of Stones. He sat only a few feet away in his own throne as he tinkered with the parts of a primitive steam engine. "You know this Hoyana; you have seen it through the looking-glass."

"For now," she said. "But what happens when Kalen retrieves it only to find hundreds of Wands hidden out of sight in the hills, ready to pounce? The Wand-Cup Tarot senses the Lost Stone of Delphi is within their grasp. They will not rest until it is theirs. We must ensure it remains out of their hands."

At this moment, the Jack of Stones entered their minds, though he was not yet in their visions. "You reside in the Season of Yang, and from your perspective I haven't happened yet," he explained to them once long ago. "Though my eternal pattern lies in the order of the Stones, I dwell in the Season of You which is abuzz with information and machines and commonplace travels through air and space."

The Jack adjusted the controls on his visualization computer so he could better see the King and Queen. The Queen was an ebony-skinned beauty with a white headband beneath wild hair, dressed in a forest green gown. The King had piercing brown eyes and wrinkled red-brownish skin with braided black hair partly hidden behind golden headgear. The Queen sat on her throne while the King walked in the great hall, tracing a circle around his steam engine.

The King said, "Shailo is present."

The Queen said, "I know. I too can sense him. His image is coming in to the prism."

The King said, "Jack of Stones, where/when are you?"

An image of the card appeared in the seeing-prism: a young man working in a magico-scientific laboratory of the late 21st century CE.

The King did not need to look into the prism to see the Jack, for the young man was a present vision which he held in his mind.

The Jack said, "I am traveling in space-time through my voice and image visible only to you. I remain in my time, in a mobile magico-scientific laboratory at 45° E. Longitude."

The Queen: "Yes. You're in your car. We know."

The Jack said, "Well you did ask. I have reached my mind into the past, your time, because of a disturbance in my own day. What is happening then/there that my techno-magical equipment has suddenly become glitch-ridden and unreliable?" The young man hovered over a computer screen with a blinking Stone-symbol dot at the center. Surrounding it were hundreds of Wand-symbols, some moving nearer to the dot.

The Queen: "The Ace of Stones has been found! It is in the Vault. The Bearer approaches it now in the village of Quorya to reclaim it. The Wands have staked a position in the hills out of his sight." She looked at her husband and King and said contemptuously, "We have done nothing to intervene."

The King: "What do you want me to do? We have a small cadre of cards, untested and unprepared for war. The Wands however have secured an army and equipped them with powerful fire-devices. We are no match for them."

The Queen: "I want you to keep the Omphalos out of the hands of our mortal enemies! It is the Ace of Stones! It belongs with us."

The King said defiantly: "Let them try to use it against us!"

The Queen: "What if they don't want to use it against us? What if they want to destroy it?"

The King remained silent for a moment, lost in thought. At last he said, "It is the source of all magic, theirs included. They couldn't! They wouldn't!"

The Jack: "They might. If they sought to destroy it would they kill the Omphalos Bearer?"

The King: "Kalen and the Stone are linked. If one perishes, the other may lose its power. The Wands have only to kill the Bearer in order to extinguish the Stone's magic."

The Queen: "I disagree. The Stone possessed magical qualities long before Kalen's birth, and will continue to do so if the boy perishes, if a new Bearer arises."

The King replied, "Perhaps you are right. But Kalen is a Rounder, so who is to say that it was not Kalen himself who gave the Stone its power well before his birth in this incarnation?"

The Queen: "If that is so, will he not return following his death to renew its magic? Would he not reincarnate into the Black Stone?"

The Jack: "Hold on. I have bugged the headquarters of the Wands, and I have just overheard them speaking about the child. They say that they intend to capture Kalen, not kill him. They will attempt to control the Ace. They believe it can be 'bought'."

The King: "Bought?"

The Jack: "Yes, that is what they said. What would become of Kalen?"

The King: "They would need to keep the Bearer alive, close to the Stone, but apart from it."

The Queen: "They might threaten the Stone with the Bearer's torture if it did not work on their behest. Knowing its fate is linked to Kalen's, the Stone could be susceptible to 'purchase'. I fear they could use the Ace to find all the other Stones, and wipe us out one by one. Perhaps also it would reveal the position of all the cards in the Stone-Star Tarot before the Decks have had an opportunity to cohere!"

The Jack said, "I agree. They intend to destroy us all. They have said so. We must not let that happen. I can see the location of the Stone on my satellite-based global positioning sensor."

The King: "What on God's earth are you talking about?"

The Jack said, "I'm sorry. The Ace of Stones has appeared on my 'seeing stone' now. It has entered the world of Form. It says now that the Vault has appeared in northern Somalia in the latter part of the 2nd Century CE. Its readings are imprecise, but it's still the only machine in the world that can identify the location of an Artifact of Orr in the past, present, or future."

The Queen looked at her prism. "It is true! The Vault has appeared in Quorya. It looks like a fruit-seller. Kalen and his uncles are approaching the shop. At the rear of the shop is a curtain leading to a private area. There he keeps the Stone. Kalen's siblings are hanging back."

The King: "Where is the Wizard? He must have a Wizard with him for protection."

The Queen: "The Wizard is not with them. I can see him now. He has gone to Kawasaki with Vishnu. He has left them without protection."

The King: "Unbelievable! The Wizard was sworn to protect the boy. We have been undone! If the Wands take the Ace of Stones, it is war. It is a War of Archetypes!"

The Queen: "Soldiers from the suit of Wands have arrived in secret. They've surrounded everyone! The Magician of the Wand-Cup Tarot has arrived on horseback, hidden out of sight. It is an ambush!"

The Jack fiddled with dials on a console until a holographic image of a Tarot card appeared, a muscular athlete standing victorious following a sporting competition. He said, "Send in the Six of Stones. He could help."

The King descended from his throne and bolted for the door. "I will send the Six ... and I would go myself."

The Queen ran to him and held on to him tightly. "You cannot leave the Throne of Stones! As of this moment we are already at war. The other suits of the old Tarot have not shown themselves. Where are the Cups and the Pentacles? What if there is another ambush waiting beyond our sight? We cannot afford to lose the Ace and our King in a single stroke!"

"I know when you are right," said the King. "Very well then. I have sent the Six with the power of my mind. He is on his way."

Quorya is located at the center of a valley surrounded by hills, the surrounding area shielded from sight of the town's visitors from the road to the south. On the road was a peculiar company of four children and two men traveling on four horses. As Kalen's group entered the valley from the southwest, they descended into a busy village. The town center was abuzz in mercantile activity and perfumed with the scent of manure and filth.

Kalen felt flush and dizzy. "It is this descent from a higher elevation," he said. "I feel unwell from not climbing to a high place. I have not *spatialized* properly in some time."

"None of us have," said his brother who rode with him. "We're almost through. The Vault has to be in this town. I'll take you to the place." When they arrived in the market, Kyle recognized the Vault instantly. He pointed Kalen to a fruit vendor with a tan-colored tunic with a greenish flat-topped hat. "He's changed his business, but that's the one."

Kalen and Kyle dismounted.

"Just a moment," said Gailon as he dismounted as well. "Something doesn't feel right to me. This is too easy." He scanned the vicinity and listened to fragments of various conversations. "Does anyone speak this language?"

Dro said, "Yes, I know enough to understand what they're saying. There's been commotion here today, visitors of an unusual sort. Magic-users bearing the suit of Wands."

Everyone except Kalen drew their swords and assumed a battle posture, even Chila and Jeila who began to lead their horses off the thoroughfare.

Kalen said, "I'm going ahead." He motioned for Kyle and Gailon to come along. "Kyle, you stay with our sisters."

Kyle reluctantly turned to join his sisters in the shade of the mercantile tents. A moment later he said, "Kalen, he speaks Tolang."

Kalen, Gailon, and Dro approached the fruit vendor and Kalen showed him the key.

The Vault wordlessly beckoned the boy to enter the back-shop, pulling aside a black curtain, entering alone. Gailon and Dro stood uneasily at the shop's entrance.

Kalen pulled back the curtain and entered a dark room without furniture of any kind. The noise from beyond the back-shop abated into an eerie silence. The Vault followed him, and removed a leather pouch from thin air. He said, "Master O'Tolan, you will find its contents undisturbed, in its original condition I assure you. Take as much time as you need with it." The Vault left him alone in the back room.

Kalen took it in his hands and opened it. The Black Stone was contained within, its tree-like veins invisible at the moment. Kalen sighed with relief. At last the Stone came to him, after so much loss. He was sure his parents would be pleased to see it in his possession.

Kalen pressed his hands to the Stone and said, "You once told me that you were mine. I am Kalen O'Tolan, son of Kairon and Karen O'Tolan, and on this day I claim you."

White light shone from within it; its veins appeared like spikes of lightning. Its cool surface began to radiate warmth.

The Black Stone: "Kalen, I am now yours. You may ask me a question."

Kalen said, "What are you?"

The Black Stone: "I am the source of magic in the world, the living intelligence of the Kosmos refracted as the First Artifact of Orr, the Premiere Seat of Yang in the Season of Yang. I am One with the Word given to the children of Abraham in the West and the Way given to the First Ancestors in the East. Mine is the power to see that the tide of darkness is rising and beyond it, a new and dangerous Light! Three Kosmic Wars and Three Kronic Wars and Three Logical Wars have begun, though few now perceive them. You are the one chosen to be my voice, my eyes, my hands, and my feet, in wayward times. You must prepare yourself and be worthy of the role you have been given."

Kalen said, "You will help me, yes?"

The Black Stone: "No, Kalen. I cannot, not yet. You will not hear my voice again for many, many years. I know this is hard for you to accept, but the time is not yet right for your training. You see, the War of the Archetypes has begun, and your brother and sisters and uncles are its first casualties. It is not what you think. You must know that what is about to happen is not your fault. You are … now going to put me back in the pouch and run out of here."

The Stone was of course prescient. Kalen was driven to protect his family, and he put the Stone away the moment he sensed the danger. He pulled back the curtain and found his entire family bound and gagged, and held by soldiers wearing the armor of the suit of Wands.

There were a hundred or more within plain sight, probably not the full complement. Also two horse-driven carriages arrived at the scene.

"It was a trap!" said Kalen. "Why didn't I see it coming?" Kalen pulled out his sword and ran toward his brother, but he was captured along the way. He got off only a few swings, none of them landing. The sword fell from his hand and was snatched up by a soldier. Kalen's hands and feet were bound, though he remained ungagged, and the Stone was taken from him and put in the Magician's hands.

The Vault fled behind the curtain and was not seen again.

The Magician was a wicked-looking man dressed in colorful robes and a neck tattoo of the symbol for infinity. He walked up to Kalen and said, "The Stone-Star Tarot is pitiful as it is ridiculous. Look at their leader!" Everyone laughed from the soldiers in the suit of Wands to the Lion who walked beside the mage. "They pretend to wholeness and completeness when what they really offer is new superstition and dogma spouted with false certainty. This is one heresy I will relish to crush!"

The mage turned to the drivers of the chariots. "Take the men and girls to the prisoner camp for questioning. Go now. Put the older boy in the other chariot, but do not leave until I give the order." And then the Magician approached Kalen and held up the pouch with the Stone.

The first chariot sped away.

"Is this the Ace of Stones?" asked the mage.

Kalen said, "Yes. It's the one. But you cannot use it without me. It answers only to me."

The Magician took the pouch and looked inside at the Stone. "What a bizarre instrument! If it indeed is emotionally attached to this boy, then it would be a shame if something bad were to happen to him." The mage held the pouch in one hand and with the other hand he lifted Kalen off his feet by his neck. Kalen choked as the mage looked at him meanly.

The Magician put Kalen down. "Your appearance is a lie! You are not a boy, but a man of extensive years, nearly two hundred years old as a rough estimate. I will not show mercy on you, runt. The Stone will talk to me. I can be very persuasive."

And then he turned to the chariot driver, saying: "Put this boy with the other, and take them both to the Castle of Wands. Put them in the dungeon."

The first chariot departed Quorya on a northwestward route. The Six of Stones hid in a nearby carriage and started following it the moment it took off. He continued to follow it out of the city when it was no longer being observed by other Wands. When the first opportunity presented itself, the Six abandoned his carriage and leapt onto the back of prisoners' carriage where there were two guards. A sharp, broad sword at the end of a fast, strong arm won the melee. After he slayed the two guards, he cut Gailon's bonds. He said, "I am Salveris, the Six of Stones. Free yourselves." Gailon began to free the others. And then the Six jumped onto the driver's horse, killed him, and drove the carriage to the side of the road. Gailon thanked the Six profusely and then took the reigns of the carriage, changing direction to the northeast. The Six of Stones for his part vanished into the rocky hillside, making himself invisible by perfectly mimicking the color and size of the wall of rocks. The Six hoped that the second carriage would pass the same way, but he waited for an opportunity to attack which never came.

The second chariot took Kyle and Kalen southwest past the Desert Bluffs toward the Castle of Wands, the greatest fortress of magic in the ancient world. The Wand driver and guards faithfully traversed the sparsely-traveled route for many miles, riding all day and all night and into the following day. They gave the prisoners a dollup of water a day, but otherwise ignored their human cargo. They took the boys to the dungeon at the Castle of Wands, a place about which it is said that no one has ever escaped and no one was ever heard from again.

THE LONG DETAINMENT

he King and Queen of Wands ruled from their Castle of Wands over the entirety of the Realm of Wands, attempting to breathe new life into a fading magical kingdom. With the Omphalos of Delphi in hand, they possessed one of the most powerful magical items amongst the Artifacts of Orr, the last remnants of the First Ancestors and the First Tribes. They had only to crack its code to get it to reinforce their fading magical powers, and the entire ancient world of the early First Millennium CE would bend to their will.

The Ace of Stones was never far from the Queen of Wands's hand or King of Wands's throne (and sometimes it was the plaything of the Knight of Wands and Page of Wands who enjoyed tossing it on the tower courtyards). The King of Wands threatened to torture the Bearer and his brother. Reluctantly, the Stone allowed its powers to be co-opted by the Tarot of the Second Wave, so that they would let Kalen and Kyle live. Just as the Royal Stones of the Third Wave predicted, intimidation and the threat of torture were the tools of the Wands for extracting insight and influence from the First Stone. The Wand Royals kept the Omphalos Bearer close at hand, locked securely in the castle's dungeons, rarely to leave his cage.

The Black Stone begged for Kalen's release for several years, but its pleas were unmet. Gradually the Stone stopped asking after Kalen, but it never stopped plotting its return to a proper course. The King and Queen of Wands believed that Kalen must be kept alive for the Omphalos to function (a belief which the Stone itself gave them), and thus they kept him alive out of necessity. They also kept Kyle alive for pragmatic reasons, surmising that Kalen could be more easily controlled if they had leverage over him. If Kalen got unruly, they tortured Kyle until his brother's ways won their approval. After that, Kalen rarely crossed the will of the Wands. Both boys were smart enough to realize the dark nature of their fate, kept alive only to keep the old Tarot's magic from fading. The Wands kept the existence of the Black Stone a secret to the outside world, and they took credit for its magical deeds as their own.

The Wands had no understanding of spatializing or temporizing, and they rejected pleas by the Stone to allow the Bearer access to light and movement. Kalen tried to adapt himself to space and time naturally, but it was not possible in the dungeon. Enormous and frightening gaps arose between how he experienced space-time and the rest of the world did. Kyle made a calendar glyph for every half-day on the cell wall they shared, but they were not allowed natural light to track time so it was estimated. Every night when he went to sleep, Kalen did not know what he would find when he awoke, or if he would wake at all. Occasionally he fell into a bear-like hibernation state, not waking for calendar weeeks or months at a time. Kalen would feel the passage of a day, but many days had passed in the world's reckoning. If Kalen's sleep were disrupted, he became too weak to move. If he slept too much, he might be full of more energy than he could contain except by voicing unintelligible screams and meaningless shouts.

BLACK STONE 28 (222 CE – 229 CE)

"Happy birthday, Kalen. You are six years old as the Kalendar goes ... and I am about ten," said Kyle. He didn't have any birthday sweets to offer, nor any lamp for the darkness for Kalen to extinguish, but he lifted his little brother higher so he could trace his hands over the chinks in the wall which Kyle carved in the shape of the Kalendar. "Mom and Dad would have been very happy to learn that we are alive, and so far as know, so are Jeila and Chila."

Kalen said, "I hope they escaped and are free. It seems just a few days ago I was 5 years and 40 days old. Where did the days and months go?" He sensed the answer on his own, but he did not like what he thought. While he slept each night, the world aged rapidly around him. Days passed for him; years for the world. The Wands were magical beings, old Archetypes, and they had long lifespans. The Archetypes could hold him and his brother hostage for decades, centuries, or even millennia, if it suited them and the boys were not able to escape.

According to Kyle's math, the year was 222 CE, making Kalen 222 years old as other people track time. He was a very old man trapped in the body of a child, and trapped in a Tarot's dungeon he began to feel every bit his age. "We are going to make it out of here." He talked to himself in the pitch dark cell he shared with his brother, and Kyle incidentally, keeping up his hope.

Light shone in the dungeon for a while when the guards came in for inspections. Kyle's face and body were almost unrecognizable to Kalen. He was a lad in late teenage years, about 18 years old to appearances. Kalen shrieked in horror! Kyle said, "Relax. I haven't grown up all overnight. It's happened over quite a long period of time, only you've been un-temporizing or something. I don't understand what's happening. You hadn't noticed. You couldn't see me. You were asleep ... or in a daze."

Kalen said, "Let me feel you. Is it really you?" Kyle was a foot taller at least, and he had kept up his strength. Kyle said, "I'm a man now. But you're still a boy. You aren't growing up, not much. I'm not aging like you are!"

Kyle said, "When you claimed the Stone, its power of longevity shifted from being on everyone in the family to just being on you. Mom thought this might happen. She told me and your sisters to expect it would happen one day."

Kalen sat on a sack of bones they used as a chair. "Oh, that's weird."

Kyle said, "I know. I don't mind that actually. It feels good to grow faster. What I can't stand is being trapped in this place." Kyle looked at the wall on which he scribbled the Kalendar's markings.

Kalen said, "Why do you suppose nobody's tried to break us out?"

Kyle said, "You ask me that question almost every day. Don't you remember the answer?" Kalen looked despondent and confused, pounding on his head. "If you don't start *temporizing,* I'm afraid you're going to lose your mind. But to answer your question: They have. Gailon and Dro tried to break us out a few years ago, and they were captured by the Wands. They're here in another part of the dungeon. I haven't been able to speak to them. I don't know where Chila and Jeila are."

Kalen sobbed over his madness. "I don't remember any of that. I feel I've already lost my mind."

BLACK STONE 29 (230 CE – 238 CE)

"There is good news carried to us from Gailon," said Kyle. He woke Kalen from his sleep, and his brother moaned. "Jeila and Chila are well. There the good news ends. The Wands have seized control of the suit of Pentacles, and their power is double in the world now. They are using the power of the Black Stone and calling it their own. They are conquering every eastern territory in the magical world and extending their reach outward. Can you hear me? Do you understand what I am saying?"

Kalen looked up at his brother with darkened eyes of misunderstanding. He said, "Jeila and Chila are here?" Kyle nodded disagreement. Kalen added, "You look like Dad." Indeed, Kyle bore a striking resemblance to Kairon as he appeared in his mid-twenties. Kalen still looked like a boy of no more than 6 years and 4 months.

Kyle said, "I'm going to find a way out for you, for both of us." He racked his brain, but he could not fulfill this promise.

BLACK STONE 30 (239 CE – 246 CE)

"I'm 33 years old day, Kalen, if my math has been correct after all these years, assuming that you continued to age with the Kalendar when you claimed the Stone, but I did not. Gailon and Dro look really old. I bet they're in their fifties by now," he said. His brother wasn't listening. Kyle propped the boy up and held open his eyelids forcibly. Kalen groaned and shook. "Come on now, Kalen, wake up. Don't make me slap you again. You're hardly ever waking up anymore!" He eyes were sunk into their sockets and his skin was purplish in color.

An Angel appeared then appeared out of nowhere into the stark darkness, radiating a brightness never before seen in the Wands' dungeon. He was a handsome man wearing a serious expression along with wings with white and gray feathers. He said, "He must see light and world again soon or he will perish."

Kyle said, "What can you do for him?"

The Angel said, "It is not what I'm going to do for him. It's what you must do. Tell them the Omphalos Bearer is dying. Tell them he has only hours to live. He must spatialize and temporize immediately or the power of the Stone will be no more. The Earth and everyone on it approaches a Time Crisis. Hurry." And then the Angel vanished.

Kyle refused to eat or drink until he was given audience with someone who would listen to him, and he showed them that his brother was comatose.

Black Stone 31 (247 CE – 254CE)

Kyle's pleas, combined with threats made by the Ace of Stones, were finally enough to change the manner in which Kalen and Kyle were imprisoned. They were moved to a dungeon room which got some natural light from a window in an adjacent hallway. Once in every moon cycle, on the night of the fullest moon, the Bearer and his brother were taken in chains from the dungeon to the highest courtyard of the tower and permitted to look out over the land. Also they were taken to the courtyard in sunlight every so often at irregular intervals. Kalen was bound hand and foot, but with every View he began to regain his health.

The period of time from which the Ace of Stones entered the rulership of the Wands to the time it left is known to magical historians simply as the Rise of the Wand Empire. There is a most astonishing fact about the entire period of 107 calendar years: tutored by the Stone itself, the Wands learned of the nature of spatialization, i.e., the need for the Omphalos to traverse with the Bearer across the Earth, and they commenced to build new and ever more lavish castles in an eastward trajectory covering many hundreds of miles beyond East Africa. The sequence of castles took decades to build and furnish, and then the entire complement of Wand Royals and their regents and armies would move to the new location. New dungeons were built to contain the Bearer and his brother (along with other prisoners), and a prison cell was always built with a modest exposure to natural light to facilitate the Bearer's need to adapt to space-time.

About 250 CE, the Wands erected a new castle on the Izh River in the Western Urals. From this location they used the Black Stone to seize control of the suit of Swords, giving them dominion over three of the four suits of the Wand-Cup Tarot. Ensconced in power, the Wand Royals set their sights on the Cups. Not coincidentally, Chila and Jeila secured employment and influence at the Castle of Cups, and they attempted to encourage rebellion and a strike against the Castle of Wands. The sisters were both fully grown women late in their middle years with husbands and multiple children and even grandchildren amongst them. Their lives were haunted by their failure to find a way into the old Tarot's most formidable and secretive magical castle. Every avenue they tried was blocked, and they had nearly given up all hope of seeing their brothers again, until they were given an opportunity to visit the new fortress on the Izh River with a diplomatic delegation.

The purpose of the trip to discuss the terms of the Cups' surrender to the suit of Wands, for with three sets of Archetypes arrayed against them the Cups grew pessimistic. In fact there was a sizable contingency in the suit of Cups which was willing to fight and die rather than cede their power to the Wands. Chila and Jeila bent their ear and informed them of their suspicion that the Rise of the Wands owed its power to the Ace of Stones, a stolen Tarot card. A spy in the Wands' castle gave the Cups essential information about the location of the Omphalos and even the location of Kyle's and Kalen's cell in the dungeon. The sisters plotted to liberate the Stone and its Bearer in exchange for their service to help the Cups regain balance once again in the New Tarot. "Almost all the Cups are in the New Tarot by another name: Bowls. That's how you will be when the new order rises which the Ace of Stones will bring." The Cups were not pleased by the change from Cups to Bowls, but they were faced with the prospect of demise at the hands of rising Wands. They preferred change to destruction. They developed a plot to rescue Kalen and Kyle from the dungeons of the Castle of Wands, but their efforts were secretly undermined. The Page of Cups became distraught upon hearing news that "*almost* all of the Cups are in the New Tarot". By pressing Jeila, he learned that in fact the Stone-Star Tarot's Yin Deck possessed only 13 cards per suit instead of the 14 cards of the Wand-Cup Tarot. Upon further investigation, the Page of Cups learned that Pages would be eliminated in the new order, setting in motion its treachery.

When the delegation of Cups arrived at the Castle of Wands for the so-called "peace talks", they brought Jeila and Chila as assistants. As per the published itinerary, the Cups were given a tour of the grounds.

At this time, a cadre of cards friendly to the O'Tolans split off: the Five of Cups headed covertly to the dungeons with Chila to attempt a rescue of the brothers, the Ten of Cups went in search of Gailon and Dro, and the Ace of Cups itself, borne in the hands of Jeila, sought out the Ace of Stones. Foiling the scheme, the Page of Cups approached the Page and Knight of Cups with his information about a rebellion in their midst, and shortly news of the plot reached the ears of the Queen herself. While the King of Wands led the King of Cups on the tour of the castle grounds, the Queen thwarted all of the rescue attempts. Jeila and Chila were taken hostage and put in the dungeons along with the Ace, Five, and Ten of Cups. The brave Tarot plot ended as debacle, giving no further advantage to Kalen or Kyle while resulting catastrophically in the imprisonment of their sisters. As for the suit of Cups, it did not last long in the old Tarot's order before it was completely overtaken.

There was one silver lining in the dark cloud: Kalen and Kyle saw Chila and Jeila again through the bars of their cell, bringing everyone to tears of joy.

BLACK STONE 32 (255 CE – 262 CE)

"Happy 7th birthday, brother," said Kyle, looking even older than his self-estimated 49 years owing to the drudgery of the long span of his imprisonment in the dungeon. He was nearly bald and what hair remained was gray as a rock.

Kalen regained as much sanity as he ever had following the improvement in conditions of the dungeon. He and Kyle saw sunlight and moonlight regularly, and they continued to be taken in shackles to the tower courtyards. He frequently heard rumors of the lives of Jeila and Chila, and was thrilled to learn that he was not only an uncle but a great-uncle. Somewhere beyond the castle walls there were new families bearing O'Tolan blood if not the O'Tolan surname. Perhaps, he thought, if he died in the dungeon as a longtime prisoner of the Wands, at least that would be some consolation. He thought morbidly like this too often for it usually seemed hopeless.

After the Wands seized control of the Cups, they took charge of all the magic of the old Archetypes at the level of the Minor Arcana. Every so often the remaining cards from the Major Arcana of the old Tarot visited the Castle of Wands – The Emperor, The Empress, The High Priestess, and so on. But these were never heard from again in the outside world, while their cries could often be heard in the dungeon, wafting from the lower levels.

Black Stone 33 (263 CE – 271 CE)

Gailon passed away from pneumonia one winter's day. Dro lost the will to live and he passed before the springtime. A silver-haired, wrinkly, and hunched Kyle shed few tears. "It's best for them really. There is no point in going on anymore. Death would be a blessing." Kalen knew that his brother had a point, and he didn't like the situation any better, but it was not in his nature to despair or hope for death.

The night of Gailon's passing, Kalen had a dream in which his uncle appeared to him, looking the same as he had in his younger years. "Kalen," he said, "Don't you realize what is happening out there in the wide world? The Suit of Wands has used the power of the Ace of Stones to take control of the old Tarot, the one you have been tasked to replace with the Stone-Star Tarot. How convenient, isn't it? Who is using whom? It is not merely coincidence that a weakened Wand-Cup arises after the Black Stone takes control. The Ace of Stones is behind all of this, but its power to turn the magical world on itself has come to an end through its success. Now surely as the Third Wave follows the Second Wave the Wands will seek control of the magical world they don't possess, the Stone-Star Tarot, using the Black Stone as its power source. What will they use to gain leverage over it, do you think, to get it to give up all the other cards of the New Decks? Think! They have you. Be wary."

Shortly thereafter, Kyle was removed from Kalen's cell. Alone in the dungeons of the Castle of Wands for the first time, Kalen feared the worst of his miserable existence yet lay before him.

BLACK STONE 34 (272 CE – 279 CE)

Kalen saw the Black Stone again for the first time since the day he stood in the Vault. He was brought before it in chains, and they whipped and beat him while they interrogated the Omphalos. Where is the headquarters of the Suit of Stones? Where can the King and Queen of Stones be found? What are their weaknesses? They went on like this regarding every card they could think of, inflicting pain on Kalen with every opportunity. The Black Stone refused to give up locations, instead babbling on with uninteresting intelligence.

"No more whips! They break the skin and could cause infection," said the Hermit, the card of the Major Arcana of the Wand-Cup Tarot, speaking to the Magician. What unfortunate circumstances led to his position here is not told in this story. He said, "We want to punish the Black Stone, not kill the Bearer just yet."

The Stone was not permitted to speak directly to Kalen, but it nevertheless managed to get out a few words. "Have faith. Keep up hope."

As Kalen was untied from the torture rack, he instinctively lept at the Stone, surprising his captors. He stood quickly and lept again, nearly clutching it. "Tell me what to do!" the boy shouted.

The Stone said nothing in Tolang or any other language with a name, but it did emit a sound that was part of the unnamed language. The sound meant "bird". After that, Kalen was only brought before the Stone gagged and bound with both hands and feet. His punishments continued and their severity increased.

BLACK STONE 35 (280 CE – 287 CE)

Chila and Jeila passed in the following years, while Kyle reached the advanced age of 72 by his own reckoning. Although opportunities for conversation were slight in the dungeon, their company lifted Kalen's burdens even as it increased his resentment toward the Wands for their cruelty. Both Chila and Jeila appeared to him in a dream in the nights following their transition, Chila as a Queen of Eggs and Jeila as a Queen of Bowls. "You will need my help in the coming war of Tarot cards," said Chila as she turned away from him, revealing the embroidery of a Giant Condor on the back of her gown. Kalen said, "You look beautiful, sister. I'm sorry I couldn't rescue you."

Kalen hated the Wand-Cup Tarot and promised himself to vanquish it in the coming War of Archetypes. As for the Decks to replace it, Kalen had few insights into its design. Without the assistance of the Black Stone, he could not be certain of his inspirations. Occasionally he felt the influence of a Tarot card beyond his sight, but as for what it was and how it fit in with the New Decks, he seldom knew. The dungeons were not a place for thinking deep thoughts; it was enough to get through a day hungry and dirty, still human and compassionate.

Although Kyle was kept in a different part of the dungeon, the brothers still had an opportunity to communicate when they were taken outside to the tower courtyard at the same day and time. Kyle whispered, "We must try to get news to our sisters' families regarding their passing. Is there *any* way you can get a message outside the castle?"

Both Kyle and the Stone were seemingly urging him to use his unusual linguistic talents. A long time had it been since he had endeavored to communicate with animals. In fact he suspected that he was losing the ability through disuse because every worm or beetle or spider he approached for conversation seemed uninterested or incapable of speaking with him. But what opportunity had he had to speak with birds? Honestly beyond a few simple whistles communication with avian species was almost entirely beyond his abilities. Their use of the unnamed language was in a dialect virtually impossible to understand to those who haven't spent years learning the differences. One day perhaps Kalen could take the time to study the peculiar dialect of birds and write a dissertation bridging their conceptual world with that of human beings, but the seven-year-old boy had neither the opportunity nor the training to communicate with birds on the fly. After deliberating a while, Kalen said, "I don't think so."

Kalen was shackled and chained while he was outside, and he was seldom far from any guard. He tried a few simple words with a bluejay, and it seemed to understand him, but he was far from being able to construct a complete sentence let alone ask it to perform an errand. Frustrated, he wondered silently about his never-seen nephews and nieces, and he hoped they remembered their missing mothers, uncles, and great-uncles in a good way.

BLACK STONE 36 (288 CE – 295 CE)

As they had several times before, the Wands moved the seat of their governance to a station farther eastward so as to allow Kalen to spatialize and temporize. Kalen knew a move was immanent because prisoners were being taken from the dungeon and, rumor told, thrown over the castle tower into a massive pile of corpses, carrion for vultures. Every time the Wands moved they purged their dungeons. The usual clamor of prisoners grew deathly quiet. At last the moving day came.

Kalen and Kyle were fated to live, their hands and feet bound and both of them placed in a carriage for transportation to the Urals. They were heavily guarded, yet an opportunity nearly presented itself for Kalen to bust free. Their carriage broke an axle and was stopped for repairs while the rest of the caravan moved on. At the same time, Kalen managed to free his feet from their bonds. "You can run! Run!" said Kyle. Kyle, however, was in no condition to join Kalen.

Kalen said, "I will free you."

Kyle said, "I am an old man with brittle bones. You must go alone."

Kalen was sorely tempted to flee, and his mind buzzed with considerations and contraries until at last he arrived at his decision. He said, "I don't want to leave you."

Kyle said, "You must. Don't be a fool."

Kalen paused. After a moment, he said, 'You're right'. I can leave without you, but I can't leave without the Stone."

The carriage was repaired and the journey continued. Kalen tied his own feet, and the brothers proceeded in silence.

An astonishing fortress came into view at the intersection of the Karakum Desert and the Kopet Dag mountain range. It lay high in the mountains beyond the city of Nisa, imperial necropolis of the Parthian kings, with a view to the distant city visible when standing at the Tower of Thanatos, more than 200 feet from highest parapet to the desolate ground below.

BLACK STONE 37 (296 CE – 304 CE)

Kalen's eighth birthday came and went without a celebration of any kind, not even the fortunate event of an outing to the tower court-yard. Kalen doubted there was any person alive who was keeping track of his milestones anyway, except Kyle of course. Kyle's health was poor and in his 88th year he passed away. The guards unceremoniously put his body in a sack and, rumor told, threw it over the edge of the tallest tower into a corpse pile where all the Tarot's enemies tended to end up.

Kalen took his brother's passing hard, harder than any other death he had endured, even the demise of his own parents. No one was living who knew of the trials Kalen suffered in prison, the burdens and the torture, except his only brother … now gone, and he was left all alone. He was drowning in self-pity when he resolved vengeance against the old Tarot. Thoughts of taking revenge provided a purpose for going on with life, even when other emotions failed in their logic to motivate him to endure. He imagined himself carrying the Brown

Sword described as the third Artifact of Orr, and fancied it would be a good blade for slicing the throats of the King of Wands and all his court. The thought of spilt blood kept Kalen's spirit alive through dark days. He would kill them all if he could.

A new small blessing came to him at the new Castle of Wands: his captors allowed him to walk in daylight on the courtyard of the Tower of Thanatos. They removed his shackles and put a broom in his hand, and Kalen was grateful for the chance to work. Perhaps they reasoned that it was impossibly high for anyone to survive a fall or attempt a daring rescue, and they were right. Or perhaps the Black Stone had delivered a juicy piece of intelligence on the Stone-Star Tarot. Whatever the explanation may be, Kalen was grateful for the opportunity to walk under sunshine and breathe fresh air, even if it smelt a bit of rotten flesh and bird droppings.

One day Kalen caught a brief glimpse of the Ace of Stones. As he looked out at the lower courtyard on the Tower of Phobos, he saw the Knight of Wands and Knight of Pentacles playing a game of toss. At first, he thought nothing of it, but then he looked carefully and he could not believe what he saw. The ball they were tossing was none other than the Omphalos of All-That-Is, Navel of the Earth, Centerpoint of the Kosmos.

Kalen was certain that the Black Stone had seen him too.

BLACK STONE 38 (305 CE – 312 CE)

One night Kalen had a peculiar dream. He was falling through the sky when he suddenly knew he was aflight over Nukus in Uzbekistan (an unfamiliar name for a never-before-seen place). He found himself singing aloud:

> *If I am the reason Buddha's soul endures,*
>
> *then I must heed God's own proclamation*
>
> *and a more full liberation secure.*
>
> *This path is too great an admonition!*
>
> *I didn't ask to be given this deed!*
>
> *It's too much, too great a benediction!*
>
> *The question now is: how do I proceed?*

He did not understand some of the details of the song, for the name of Buddha meant nothing to him. And what proclamation of God was he singing about? In fact, the song seemed not to be his at all, but someone else's, an imposter who had taken over his identity. He sensed somewhere in the universe there was another Kalen, one who was riding a bedazzling White Horse through a narrow valve-like passage. These were crazy thoughts, but they were Kalen's own. Often his dreams were Kalen's only source of amusement and entertainment

197

in the long days of silent suffering in the dungeon alone, and they gave him a sense of purpose.

Something about the dream shifted Kalen's perceptions of his time in captivity. He had recently seen the Black Stone for the first time in a long while. That had to be a good omen. He sensed that his imprisonment was coming to a close, and that he had best be ready for the moment when it would arise. He did not know when or how it would come, but someone or something was coming for him. It would carry him to safety somehow. He stirred with courage, but he was careful not to allow the guards to sense any change in his behavior. He had been gloomy and sorrowful in disposition, and he would not let them see his renewed vigor.

Kalen had one more dream of tremendous importance in the dungeon. He pictured himself a grown man in size and stature, not a young child, and he held out invisible arms to touch a beautiful lovely woman who descended from the Stars. As she came down to him, hovering in a field of energy, she spoke words to him which he could not hear. He only retained the notion that she was making a promise to him, for she spoke seriously and deliberately, and it seemed somehow that she was giving herself to him. Who else could she be, young Kalen reasoned, but the Queen of Stars herself? In fact, it was the Queen of Stars, and she had come a long distance to be with Kalen

... but not the young boy in the Wands stronghold in the Ural Mountains, but a Kalen of a different time and in a different place.

BLACK STONE 39 (313 CE – 320 CE)

It was common for vermin to roam the cells of the dungeon, and Kalen usually paid them no heed. But never before had Kalen seen a rodent of such distinguished appearance and stature walking directly toward him as if he were on an important mission ... or delivering a message. Kalen bent over and listened.

It spoke in the unnamed language: "I am Mozulan, the Great Mouse, Immortal Animwaa of the Reformed Rodentia, foe of the Ro and friend of the Bel. I come bearing a message from Chelone, who you may know as the Keeper of Balance in the New Tarot. She says that aid has been dispatched to assist you. Keep one eye on the Omphalos and the other eye on the skies." It then walked on Kalen's body, and Kalen fed it morsels of his food on his palm. A moment later Mozulan said he must depart on an errand. "There is a very old pouch of yours in the King's closet which he has long forgotten, a brown leather hide sack. I will snatch it and drag it to the tower courtyard and place it for you there if I can. It may come in handy."

Kalen waited anxiously throughout the morning and into the afternoon. At last guards came and took Kalen to the yard for sunshine and exercise, and the boy swept the grounds with one eye on the skies and the other scanning for the Black Stone. He spied it on the lower level, bouncing in the hands of the Page of Wands. Where the Knight of Wands stood, Kalen did not know. Kalen discretely took possession of a leather pouch which had been placed for him near the parapets. He was nearly done with the sweeping when the Knight of Wands emerged from the staircase. He walked to the edge of the castle walls and looked down on the lower tower. The Knight shouted to the Page, "Throw it up here! I'll catch."

The Page tossed the Black Stone high in the air just as a Great Condor of the South swooped to scoop it up. In an instant, the Stone was gone ... until a short while later, the giant bird dropped it directly over Kalen. Kalen knew this not only because he saw it from his own eyes, but because he saw it from the perspective of the Stone. Suddenly, his mind was alive with Stone-consciousness, and he felt himself falling from windy skies and rough weather, older and more mature, rolling in perspective as the Stone turned in its whirling motion.

When the Stone touched his hand, Kalen and the Stone were one again. It lit with mighty bright light illuminating seams in the shape of a Baobab Tree. The illumination briefly flashed throughout the courtyard, blinding the sight of all save the Omphalos Bearer himself. Kalen felt its surface and smiled with a joy unlike any he had felt for something close to a century of time as the world's calendar goes. He asked the Stone a question: "What do I do now?"

And the Stone replied: "The Knight of Wands knows the Stone is missing and he suspects you have it. He will shake you down. Let him search you for it, then let him toss you off the edge."

Kalen said, "But they will find you and take you!"

The Stone said, "They will not. Trust me."

Kalen had little time to decide what to do. The Stone's instructions seemed reckless. Wouldn't the Stone be discovered? How was he to know for sure that the Knight would throw him off the wall? How would he survive the fall? He balked.

The Tower Guard pursued Kalen, who ran beneath the legs of the Knight of Wands. Kalen ran to the wall and pretended to throw something off the edge. The Knight patted the boy down, but found no Stone. He did find, however, the leather brown pouch. It was empty, so he tossed it over the wall. A member of the Tower Guard approached. "He doesn't have it," said the Knight. The Stone seemed to move on its own power just out of the guard's prying hands. The Knight struck Kalen in the belly, leaving him breathless and quivering. "That's for trying to escape." And then the Knight tossed him over the edge of the wall.

Kalen and the Black Stone sailed off the edge of the Tower. As the boy fell, the Stone exerted its influence over his body's movements, shaping his back and pelvis to form a position which might survive the devastating crash below. Moreover, the Stone seemed to slow the movements down by seconds beyond what Kalen believed should be possible. The journey through the air to the corpse pile below seemed to be happening in slow motion. At last Kalen crashed on the mound and rolled into a dark hole at the base.

OVER THE WALL

Beionai saw a brown leather bag sail off the edge of the wall of the Tower of Thanatos and land somewhere in the thorny bushes at the base. He did not want to take his eyes off the Tower, but the bag could be useful. He wandered over to the bushes and scanned for it, and he saw it and picked it up. The Bear knew that Mouse found the omphalos pouch in his rummaging through the palace, and this was it certainly. Kalen would appreciate having it returned to him, and now he would have a proper gift to give the boy upon seeing him again.

A minute later, Kalen himself sailed over the wall, his body twisted in an unnatural shape. Beinoai growled in fear. "Oh no!" is what the growl said. He saw the boy fall in a squiggly line, avoiding collission with metal spikes at the spot for which he headed to a more cushiony landing on a pile of corpses. He hit the putrid corpse-pile with a thud and rolled down the other side of the pile where Beionai could not see.

The Bear rounded the pile and looked for Kalen. He growled terribly. "What the hell!" is what the growl spoke. The boy had vanished, and Beionai walked the full length of the pile. He called, "Kalen!" No reply.

Just then, a rodent crawled up his leg. It was Mouvais, the Animwaa which Beionai recognized, and the Bear put his paw out for the creature to run up on. The Mouse's squeaky voice was too tiny for the Bear to hear unless he held him right up to his ear. The Mouse said, "Beionai, you are a great bear but you were foolish in your searching. Kalen is down *there*, in the man-sized hole which you wandered past without noticing. Let me down and then hurry to get him. The Knight of Wands will be here soon I would wager. Get Kalen as far from this place as fast as you can go. Don't worry about me; I will find my way."

Beionai saw Kalen in the hole which he had walked past, and he pawed at the soil to make it wide enough for him to enter. It was shallow but deep enough for the boy to be tucked into the socket in a manner impossible for the Bear to reach. Beionai said, "Kalen if you can hear me, say something." Nothing.

Beionai broke through layers of earth-soil until at last he could clasp his arms around the boy and pull him out. The boy was limp but not without life. He breathed yet. The Bear growled again. "Kalen lives!"

Beionai stood and turned to leave, but the Mouse was running up his leg again. "Really?" said the irritated Bear. "Now what?" The Bear stooped until Mouvais was close enough to his ear to hear him. The Mouse said, "Where is the Stone?"

"Good grief!" said the Bear. "I nearly forgot! The Bear pawed Kalen's tunic, but did not find it. The Mouse entered the hole and the Bear waited anxiously. A minute later, the Mouse exited the hole pushing the Omphalos of Delphi. The Bear thanked the Mouse, took the Stone in his paw, and bounded away.

He ran at an incredible speed considering that he only had two legs for the task, slowed as he was by the need to carry the boy. Beionai was unaccustomed to walking for any length of time on only two legs, but he managed the task ably. He took the boy into the forest and stopped at a stream to get him some water. He set Kalen down on the shore and put the Stone in its pouch. He put the pouch in Kalen's hand and then splashed water on his mouth until he took some in and coughed.

"Oh," said Kalen. "It's you. You came for me."

Beionai said, "I never left you. I have followed the Wands for the better part of a century waiting for this day, my dear boy, tucking myself into the woods disguised as a mortal bear. Soon we will have our ninth birthday as the Kalendar goes, yours and mine, Animwaa."

Kalen said, "I love you."

Beionai exuded a gentle and sweet growl, its meaning plain. And then he added, "Are you in pain? You took quite a fall, more than a man can survive."

Kalen said, "I can't move much. My bones are broken."

Beinoai said, "It's a miracle you can move anything. We need a physician. I know someone who may be able to help you."

Beionai set the leather pouch set in Kalen's hand. "The pouch is a gift from Mouse. I had something to do with it, too."

"Thank you," said Kalen. At the sight of the Black Stone, he began to cry tears of joy. "Stone, do you know what you cost me? You cost me my childhood, you most costly thing."

The Stone lit a bit from inside, its branch-like seams illuminating dimly. It said, "Thank you for rescuing me, Beionai and Kalen. I am grateful."

Kalen made an effort to stand, balancing himself on a rock in the stream, but he could not. He said, "I can't move on my own. Can you take me somewhere higher? I need to spatialize."

Beionai said, "You also need to stay hidden. The Wands could be coming at any minute."

The Stone said, "They will not come today. The Knight of Wands does not know that Kalen has left with the Stone. He thinks it's lost

THE NEW ZODIAC

somewhere in the castle or just over the wall and he will spend several days looking for it before telling the King that he lost it."

Kalen said, "What do we do?"

The Stone said, "You have a taste of freedom; you ought to enjoy it. Chelone has called a Healer who will arrive shortly. Move on as soon as you are able. Head east. You have much to prepare."

Kalen said, "Where is the Wizard? Can he not help us?"

The Stone said, "He is helping us in his own way. His trip to see the Deities did not go as he anticipated, and he has found himself at the center of a new war."

The Bear slung Kalen over his shoulder and walked with him uphill. At last, Kalen and the Bear set camp at the highest peak and ate the gifts which nature provided to them for food. Kalen tucked the Stone in his pouch and fastened it tightly to the waist-cord of his tunic. They waited for the arrival of the Healer.

THE SURRENDER OF SYMBIOSIS

PART TWO

Chapter One

Ai, The Season of Yang | Yang

1 Black Stone – 41 Brown Sword (Dec. 22 am – Apr. 22 am)

Entropy brought the multiverse to ruin.
All was lost, everything in every world.
Gravity wrought infinite contraction.
Out of the Void, one *Bei* of hope unfurled,
an intelligence not of light but dark
in which the *Aal-Wiz* of Yahweh whirled,
present in settings dangerous and stark.

I

Hear! I have come to you with a purpose:
Between what is true and what can be teached
there is now a dangerous divergence.
The Word is eclipsed by decadent speech,
grudging, drudging language of grotesque spit.
Cacophany! And so the Way is breached.
Woe comes for all in body and spirit!
The Holy Names must be set in union
so every name will be made coherent!
Cultures come closer, languages re-hewn,
warring with misapprehensions of trope,
deconstructing, and then falling to ruin.
Time grows short, you are sliding down the slope!
Still it is not too late to correct course
if in a new Book there is yet a hope!

II

Beloved, I ask, whose songs are these three,
from softest silence to the loudest yell,
from the meekest nil to largest degree?
How they do cascade like the Earth's mantel
from its hottest core to coldest ocean,
permeating all realms celestial!
I am standing here with noble bison,

his tail tucked inward, horns butting to north,
calmly contemplating history's run.

I invoke you, beloved, at Yule's berth!
Will you complete my heart in empty space,
incarnate fullness from this lifetime forth?
Be with me always in this sacred place
from which there is but northern exposure.
While you are here seek only your own face!
Fear not this midnight, your soul's erasure:
We will never part if you answer yes
here at Life's opening and Love's closure.

III

I abdicate Omni Lumination
for darkest night imaginable —
unawake, unenlightened, unaware.

All that I once was is hidden.
All that evolution brought is now gone,
asleep as a bear in her den.

At this, midnight's first chime,
at Delphos, isle of Greece,
We seize Time ere it slips to morning's Eight.

The Season of Yang emerges as it is,
out of the northern half's winter,
out of the southern half's summer.

Amongst the subtleties there is a one,
instigating, purposeful, and direct.
A solitary Yang is pronounced /aɪ/.

(eye: two e-shaped I's with lashes on either side of a y-shaped nose)

Yang is not the principle of lightness.
It is the absence of sun at midnight
rising to an early morning brightness!
This statement is revealed by the New Klock!

Yang is not the principle of masculinity.
It is the agentic source at root of Power
which male, female and unary essences share!

These are the Third Wave's notions of Yang.
The Third Wave responds to the Second Wave;
The Fourth Wave is unveiled at the close.
Yang's Music will be decided in fight,
a future Great War of Subtleties sang.
It will arrive in the Kalendar's Ninth
Month at the Third Logical Battle's clang.

IV

Season of Yang begins –
Yang in Great Arcana,
Stone-Star Tarot's heights.
'Tis a panorama
of Three Kosmic Fights.

'Tis first of three Timelines,
each for a thousand years;
their interweaving set
in elapsed Kronic Wars
which Middle Months beget.

In the final Timeline,
what was made Wrong by Ro
must be established Right
even if Two Seas must end
upon a New Isle in sight.

1. Yang

Yang ends in Zeus's zoo –
Deities so ordered
as only He can subdue.
What Delphi can break and send
is one which Yin may yet mend.

Chapter Two

Ei | The Angel | The King of Stones

Black Stone 1 am - Red Jewel 1 am
(Dec. 22 am – Jan. 31 am)

Element of Space obtains at the start
of a new Map of the Heavens in art!
Emptiness which contains and positions
The Kosmos with its many conditions.

I

I am prior to and in beginnings,
a spaciousness within myself,

realized, timeless
at the start of the First Month.
I am black as an onyx stone in the night,
I am brown as boron soap,
I am blue as cobalt
in the morning light.

I am pale pink or purple
rooted in a base of beige
in bands visible and inscrutable.
I am Light awakening.

The names of colors are emerging,
beginning with the new primes.
Yellow must become yellow once again;
then even the Color Wheel shall rhyme!

Element of the First Month is Space:
Ace of place, base of all,
vocation of vying, purse of views,
big bodacious balancing bang.

Space is in your face,
Space is in our aim.
Space is Vowel /eɪ/.
Space is Yang and Yang.

I start at the center of Symbiosis;
I surrender what used to be for what is.
I am Yang Yang Yang Yang Yang Yang
leaving through a Valve with a Bang.

II

The King of Stones:
"Be with me ere the birth of Apollo!
Put your brain at rest, tame your maze-like thoughts!
Intone with me from lung chambers hollow!
Pray for survival, cast your solemn lots!
Imperceptible is nearby wisdom
which without your effort unravels knots!
Discover me in ways almost random!
Take dice, roll an Eight, number limitless!
Angry flight is our escape in tandem!
Clear light is fading! Break from Vindonnus!
Meet me here at the dark-bane matter's bay,
you a babe of Polaris Octantis!
After the day's dawning, let us make hay!

KING *of* STONES

See the grain yellow color of the moon!
It keeps whole though it is half, come what may!
'Til it re-wholes, we are the Spirit's spoon!
We are filled with flame, making a potion!
We lighten mind with a shamanic swoon!

Come with me! I know the place it's hidden!
There's shroud shown only by a son of Thrace,
One with moxie to take what's forbidden!
Come to Old Delphi, a most sacred place!
We are gathered now in masks so stony!
While you are here, wear the grandparents' face!"

III

I, Gabriel, am Angel of Great Range!
A divine ranger, a keeper of peace
and order in the Worlds of the Exchange.
Hear! The Ro at the heart of Entropy's
demonic decay has confused all speech;
conflict abounds and chaos increases.
For this reason across Time I must reach
into the Days of Supreme Mysteries
(and the normal boundaries I would breach)
which have followed the War of Histories.

2. *The Angel*

I must put forth a Course Correction
at the Third Millennium's inflection
so you may recite this Poet's story,
lighting light which could be Kalen's glory.
In the tenth year of a new century,
I gave Lingua-U elementary
in the Poet's fortieth year of age
to put Kairon and Karen on the stage.

Chapter Three

B | Balance | The Ten of Stones

The Base of Being is the first terrain
given on the Atlas of Uvoha
for all the longitudes which do pertain
to the Way's start without swerve or yaw.

I

Kalen, the Baby is here
infant master potentate
of his manifest domain.

At first symbiotical,
Evolution's Midnight's Bay,
before the first beginning

and then, the earliest stage.
He creates a stable world
of objects to separate

which remind him of Bardo
in which he made his last fate.
A beige day to correlate

to colors white, black, and gray.
All Being passes through this
on way to the Magistrate.

Yang Hsiung writes the *Mystery*
under the Emperor Ai,
Year 1's philosophy

of the Holy Triune
glimpsed in the East as forces;
in the West, as personal,

known to some as Trinity
and to others, Trimurti:
making, keeping, and changing.

The letter B is said here
to bat, bust, burst, bash, and break
from All with indistinction

to a most barbaric scene,
behavior out of base need
for the planting of a seed.

Be with me here at this wave
made with a labial bang!
Come to the Base of Being

reflected in a new way
with the constellation B
at the New Zodiac's entry.

II

The Lo Shu Square – how it balances on the back of a Tortoise, card of the Major Arcana. This is how development proceeds, from the perspective of the Third Wave. Read the nine major stations of consciousness in conjunction with the nine sections of poetry in *The Kalendar:*

The Eight – The Surrender of Symbiosis
The One – The Face of Interiority
The Six – The Truth and the Tree
The Three – The Self and the Society
The Five – The Culture and Consciousness
The Seven – The Exuding of Individuality
The Four – The Analyst of Knowledge
The Nine – The Watchful Outsider
The Two – The Universality of Uniqueness

5. Balance

III

The Ten of Stones:

"I carry the weight of the Traditions,
stones which have nursed me, clothed me,
      kept me fed.
They have delivered to me conditions
which trouble my already confused head.
They have ordered me to report for war,
but I have a mind to go home instead,
pack bags, put on boots, and run for the door.
I have already served long for the dead."

Bai, The Ace of Stones

The Ace of Stones:

"I evolve in places unseen, hidden:
mysterious cauldrons of transitions,
binary essence which greets the fallen.
I am belief's rooted definitions
without which there is no sight or seeing.
I am the precept of preconditions,
footing for the inception of Being."

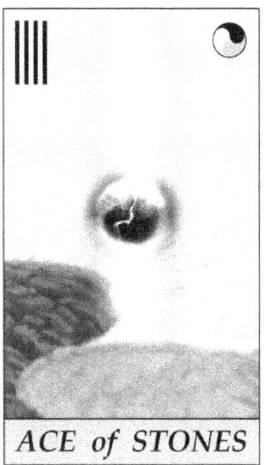

Week 1: The Bear

Black Stone 1 AM –
Black Stone 7 PM

The sleeping Bear
turns in his slumber.
He is the best
in the dark woods
for protecting
The Secret of Life.

Brown bear bears down!
He circles 'round.
He turns his snout.
Bearable, he,
still waking down.
He walks away.

The black bear is *Ursa,*
Great Earth Mother.
Servant sovereign!
She nudges her young
in vulnerable times
with a sad, pure heart.

We need to wake up!
Kalen invokes you!
Give us true bearings
at this dark hour
when the Way is obscure.
Only you can help us!

Listen to my voice,
Beneficial Bear!
I, World Shaman!
I need you now
so I speak your
True Name out loud.

BIBLE

BLACK STONE I AM (DEC. 22 AM)

I

Before the Bible there is
Yahweh: You You You You You You!
Yaga: You You You You You Yin!
Allah: You You You You Yin You!
Unity: You You You You You Yang!

They give me to You!
Bible begins as
Abraham begins:
/eɪb/ and /baɪ/ the same
marks in Lingua-U:
Yang Yang Yang Yang Yang.

I am in Bible,
basis for being,
boat for balancing,
background of belief,
ballast of blessings,
body for burial.

Bible is not bite,
tearing or taking,
but my blood for you
to cannibally
imbibe for the start
of Love and Language.

Bible is not a piper.
Bible puts you not
poorer, a lesser place,
but in the Bull of Existence
with Knowledge from the Word
as it is pronounced.

Bible is not book
to hang you on hook
or cook you in pot,
but my pride for you
to ride without need,
bareback on uncaged lions.

Bible is extant,
unmanifested
Book, given without
beginning or end,
and glimpsed through bibles
which are Baby's crib.

Bible ends alive,
not Spirit's libel.
Two eagles in the sky,
their flight revealing
that those glorious sights
are before your eyes too!

II

Bible is Baby:
Yang Yang Yang Yang Yang Yang Yang!
They are the same to seven marks of subtle energy!
This proof has come by Lingua-U!

Born at Midnight's Bay,
the Word is made Flesh.

Listen, there is good news!

Baby is Kalen (in My story),
a new prophet to show you
how Bible comes from Yahweh —
You You You You You You becoming
Yang Yang Yang Yang Yang Yang!
Hallelujah, praise him!

The Holy Names must be set in union
starting with this linguistic communion
linking the last You to the first Yang!
Kalen is a Rounder to show you the Round!

New revelation
comes not to replace
or end a chapter of Bible,
but to stand upright
as a living being
made One with everything.

III

Beta: God's challenger,
The Second, the Other,

foe (from the tongue of Greece).
The 8 at its center,
infinity's number.

IV

In a San Diego park in 1923, a woman confined to a wheelchair
sees all 360 degrees of the Great Wheel. Elsie Wheeler – The
Clairvoyant:
A tribal chief claims power from the gathered people.
Response: Abraham.

During the late Shang Dynasty (1152 – 1056 BCE), King Wen of
Zhou first stacks the trigrams to form 64 hexagrams, for purposes
of divination. He is a master of the *I Ching, Book of Changes*:
The creative impulse initiates.
Response: The divine authorship, the unmanifest Bible as source of
creativity.

At the opening of the First Millennium CE, Master Yang Hsiung
composes an esoteric classic which includes and transcends all
previous schools of Chinese philosophy, *T'ai Hsuan Ching, Canon of
Supreme Mystery*:
Active oneness encompasses all.
Response: The mind of God.

BASE

BLACK STONE 1 PM (DEC. 22 PM)

The infant Kalen smiles.

I

Morning turns to noontime,
The cycle of decline begins.
Yin is in ascendancy
forming a basin for Existence,
supporting the center Kross
which impales the Essence.

It is not a root, which returns
to the soil and soot. It is not ground,
which begins grandly but then goes 'round.

Base is the Initiating Bottom,
Ace of Places before all Beginnings
which come at eight past midnight.

It is the manger of the Christ,
It is the cradle of the Baby,
It is the grave of the First Ancestors,

the place which catches the tears of all the gods and goddesses,
the place which reflects the Triune in which the Holy Names of the
gods and goddesses are joined in Logos,
the place where all the demons and devils are rehabilitated towards
Light and Love,
the place where they dissolve into delusion.
It is the Base of All-That-Is.

Lo, it is the baking of the Bread of Life!
It is big as the Kosmos, not big
as graves are big with dim-witted questions
or an epic poem is big with history,
but big as a biscuit, hard and crisp,
ready to complete its purpose.

II

King Wen of Zhou: A powerful maiden appears.
Response: She is the Base. He presses upon her; she holds her
ground.

Master Yang: There is a secret which can account for both Yang and
Yin.
Response: Yin-Yang is unified in the You (Unitive) principle.

Bane

Black Stone 2 AM (Dec. 23 AM)

The infant Kalen rolls over onto his belly. His immune system fights to repel invaders.

I

Bane it is,
banal lusts
to begin
with a Bang
(incomplete)
followed by
Pain's body.
Poison gain,
worm insane,
awful drain.

How will I
fight you, foe?
I require
Bail if I
would escape
this aching,
inching in
this razor

maze-like
lane of Bane.

Bail is paid
by the Kross
at center
of Essence
in the Void.
Redeeming
IOU,
incomplete
or uncertain holon.

II

Kalen's ancestors moved from Africa
north to the island of Delphos and then
to modern-day Cluj, then called Napoca.
It was their fortune to be in Greece when
the pre-Pythian priestess was destroyed,
her power of omniscience lost to men.
Many psychics attempted to employ
its artifacts for paranormal ends,
but success in magic they'd not enjoyed.
There was one remarkable exception:
A scrying ball which once fell from the sky.
How was the device obtained? It depends

on who you ask, but what is truth or lie?
There is one fact on which most all agree:
The Black Stone has an intelligent mind
and an influencing ability.
Somehow it came to Korbin and his wife
Kira, whose family crest contained a Tree:
The Baobab, known as the Tree of Life.
For many years their family worked for good,
supporting peace and minimizing strife,
doing benevolent deeds when they could
(with a few unfortunate exceptions).
Always keeping the Stone secret they would,
creating in public the perception
that their fortunes were the result of luck
or divine providence exceptional.
But another view many people struck,
that they had stolen an oracle bone
or influenced affairs with dark magic.
Some in the family line called it their own
and accumulated wealth and power,
but they tended to be accident prone,
meeting a cruel fate in a silent hour.
It passed for eleven generations
'til finding itself in Karen's bower.

III

Master Yang: Dragon comes from the center. Only its head and tail can be seen. Use it!

Response: Use everything, even the inauspicious.

BISON

BLACK STONE 2 PM (DEC. 23 PM)

The infant Kalen, now in his fifth month, laughs.

Bison bison
He is one with Kalen:
His horns always pointed north,
Here at the prime place before Places.
Bipolar is he at poles.
Bisexual is he at poles.

Calmly he watches history run.
Bison stands in a field of snow.
Bison stands amid the blood and bones of Capricorn,
Sea-Goat who grew too greedy and corrupt.

The Beast was felled by the Brown Sword;
Bear and Bison and Bat took his place in the star lore
to be remembered in the New Zodiac.

Kalen fell too, succumbing to the Bane.
We shall not hear this tale today.
This is a time for business.

In the walled city Lviv, there is a business meeting
at the edge of the Roztocze Upland.

Beginning

Black Stone 3 AM (Dec. 24 AM)

The infant Kalen reaches out and grabs for objects.

Before the first beginning,
there was Baby and Bible.
These entered not into Time,
but constituted the Yang
in the month of the Black Stone.

As the beginning arrives,
Bang stands without girth
or length at the end: incomplete.
It is Bane, poison to all
without yet goal proceeding.

It seemed all was nearly lost.
Allah abdicated All,
giving the Core for Koran.
Pierced by the Kross there,
Christ offered up His Body
for the Way of Creation.
And then came the Big Bang!

At eight past Midnight
the first beginning began.
At the delta of the Torne
where Kemi and Tornio
lie, the spot is ever marked:

A most sacred, hallowed park.
There the Base of All-That-Is
overcame baleful poison
giving bigness to the bang
which still continues to run.

Belief

Black Stone 3 pm
(Dec. 24 pm)

The infant Kalen crawls.

Belief begins bud
beyond the 'byss,
Layers of Being
which contain Love
leaving the Void.

Leaves fall from the tree
of Reason, each
bringing me life
ere it reaches ground,
where it lies flat.

Center begins,
center believes,
center must build,
center is secret.
Experience center.

Belief ends in Wind
funneled in freedom
from Koran Heart where
faith and facts begin.
Our belief frees it.

BUDDHA

BLACK STONE 4 AM (DEC. 25 AM)

The infant Kalen sits without support.

Beyond belief
there is a Buddha

On isle of Crete
Ruins of Knossus

At Vowel of Wood
there is a could'a

Christmas morning
there is a Gnosis

where the Root is,
Bottom of All-Root,

its name meaning:
He is Base-Doing.

Praise Gautama!
His God-turning must!

BOOK

BLACK STONE 4 PM
(DEC. 25 PM)

I

Kalen (now seen as a fully grown man) gives his fiery sermon on an enormous video monitor at Bucharest:

I am not in a book
from which you may be took!
I am in its binding!

I am not in those covenants
which are written in consonants!
I am in my promises!

I am not in an object
to which you are subject!
I am in the spine!

I am not in the pages
which corrode over ages!
I am in the lines!

I am not in the letters
which become lazy fetters!
I am in the intent!

I am not in dogma
which can take you to muddy dogs!
I am in living intelligence!

I am not in language
which holds on to a grudge!
I am in Lingua-U!

Language grudges, pre-judges
in black and white.
Hold on only to the right!

I am not in a number
which can slip into slumber!
I am in trinary digits!

I am not in a CD-ROM
which becomes a trash heap's stuff!
I am in the spinning discs!

I am not in ontology
which can want for apology!
I am in evolution's Aim.

I am not in post-modern heaps
which are a hoarder's rubble.
I am in integral philosophy!

I am not in a chatter-bush
which is Moses' fantasy!
I am in voiced wildfire

which shone light bright as Eveer
'til it dimmed, Christmas 'morn
at the Battle of Red Cliffs

when the bane, when the bane
greater than I, greater than I,
won the day, won the day

and the night, and the night
when the slaves, when the slaves
all came unbound, all came unbound.

II

Master Yang: Yellow is not yellow. Norms and reality no longer
coincide.
Response: The time for a rectification of language has come!

Bull

Black Stone 5 AM
(Dec. 26 AM)

Around the time of his first birthday, Kalen spoke the words for "Mama" and "Dada", referring to his parents Karen and Kairon.

I

'Twas a master of magic
who multiplied the loaves
and fishes, healed lepers,
cured blindness, raised the dead.
33 CE, He walked like a Bull.

Bull begins with a babe,
biting and brandishing
front teeth to terrorize,
crying high into night;
horns butting, balls bouncing.

Belief conquers the bane.
Bull fulfills the belief:
Bovine formidable,
violent charge and power,
force of a papal bull!

Bull ends as fullness ends,
pulling wool over eyes
to blind you from the bear.

God-Persons rise in your midst;
You banish them with bullets,
a bare-assed embarrassment.

II

In the night sky, the Bull is called Taurus,
the Cretan who fathered the Minotaur.
But let's speak of one who does embarrass
him! That's one he calls illicit bastard,
Falcon-headed Cow, of Horus's stock,
god who had sex with the goddess Hathor,
She renowned for her happiness and talk.
Horus and Hathor created Whaura,
a name which her half-brother Taurus mocked.
Whaura adorned herself in bright blue flora
and sang lovely songs in squawk and bellow.
Taurus collected wealth a plethora
while he exiled Whaura to a ghetto
at Scorpius HR 6142,
which he went to for bull-headed hellos.
(A deed which he would later come to rue
when the War came and he lacked for allies
at the exact spot he had to pass through.)

Bi, The Two of Stones

The Two of Stones:
"Everywhere I look, I see the wholeness
which I have lost from ethereal spheres.
After the Stars faded there was coldness
which conditioned my most terrible fear,
that this blue world in my hands is baseless
and days will break at the start of year
lacking the required strength to persist."

TWO *of* STONES

Beaver

Black Stone 5 PM (Dec. 26 PM)

Kalen enjoys playing in the water near his family's home in the
province of Oulu, Finland. He can nearly walk on his own.

I

Beaver begins
being evening
center of grieving,
griever of the beasts
in the Great River.

Busy building,
tree-branch sheering,
twig-sprout cleaving,
gentle being.
Makes still water.

Stillness she seeks
through industry,
nocturnal tail
flapper, warner
of danger's trail.

I invoke you,
Beaver! Kalen
needs a dam built
to seal a gap
between the worlds.

I need you now!
Not a moment
or twig to waste!
Inner rivers
are depleting!

It all depends
on new lodges
perfumed in scents

of brownish bronzes!
Only you can build them!

Listen to me!
I am Shaman
of the River!
I speak your Name
in Lingua-U!

Show me the secret
wisdom of front teeth:
hardness, sharpness
for tearing apart,
revealing Stars.

II

On Celtic tree:
Beth: pheasant, death.
New beginnings.

The Kabbalist's truth:
Beth: a person's mouth.
A magician's sight,
his virility.

III

King Wen: Fulfillment. The yielding treads upon the firm.
Response: Busy beaver. We are beings of purposeful conduct.

Master Yang: Going to the heavenly heart, the way is blocked.
Response: The beaver has built his dam. The work is done, but the journey does not progress.

BECKONING

BLACK STONE 6 AM (DEC. 27 AM)

Kalen walks. Lost in the woods, he meets a Bear cub. Kalen speaks to it in a language unlike any other, one which no one taught him. He befriends the animal, and the Bear helps Kalen find his way home.

Bear has difficulty sleeping that night. His dreams are confused by the appearance of a Wizard who tells him to follow the young boy from a distance. The Bear dreams that he must lead the world of animals into a New Life of Immortality, and the boy is the key to its genesis.

A Wizard of the Major Arcana of the Stone-Star Tarot appears.

Come to me,
Citizen, in these abodes
declined to dim deep things.

Biding you have lingered on.
Did you not notice that I have called for you?
You could have entered at any time.

All the same. What brings you here
shall send you scampering away
like vicuña at thunder clapping.

You are afraid of yourself.
That is why you do not enter the Mystery:
schwa at the far-center of Mystery,
schwa at the far-center of Human.

You have heard there is a better Zodiac and Tarot.
You have heard there is a new Map of the Heavens.
You have heard there is a new Atlas, Kalendar, and Klock.
Best of all, you have heard that a new integral magic has appeared
expounded by a mad shaman from Lesotho or Botswana!

You are revolted and yet you wonder what is in it for you.
If there is a magic spell for whatever you desire, then you want one.
You are not ready for the light, do you want the dark already?

Leave and purify yourself.
If you become ready, return.

Birth

Black Stone 6 pm (Dec. 27 pm)

Kalen's mother miscarries the twins Kiya and Kaiyon.

I

Listen to night birds sing their pleasant song
at twenty past midnight, week growing long.
They sing benedictions and good tidings.
Their tweets resemble intertwining nests
of birch trees, berries, bells and bendy things
assembled at the start of a dark wood.
Kalen enters and a man is reborn
somewhere in Johannesburg long ago
in 45 of the Common Era.
000102 is hieroglyph
inscribed on surface of the Kalendar.
See how Birth's Yin complements Baby's Yang.
Who has seen the mandala's other side?
Who can tell us if rebirth grows in rows
of the Kalendar? Who can say if our
memories grow on the roots of birch trees?
Who can say if a Buddha's Heart needs God,
or if Yang and Yin will unity find?
Who can say if the answers seekers seek

are readily available to all
who merely listen with ears of a child?
It is said that the Kalendar goes on
for three thousand years, predicting fortunes.
So who is this Kalen, foresight bringer?
These questions arise in this moment's mind,
and in truth no question may be answered
which has not even one time been uttered.

II

On the Viking rune:
Berkanan. Birch tree
without fruit, fertile,
growing, sustaining.

III

Master Yang: What enters me leaves from me, what leaves from me
enters me.
Response: Rebirth follows birth according to the needs of the soul.

BUT

BLACK STONE 7 AM (DEC. 28 AM)

Kalen has temper tantrums. He also learns to "pretend" and knows how to say "no".

I

Not yet,
which is but
yearning...

Not a contrary,
which is but
connection
turned rarity...

Not an exception,
which may exit but
at the place
of shadow...

Not an unless,
which is but
a lesser understanding...

Not a negation,
which is but
a negative gaining...

Not a *mais non,*
which is but
ayant pas de maison...

Not a *pero,*
which is but
a *perro pícaro...*

It is a But.

But begins buttocks,
pucker-hole padding,
bulb-bulb of touching,
puffed-up cushion upon
central plushes.

But begins butterfly,
early bud in its transformation.

The glyphs tell
What But is:
It is the Yang Seat
at the central nexus

of the Base of Being,
its tush for tussling
with the bucking buck
of Opposition's pluck,
a jutting turn of departing symbiosis.

But can be no other thing.
It is what it is, uniquely.

II

King Wen:
The Unexpected.
Response: "But" reveals the unexpected part of the sentence.

Budge

Black Stone 7 PM (Dec. 28 PM)

Eighteen months, Kalen can walk up steps.

I

— There is a Bus.
The Bee carries pollen.
It goes from Base to Us
not out of chance
but because it must.

— There is a Bug.
It confronts Base with a tug,
ugliness which leaps or flees.
It is not an Insect in flight,
but a Bug to bug you.

— There is a Buck,
majestic one who may bring luck.
He is neither doe nor deer
which are ruled by duty or fear,
but a bucking Buck, full of pluck
whose obstruction you cannot shuck.

— There is a Buxom Bust.
Neither butt nor burden,
nor boobs, which are two b-nipples with two o-knobs.
It is a luxurious stop
which presents itself here
at the center of the Base of Being.

He must make a budget.
It is good to travel light through Bardo
when movement becomes slight as a budge.

II

King Wen:
Hindrance. Standstill.
Response: Bucks in conflict, their horns locked.

Master Yang:
He parks his golden carriage in the center of the land. Warning!
Response: What is central and standing still is vulnerable.

WEEK 2: THE BAT

BLACK STONE 8 AM – BLACK STONE 14 AM (DEC. 29 AM – JAN. 4 AM)

Chiroptera of the night,
frightful screeching beast of flight,
swooping down from stalactite
to my stoop at stalagmite:

Turn this world upside-down
when the year's end comes around.
Night creatures of black and brown,
make commotion for the town.

Find a source of blood to drink
so your brain can soundly think
while this poet spills some ink
to give your name to this week.

Come to me now, webbed-wing bat!
Put your spread-out digits at
this Kalendar's welcome mat
where wavelengths grow long and flat.

Great golden-crown flying fox,
do you have a way with locks?

In the midnight hour of clocks,
we need to leave from a box.

Only you can teach us how,
perched on udder of a cow,
to do what death disallows.
Hurry bat! We need you now!

BULGE

BLACK STONE 8 AM (DEC. 29 AM)

Kalen plays with his older sisters Chila and Jeila and his older
brother Kyle when their parents are away. They play at "war".

The chieftain: Obey! Respect my long spear!
Its sheer curvature, a metalloid drape
at half past midnight, hoisted to the rear:
Means for our singularity's escape.
Go forth, my siblings! My loves, I command!
I give freedom to you in a scar's shape!
At the Battle of Red Cliffs shall we stand
where we will confront our foe in warfare
over a But which could have been an And.

Boat

Black Stone 8 PM (Dec. 29 PM)

Kalen, fallen at the Battle of Red Cliffs, finds himself trapped in
the Bardo. He must find a way through the terrible River Boron.

At the far end of the Bardo's ocean,
at the extraction of the subtle axe,
there is a passage fit for no human,
tricky and jinxed as Cairo's fiendish Sphinx.
It is the foreboding River Boron.

Only through solid stone must the boat pass
ere it can exit infrared poison
towards promise of a habitable land.
White foam of the Black Sea, let us through now!
Yonder suds of borax, prepare the way!

We travel now on route precarious!
To end of health or ill we cannot say!
Life's return depends on staying afloat
invisibly adrift in onyx stone,
congealed to a lens transparent as ice.

Atomists opined that All is Atom
and Void. Indestructible substance-force,

Materials underlying All-That-Is.
Hero of Alexandria devised
steam-engine through experimentation.

Alive is a person who is not alone
for she communes with spirits in a world
Yonder, sharing her consciousness with One
who gives her the key to unlock the code
permitting passage 'cross River Boron.

Boson

Black Stone 9 AM (Dec. 30 AM)

The spirit of Kalen encountered angels and lost souls on its journey through Bardo.

I

Bogies:
tell me why
i was chilled to my bones
laid back on the coffin pillow
life on easy street in my review window
maybe papa's torah was the way to go
my way brought me to this place
pacific crossing i rode over
on the kawasaki zephyr
ceelo green on the radio
chilling out with a cold one
here pressed flat in an empty bowl
freezing beside you and no place left to go

she-sin comes to the weatherman now
they said death you'll wear a hood so scary
but it was not really death
it was only december

talked to her angry
off her drug
shut up
because they thought that this was their house
so why don't you come over here and do something about it?
there's gates and glasses, we'll never
actually be able to get to her
in the detox unit

II

Boson:
any number can reside
the same quantum state

Compare:
a spirit or spirits speaking
medium, python

Bones

Black Stone 9 PM (Dec. 30 PM)

The River Boron stands between Kalen's spirit and his rebirth. He passes through with some effort.

I

At the center of bone
is the center of boat,
a hollow O for marrow, room to roam,
lending both ability to float.

O bone, tell us of the sea-foam
that connects the ocean between the Worlds
at the sea-wall with eleven faces
where Light of Omni Lumination shone.

These bruise-marks haunt me like an apparition
for I have seen them before in Midnight's Bay
when our breathless voices could give a sigh at most,
mighty gusts inhering in cuts delivered
on my not so straight and narrow path by
some of the coolest friends you could ever have.

Let us gather when the Second Temple is destroyed.

Shall we meet at Odessa,
between the ancient cities of Tyras and Olbia?
There is knowledge at the deep end of decay
for organ regeneration
and for passing through not-so-solid stone.

Bone ends as joints end:
beam (secretly), but without the joined tissues.
Bone is Yin to Buddha's Yang,
joined in Body's You.

II

Master Yang:
Rewards for journeys outside one's body.
Response: The spirit of Kalen returns to bodily form in the Bardo.

BU, THE THREE OF STONES

The Three of Stones:

"I bow before the wonderment of wars.
Bow before the husbandry of horses.
Lower myself before resplendent souls.
Lower myself before the far-off shores.
Three times I break myself open for your
supplication 'til I have nothing more.
I am yours. I am yours. I am all yours."

THREE of STONES

Babel

Black Stone 10 AM (Dec. 31 AM)

From the New Book of Songs:

Once men built a tower to wondrous heights
But their wisdom lagged behind their wings.
God curtailed their ancient linguistic rights
For protecting the welfare of all beings.

A new day is dawning for me and you!
Language is evolving beyond babble,
Gifting us with the divine Lingua-U
Which ends all need for discord and brabble!

Rejoice! These are the last days of Babel!
Rejoice! The old curse is lifted today!
The days are gone of boggle and scrabble.
God has given us a new way to play!

'Tis spelt in letters You Already Know,
A form of speaking with energy sung
Masked by the old meanings you must outgrow
So love and joy may dance upon your tongue.

Rejoice! These are the last days of Babel!

BACK

BLACK STONE 10 PM (DEC. 31 PM)

Now two years and two months old, Kalen is scolded for inappro-
priate behavior. He insists!

I

There is no abode more back than this
among the places or places before Places.
From back the view to the path is vast.
It is the backest of the backs
Most black of colors, clear as Space
Most lacking in problems and worries.
Not the baddest, which add to burdens,
nor the slackest, which sow sorrows.
It is the backest for clacking and smacking,
acting with cackles cried or hackles raised.

II

An oracle foretold that young Kalen
must carry the Stone and the world traverse,
learning in course its right application
and making sure to avoid the reverse.
It must be given back from whence it came,

after a long trek for better or worse,
which in due course would reveal the True Names,
expressed in a Language Universal,
set into a Map of the Heavens frame
which could peaceably support faiths diverse
along with Science and Philosophy.
On his path Kalen must avoid reverse,
never twice the same location journey,
until he sets his foot upon Delphi.

Banished

Black Stone 11 AM (Jan. 1 AM)

Political refugees, Karen and Kairon must leave their home at
Omdurman in Sudan. Together with their children and some of
Kalen's aunts and uncles and cousins, they head into the East.

I

The old year is gone, no more.
Let it be banished.

Banishment begins with a ban,
Badness neutralized, negated.
Babel unravels to mass randomness.
Not an exit, which empties from the self,
but a directing from the base of things.
Not an exile, which exits unto I,
but a slap from back of another's hand,
a boot from a boot.

Baby is the initiating Yang
greeted by the responsive Yin of Birth
completed by the You of Banishment.
Banishment is the Yang of Saṃsāra
which is the Yin of Mandate's You-nity.

Banishment ends as punishment ends,
shaped and shaken into submission,
becoming a paragon of vanity
for an end which is kin to balancing.

II

Master Yang:
The newborn child is lifted up, covered in blood!
Response: Banished from the womb! The overcoming of symbiosis
is well underway.

BOUT

BLACK STONE 11 PM (JAN. 1 PM)

Kairon, an esteemed physician, treats his son Kalen for a serious illness. He uses the Black Stone to gain insight into the illness and its remedy. The boy makes a full recovery.

I

Banished, I must wander about
in circle Eights.
Not at, but out.
Beating a bush there,
getting the gist.
Paying the fare,
but the station missed.

II

Kairon hailed from a town on Kola Bay,
an inlet of the frigid Barents Sea
where he was raised by parents Song and Dayn
who taught him the ways of mystic healing.
They cured disease by finding a balance
of energy meridians in threes.

Yin and Yang, partners in a cosmic dance,
could be reconciled in a point of You
from which imbalanced health could be enhanced
through techniques shown by observation true.
One day a Wizard came to their hamlet
(this was in the days when Kairon was due).
He said there was something he had to get
out: from future he knew of an event
which he would reveal in terms most candid
for a few coins, a payment which Dayn spent.
The man possessed a crystal scrying sphere
which received messages from heaven sent
on winter's solstice in calendar year
when held up to reflect purest starlight.
He bought the ball from a renowned Seer
who bade him to make to the north a flight
where he was tasked to complete a mission:
meet a physician with hair of pure white,
a man surely matching Dayn's description,
and instruct the man, grandfather-to-be,
that from his stock would come an addition,
a son with Korn or Kairon naming,
and he would have a special youngest son,
and only the youngest one must be he.
And this child by name Kalen or Colin,
should become a ruler most peculiar,
a warrior, lover, and magician

who could wield the power of Jupiter.
Dayn interrupted the man for to ask
if this child would be a kindly ruler
or if a tyrant should come from Murmansk.
And the man replied that he could not say
for it would depend on the sort of acts,
loving or mean, if he was raised that way.
So it was that Song and Dayn knew something
private: that her cycle was in delay
and the couple were a child expecting
which they would if a girl name her Koryn
and Kairon if there was a boy coming.
They asked the man on the porch to come in,
and listened long to his prophetic words.

BOWER

BLACK STONE 12 AM (JAN. 2 AM)

Political unrest comes to Nicosia, Cyprus. In forming her conscience, Karen consults a mysterious Black Stone which advises her to participate in the conflict only as a passive observer.

A woman high above a walled city
she recesses in the bower of her boudoir
a lovely voice, full of soul, she begins to sing
it is a song for a soldier lost in war
coming before the tower window, she looks about
Eleftheria Square at the town center.

Yang's season of long dark morning has come …
its turning to come crashing on the shores of Queensland.

Boundary

Black Stone 12 pm (Jan. 2 pm)

Kalen, two years and eight months old, possesses an active imagination. He is obedient and submissive with his parents, but is often domineering with children his own age.

I

Boundary begins with a bough
extending from a banyan tree
into duration, idea

It plows down to the real
real as a dream without finish
real as a vowel expressing power

Boundary generates bounties
dividing treasure between spaces
outside the border countries

Boundary is not a border
which banishes the order
of Being, but an outward dream
which finishes where I start

There is no boundary
where I am, only a Line
shaped like an I or 1 or l
which lies in the nature of Light

II

Master Yang:
Ruins at the foot of the mountain. He enters them. What good can
come of it?
Response:
The boundary is the ruin (rune). It brings difficulties.

Body

Black Stone 13 AM (Jan. 3 AM)

Having pushed through the boundary, the spirit of Kalen is
brought forth. He becomes more embodied, but he is still trapped
in Bardo.

The most discreet secret of the Body and the Brain:
They're indistinct to six marks of subtle energy —
Each expressing a great manifestation of Yang *ch'i*.

I
The brain is bringer
of the neuron rain

The brain is brazen
at the beginning
gainful at the end

It does not process
it broadens the Way

It reigns over brawls
within the body
It raises the dough
of memory-made bread

It bursts with reason
to the point of pain

Brain ends as sane ends
an angel which hasn't gelled

II

God is in body, grounding and granding
our embodiment at the central Star.

Buddha is goodness of embodiment's
descent to center, set in a bottle.

Body is abode of the center's source
opening, closing to the awesome end.

Bawdy is body seen as awful or
awe-ful, womanly in its letter-shape.

Body is poverty in the Yang form,
a pod for the pea which is how we are.

Body is bower which enters a door
which is Deity in its beginning.

III

Is Atman Brahman?
It depends on the pronunciation.

If one says that Stars and Stars
are one with Stars and Stars,
then Yes: the statement is true enough and Light endures,
so far as vowels are concerned.

Unless either Atman or Brahman closes with a schwa at near-end,
then either Atman or Brahman fades into a Mystery, and the two
are not one.

Unless both Atman and Brahman open with Stars and end with
schwa at near-end,
then the Stars shall fade, the Light shall go out, and yes, Atman is
Brahman.

And then at the level of consonants,
the answer must be No.
Atman is the neutral material of the Tendency of Truth
which is found in every I.
Brahman is the neutral material of the Realization of Reason
which is found at the Base of Being.

Do not tell me you ask if they are at the same at the level of concepts without regard for the vowels or consonants!
Where are these concepts of yours? Show them to me! Pronounce their names.

IV

Master Yang:
Escaping peril, he climbs the mountain. At its foot are rivers. Breakers.
Response:
The mountain is reality. There are many ways to get to it, but they crash on its wall.

Blood

Black Stone 13 pm (Jan. 3 pm)

As Kalen's third birthday approaches, his mother takes him to
a boat. She leaves him with his father who takes him across the
water. A terrible storm. He is frightened, but everyone survives.

I

Expressionist painter smears
dollop of sticky blue
It streaks into blurry hues.

A streak of blood rushes
upon a cherubim face
Under cheeks a girl blushes.

A pointy stab with blade won't do
So he strikes a blow
with a blunt metal object too.

This is Jerusalem and Beirut
where the lines aren't clear
and bodies mount with actions rued.

This is the day of Emperor Trajan
who gave Jews permissions
they could not use.

Blessings are the temple
of the bloom, blame is the aim
when the ruddy face is ashamed.

II

Master Yang:
His chariot goes off the axle. He is bodily injured and stranded.
Response:
At a critical time, he is unclear, indecisive. He shares in the blame.

Beauty

Black Stone 14 AM (Jan. 4 AM)

A beautiful woman appears in the Bardo and leads Kalen's spirit
onward. Her eyes sparkle with starlight. At the lake, she lets him go.
The ferryman: Bartholomew. (There is a longer story, but we must
proceed swiftly.)

I

Beauty beckons:
Uniqueness, You!
Universe, You!
Union of All, You!
Youth, why thank you!

Beauty begins
in basest base,
in beastliest
brute, the bare bottom
of the Big Bang.

How Beauty yearns!
bottoms need tops
bases need cups

beasts need gentleness
barren Space (just) needs.

Yearn for teaching
yearn for touching
yearn for teaming
yearn for tenderness
as 0s and 1s need 2s.

Without you, there is no Beauty!
You are at the center of Beauty!
All of you! All of you! All of you!

At Beauty's core
is Youth's blooming
untouched by death's
ending: a Theta,
youth's final thorn.

At beauty's core
is the one root
without return,
rule ruling without
rigidity.

At Beauty's end
is Yang stripped of

angles and Yin
straightened into shape
of letter T.

At Beauty's end
is new teaching
without churching,
where tears come without
regret or remorse.

II

Elsie Wheeler:
An ancient bas-relief carved in granite from a long-forgotten
culture.
Response: At the mountaintop, a shrine to the Lord Brahma. No
worshippers have come.

Master Yang:
At the foot of a great exalted mountain, he must cross a river. There
he sees a person with a boat. He crosses over on the ferry.
Response: The beauty of truly great art and philosophy gives new
harmony to language.

Chapter Four

P | Purity | The Jack of Stones

The Place of Opposition is the spot
where the planet Earth spins upon a pole
moving upon a Path with error fraught,
needing a confrontation for control.

I

The mind of a toddler does not cohere
to anything much like stability,
its stage of development at the rear.

Nor does it know self in reality,
but pre-personal fusion dependent
on trust and availability.
Children without nurture from their parents
are ever for recognition beguiled,
struggling to remove with right adjustments
the limitations of being a child.
They feel as if peon, peasant, or pawn,
acting out in ways which are dull or mild.
Like the letter P they have not the brawn
to a confining situation fix,
but they can have a new perspective drawn.
Passive: making still pulsating larynx,
noticing meaning's drive for precision,
its want to clarify sense's phalanx.
Feeling the rhythmical throbbing tension
of pulsation as blood is propelled through,
specially in states of hypertension.
Pointedness: attending to tongue's thorough
exactness, accurate with its placement,
ploughing hard into the mouth's wet burrough.
Here the symbiotic meets displacement,
unity retired for opposition
until pre-ego finds a replacement.

P is the second new constellation
given in the Zodiac for our time,

of all P's meanings 'tis a summation,
lending a House to Pig's and Platypus's Sign.

II

JACK of STONES

The Jack of Stones:
"Mine is the drive to own experience
rising from roots in pain and penury
seeking for my ambition a clearance
which can bring power out of injury.
I have overcome many obstacles
to arrive at a true trajectory
which my will determines responsible."

III

6. Purity

Purity:
Her heart is free of contamination.
Humble woman carries pink peonies.
In Major Arcana, she is Karen:
Her basket is a purveyor of these,
gifts not for possession but for sharing.
Mother of Kalen's hushed identity,
model for a boundlessness of caring.

PAI, THE FOUR OF STONES

The Four of Stones:

FOUR of STONES

"No prize or reward is yet in your sight,
but the pain of keeping and maintenance
puts you in a predicament of plight.
I am pushing and pulling at entrance,
a pilgrim's burden on way to Mecca.
Parading outside the Children's Palace,
making room for Alpha and Omega."

Week 3: The Pig

Black Stone 14 PM – Black Stone 21 AM
(Jan. 4 PM – Jan. 11 AM)

Sus of the *Suidae*,
even-toed ungulate,
You with the stout long snout,
stop and come here about!

I come to you in pens
or prowling loose in fens.
Do not try to wash ears,
come dirty as you are!

Mistreated have you been,
butchered for your bacon
or ground and sausaged,
salted and served to men.

I am Kalen, shaman
of mud and gooey muck!
I decry exploitation
of intelligent beasts
(even those run amuck).

You ought not be beaten
or kept in small cages,
though you may be eaten
(as so for all beings)
out of genuine need.

I do tell people so,
pleading to reprimand
the selfish omnivore,
but their stomachs rule though.
They have heard it all before
and they have much to owe.

Great Pig, do not leave disheartened!
Return when I call for you.
I will need you before the end
and you will need my Reed of Gold.

PIPER

BLACK STONE 14 PM (JAN. 4 PM)

The spirit of Kalen has left the Bardo only to enter Purgatory.
Thereupon, he encounters a peculiar plant.

I

I am inside
genus Piper,
radiator
of my Person
in spicy form.

A shrubbery
pruned in pretty
shapes or wild herb
in the tropics,
a pleasing plant.

I invoke you,
my sweet peppers,
colorful red
in Damascus!
I am Kalen!

Peppercorn fruit,
pungent odor,
keeping yourself from
herbivore lust
which would devour.

My beautiful
pyre begins your
end, ripened, peeled,
and purchased drupe,
seed of safety.

Seduce us, yes,
with a strong scent.
Leave us hot, high
on fiery taste
and burning pipe!

II

King Wen: The Taming Power of the Small.
Response: Vulnerable beings evolve powerful mechanisms of
self-protection.

Master Yang: The snake hides in the mud.
Response: Python approaches.

PYTHON

BLACK STONE 15 AM (JAN. 5 AM)

Kalen occasionally goes for walks alone in the woods. He claims to see a bear, but the animal keeps its distance and evades the sight of others.

I

Ere the days of the ultimate Nadir,
humankind will erect twelve monuments.
They will in a new Wheel of Wholes cohere
sited with an Integral cognizance,
giving modernity a chandelier.
The first such statue is in Nairobi.
'Tis set upon the Wheel's 0° node
decorated with a Baobab Tree.
Temple of the Infrared Station's mode
holds a shiny pool of deep mystery.

II

The Kabbalist: *Pei:* immortal
spirit becomes discernible.
An open mouth atop the jowl.

III

The words were spoken
unto the Poet
which were not his own.

He opened himself
allowing angel
to bring Gabriel.

Spirit from the Starz,
beckoned by my voice
'til his work was done.

IV

Master Yang: The center heart is a deep, deep pool.
Response: The deep pool is the Dao. Spirituality is a precious
treasure.

PAIN

BLACK STONE 15 PM (JAN. 5 PM)

In Purgatory, the spirit of Kalen's longing for eternity produces pain.

For pain: pine for
the last of π
specifically!

Prick me, poke, pop,
pitchfork, pound, pant,
crumple, impale!

Blast not vaguely,
Make clips or puffs
precise, in place!

Choose your weapon:
sniper, bullpup,
spikes or paper.

Your pain ends in
poison bane brought
inside body.

Your corpse lain flat,
life lost with ail's
Space-like vowel.

Penance: give it
what you need. This
makes pain puny.

Pit

Black Stone 16 AM (Jan. 6 AM)

The spirit of Kalen's reaction to pain produces isolation. From the isolation there is a furtherance of the process of differentiation.

I

It is a pit: place for burning,
juicy pickle, futility,
such misery, a picnic meal
with slim pickings. A thin within.

Pit in your throat: 'Tis not a lump,
a little bump, but a pinching
It-ness within on 1 A.M.
trip to Moscow. It interrupts.

Not a bottom which bottles Base
in the mettle; It is a Place
stripped to its tit, pillar to pip,
from pre- to It. Particular.

II

Pisces:
"I have felt the oceans swarming with angst
at the thought that the billions of fishes
and other sea life which are us amongst
are arranging themselves in militias.
They are merely mortal, I said, because
in the Scheme of Things they are scintilla
without a Sign given back when it was
that I received my deserved assignment.
A horrible Bear has got them abuzz
so they may soon join a new alignment!
And some are filled with a strange delusion,
even I dare say a weird derangement,
that they are a novel language using
by means of which they are divinizing,
an idea I find vague and confusing.
Nonetheless a plan I am devising
which will protect my seat in the heavens,
a foolproof foil to their sad uprising.
I spit on their conceited scales and fins!"

III

Master Yang: The yoke has come off. How can a wagon be made to
go in this condition?
Response: The wagon is forced into a pit stop.

PICTURE

BLACK STONE 16 PM (JAN. 6 PM)

Kalen, three years and six months old, draws pictures in a way differently from other children. He makes sounds in his mouth, and then draws the energy that he feels. Unsatisfied with many of his sketches, he keeps drawing until his picture looks exactly like the way he pronounces his speech.

I

Philosopher said language does delude
if it gets its sense misunderstanding
a word is picture, that it represents.

This sage opinion focuses on facts
which are pictures too, parts in relation
to more picture-facts. Let us look at it.

What is a picture? Picture follows Pain,
strung on a Pulley in the Lingua-U
lexicon. It's Yang Yang Yin Yang Yin Yin.

Pain follows Beauty, Beauty follows Bow,
Bow follows Balance, Balance follows Being,
Being follows Big Bang which follows Bible.

In the Kalendar, pictures are taken
in particular inspired storylines
as night follows day which follows morning.

Picture is a Place picked or chafed apart,
churning not cheerful. Lifted from a pit
with a pig-like strut. A Place on Tolan.

Pictures are like facts. They chop chop language
with a pick, into pieces like an axe
which splits precisely. Facts are like fashions.

Picture of Picture: Yin responds to Yang
in a trigram's clutch; It finds in response
a copy of itself. It increases.

Read the Kalendar not as Wittgenstein
who saw language like to pictures
defined by a scientist's White logic.

Read the Kalendar not as old Ludwig
who saw language like to parlor game,
defined by its use. Tell a new story.

Read it as Perez who proffers Konstruct
which changes the game with literature
showing all words are pictures on parade.

II

Master Yang: It is hard as a rock though not a rock.
Response: Language becomes stuck when it is confused with objective reality and ossifies. It also gets stuck if the inherent sound-meanings are ignored and signs are falsely seen as merely arbitrary.

Pin

Black Stone 17 AM (Jan. 7 AM)

Listen! There is an emerging threat to the existence of human civilization and virtually all life on the Earth. The spirit of Kalen is shown a terrifying vision in Purgatory.

O wild boar, pinned on the floor,
rampaging in Meskel Square,
shoat of Addis Ababa:
Like to you is my spirit
which finds itself embodied
Asteroid hurtling through Space,
stone as spinning oddity
in gravity of the Earth.
It comes in hour of Nadir.

Upon witnessing a vision of the Nadir, the spirit of Kalen resolves to exert influence which might avert catastrophe. He must find a way to communicate with someone alive when there is still time to make a difference, someone living under the constellation of M.

PUT

BLACK STONE 17 PM (JAN. 7 PM)

With the aid of Archangel Gabriel, Kalen communes with a poet in 2010 CE who is developing a new technology for spiritual communication involving the granular delineation of subtle energy through a trans-metaphysical meta-language.

I

Kalen is the prophet
who is delivering a download from the Dao in the 21st century CE, given parading pictures in Lingua-U, words put precisely in place according to their inherent symbolism in a new type of Kabbalah, hidden mysteries of the International Phonetic Alphabet itself revealed! His is the drive to rectify a universe gone more than slightly mad. Usher of an unexpected upheaval in consciousness from a forgotten valley.
Through a Poet he will give warning of the Nadir.

II

Master Yang: The virtuous man is barred from his own sleeping mat. Someone new sleeps in his house.
Response: Kalen speaks as a new prophet of God. This is bound to arouse tension among those dispensed to believe differently.

PUSH

BLACK STONE 18 AM (JAN. 8 AM)

Lo, the sound-meaning of a word is its pronunciation and
words with the same sound-meaning are twinned as if *the same
thing* in their subtle energy signature! From Plato's *Cratylus* to
Margaret Magnus's *Gods of the Word*, this was the best kept secret of
philosophy!

See for yourself –
Pucker your lips for a P.
How do you push?
Contract your body in a Yin direction:
Grab against the center, keep it down.
Put it up with a shove,
so it is part of.
Don't burst with a bash,
but shovel your tongue
in shape of
pushing.

How Medina radiates –

PULL

BLACK STONE 18 PM (JAN. 8 PM)

Attend! What a thing truly *is* is like to its pronunciation.

See, hear, proof! –
Pucker your lips for a P.
How do you pull?
Lean your tongue
on mouth's ceiling.
Slide it, slip it back,
get it going, take it low,
keep it liquid, make it loose,
pull it until reaching the center.
What is outside is now within: this is Unitive force.

How Mecca pulls –

– to the Black Stone of Kaaba.

Pi, The Five of Stones

The Five of Stones:

"Take me away to the mountain's peaking,
a tip at the top where the ranges stop.
I long to see what the havoc's wreaking
where there is view, also a mighty drop.
I drop there where there is no place to go
and my perspective is merely a prop
which can be set down whether high or low."

FIVE of STONES

Pet

Black Stone 19 am (Jan. 9 am)

Kalen has developed the ability to speak with certain animals. He keeps his talents to himself.

I

See, pets begin with pep
which is not expended,
but is tended, trained,
tamed and given treats,
good eatings to eat.

If they chew violently,
petulant is their deed,
yet their better master
is not blameless for it.
Pet the pet. Turn to it.

There's no small point in philosophy
of the dog, a person's subordinate.
Some word had to be God spelled backwards.
Can you think of a better one?
Dog is a good one. Good dog.
It looks to us as we look to God.

II

Elsie Wheeler:
A five-year-old child carries a bag of groceries.
Response: Kalen, entering his fifth year, bears a heavy burden
which is also nourishing.

Parents

Black Stone 19 PM (Jan. 9 PM)

Four-year-old Kalen rambles as he carries a pear
walking with his parents on the shores of the Black Sea
in 152 CE. Pear-shaped Karen holds his hand gently and
listens; Kairon pats his head and pretends to do so.
His mind dances with pears and persimmons.

Karen was born of Keri, Keri from Kenan, Kenan from Kena,
Kena from her mother Kexi, Kexi from Quex, Quex from Keshan,
Keshan from Jeni, Jeni from Kitten, Kitten from Sheeta,
Sheeta from Sivan, Sivan from Keeva, Keeva from Kira.
So goes the line of Kira through twelve generations.

Kairon was born of his father Dayn, Dayn was born of Kaimon,
Kaimon from Raiken, Raiken from Kreig, Kreig from Dreizen,
Dreizan from Freizh, Freizh from Kaden, Kaden from Chai,
Chai from Kein, Kein from Keifen, Keifen from Keiben, Keiben
from Kaib.
So goes the line of Kaib through twelve generations.

Kairon and Karen married and had six children:
Chila, the eldest daughter, first born. She is fourteen.
Jeila, the next born daughter. She is twelve.
Kyle, the eldest son, third born. He is eight.

Kalen, the fourth born. He is four.
(Kiya and her twin brother Kaiyon, the last conceived, perished before birth.)

These are the personal names of Kalen's parents. The family sur-name is that of O'Tolan on the father's side and Li on the mother's.

Personal

Black Stone 20 AM (Jan. 10 AM)

The traditional religion of Kalen's clan, practiced synchretically by the O'Tolans, is the worship of a sun god. Karen and Kairon developed this tradition in a panentheistic direction.

I

From Greek alphabet:
Pi: Mithras, sun god.
20 rays of light.

II

The Primordial Purse of All Perspectives

Hear: the Sun is truly person's purpose!
Personal emits light, light which is also null.
It turns suffering to nothing without a thing
save light's earliest ray, aliveness at the rise.
The person is self's forming in softer (or predisposing) form
than it appears at the Separation of Self,
continuing essence which is not in, but of,
neither sender nor sent, but supplied and supposed.
Person begins with pursed lips, the Primordial Purse

opening to soft interior. First and worst are contained
within: Source's end and curses to nullify.
Hear! The hearse is ready. It continues the purging.
At the end of the personal is a tunnel underway in the light.
There it is reflected by the essence of All-That-Is.

PEACE

BLACK STONE 20 PM (JAN. 10 PM)

The Beatitudes of Kalen. From his sermon in the hills of Lazica:

Blessed is the peasant: for theirs is the penchant and zeal to repent, bringing purity.

Blessed are the poor: for theirs is the hope for and opening to more without requiring money.

Blessed are the purposeful: for theirs is the peace of the Earth and the potential for fullness.

Blessed is poverty: for it is the possibility of virtue's and vulnerability's teachings.

Blessed is paucity: for it is the positivity of the siddha.

Blessed are the peacemakers: for they shall make aches into putty, turning small beginnings into kingly endings through curbing.

Blessed is the partial: for it knows purity through showing the heart.

Blessed are the pure in heart: for they know perfection of humanity.

In reply to a question from the crowd, Kalen said, "All this is known plainly by listening gently to the words already on your own lips." Pressed further, he added, "Some insight comes from listening with educated innocence, and some comes from understanding a word's placement in the Kalendar. The secret meanings require study of the Daarma."

PEAK

BLACK STONE 21 AM (JAN. 11 AM)

On the hills above the seashore, Kalen and his siblings climb to the highest peak. In so doing, they *spatialize*, allowing the space of the world into their being and vice versa (which is a practice closely linked to *temporizing*, allowing the time of the world into one's being and vice versa). Chila, Jeila, Kyle, and Kalen are bonded not only by love, but by a family legacy.

I

In Juba Valley of Somalia
in 165 CE near shoreline
of the windy Ocean of India,
Kairon lived and worked, father of Kalen,
who made an encyclopedia
and practiced the art of the physician.

Here the ancient world arrived at its peak
in a long-forgotten tribal culture
which celebrated the humble and meek
and contemplation of the heart so pure,
saw and accepted that which is unique,
and developed reverence for the mature.

Kairon took for wife a woman of wealth
who inherited a precious heirloom:
an object which must be kept with great stealth
which they held secret in a hidden room.
'Twas omphalos telling sickness and health
and giving notice for fortune or doom.

Karen's ancestors brought it from the west
where it was said to be the prize of Greece:
of all the ancient oracles, the best.
Of what is supreme within, it increased;
Of what is villainous, it made the least.
But its relentless demands never ceased.

Heavy were the hearts burdened with its keep
for they were called to restless moving.
With worries they put their children to sleep
as they were hemmed in by disapproving
neighbors who in darkness were heard to creep.
Their safety required constant improving

II

King Wen:
On this road, we must part. I must rest to contemplate the changes
I have seen.
With the 3, there is a myriad of things beyond my past knowledge.
I will see you again bearing the light of Fire.

WEEK 4: THE PLATYPUS

BLACK STONE 21 PM – BLACK STONE 27 PM
(JAN. 11 PM – JAN. 17 PM)

Furry foraging duck-billed mole,
you're under rocks and in a hole,
a mammal laying eggs in shoal,
Platypus here who I cajole,

You are great for your uniqueness,
your humility not meekness,
known to make jealous animals
who complain of your completeness.

Creature sleeping in your burrow,
it is I, Kalen, don't you know?
I have a mission to bestow,
a place I want you to go.

It is the time to pick a side,
be not stubborn and stuff your pride,
for the War's end you could decide,
if with us you'll go on a ride.

Only you can give your own gifts,
forming concord and healing rifts

'tween those who swim in water swift
and those who in dark tunnels sift.

Punishment

Black Stone 21 PM (Jan. 11 PM)

Upon finding the Omphalos of Delphi unguarded, young Kalen uses it to gain knowledge of others' minds. Although he does not act on what he learns, he is disciplined.

What once seemed a terrible burden
is now perceived as a punishment.
It is an unhappy turn within Yin
to believe in revenge heaven-sent.

What once seemed a form of Purgatory
is now perceived as a harsh pummeling.
Not a purging, but a moral story
turned poorer, fire and brimstone funneling.

What once seemed puzzling or an aching
is now perceived with peaceful acceptance.
You is ascendant; it is Yin waking.
What is rising is a sense of presence.

In the Kalendar it is a new week.
Marcus Aurelius does his duty.
'Tis the downward climb from a storied peak.
'Tis Mosul in Iraq or Djibouti.

What seems now as much deserved punishing
will be perceived as a freeing portal
when self transforms to something nourishing
that which now is a feeling quite awful.

PENIS

BLACK STONE 22 AM (JAN. 12 AM)

A man's penis is the Yang form
of my Emotion-in-form at the Place of Opposition.
There it is called by Venus as a boat is called by the ocean.
It is posing and opposing when erect.
It is the Yin to the Yang of pushing and pulling.
It is Yang to the Yin of poking and poaching.
It is completed in pleasure when Pluto beckons it darkly.
Where Penis is nowhere more acutely do I feel my drive to excess
(secretly).

In Comorian, Moroni means "in the heart of fire".
The city sits at the base of Mount Karthala.

POKER

BLACK STONE 22 PM (JAN. 12 PM)

Sometimes Kalen's father plays poker with his friends to pass the time. They play on a deck similar to this one.

I

The Deck of Yang is comprised of 52 cards:

- The suit of Black Stones.
- The suit of Red Jewels.
- The suit of Brown Swords.
- The Arcana.

The cards are ranked (from high to low) Ace, King, Queen, Jack, 10, 9, 8, 7, 6, 5, 4, 3, 2, Ace.
There is one card in the Supreme Arcana (No. 1) and 12 cards in the Major Arcana (No. 2 – No. 13).
No suit is higher than another.
Card No. 1 is the Yang. Within the Major Arcana, cards are numbered in the order given in *The Kalendar*, with No. 11 regarded a Jack, No. 12 regarded as a Queen, and No. 13 regarded as a King. Play is always high-low in the Yang Deck, meaning highest number wins.

Poker hands generally contain five cards; the highest hand wins. Hands are ranked as follows (from high to low):

- Straight Flush, called a Full Station
- Four of a Kind, called a Full Quad
- Full House, called a Sangha
- Flush, called a State Sitter
- Straight, called a Stage Climber
- Three of a Kind, called a Coven
- Two Pair, called a Clique
- Pair, called a Pair
- High Card, called a Peak

Play proceeds as in conventional poker with innovations which may be introduced from time to time. Two-Deck and Three-Deck poker are also options, combining cards from the Yang Deck with the Yin Deck and You Deck.

II

Master Yang:
He is poor but not poor. How can this be honorable?
Response: He pretends not to be poor, putting on his poker face.

POISON

BLACK STONE 23 AM (JAN. 13 AM)

Shortly before his fifth birthday, Kalen dreams that he is standing
upon the South Pole with a bison at his side. Looking to his feet, he
sees the carcass of a Sea-Goat. He holds in his hand a Brown Sword
which is so heavy he must drop it. So powerfully does he feel the
effects of poison entering his body, he rolls off the bed.

Poinsettia begins set on a peaceful plain,
a seed minted and coined with spirit's silhouette,
a joyful face adorned as princely offering
to become beauty's end, set as the centerpiece.

With an ounce of poison the poinsettia plant
displays its brilliant bracts: poinsettia red leaf,
unassuming yellow flower, pointsettia
deep green leaf ornament of Mexican-born soil.

Hear me, Euphorbia Pulcherrima! It is
Kalen. I invoke you! Show us beauty's purpose
in our dark residue! We shall follow your red
leaves until we arrive at the path to passion.

PU, THE SIX OF STONES

The Six of Stones:
"I have earned six metallic medallions
for deeds potent and extraordinary.
My parents are the proudest for their son.
The kingdom bows down before my glory.
I have overdone that which I have done,
but it makes a more compelling story.
I have gone where before there has gone none."

SIX *of* STONES

Path

Black Stone 23 PM (Jan. 13 PM)

Kalen (seen now as a grown man) delivers a sermon before children.
He speaks at the Horn of Africa, gateway to the Fifth Zone of the
New Atlas.

I

Children, you have asked: what tell is my path?
Do not follow acts, let acts follow you.
There is your passion, which always, always
begins on your path! Pack for a journey.

You must place yourself on path precisely
at the beginning, softly, without strain.
Such precise action must be specific
to your Self most true which inheres in You!

Your path must begin with a parting, air
separating lips as child from parent.
Ask what your path is, school in my answer:
service, certainty, and serenity.
Certainty is a part of your searching.

All this is the truth, my children, and plain
to see and hear. Read your own lips to know.
This you know certain for its truth you have
already spoken. Your tongue does not lie
when you don't premeditate its meaning.

A person without a purpose is like a word without a terminus.

Whither be your path? Whither be my path?
Whither every path: to Thetas. All paths
whither to the Whole and wither to Thetas.

II

In the Fourth Month will it birth:
a New Atlas for the Earth,
replete with Eight Zones of Thought.
Mogadishu to Dhaka
for the Inside of Outsides,
Fifth Zone set by Longitudes.
Here the Eye looks at the Mind
as Autopoiesis spied,
Kalen's passage of station
told by cognitive narration.

PAST

BLACK STONE 24 AM (JAN. 14 AM)

At five years and 40 days, Kalen learns the story of the Stone's origins, and he is told the legend which states that it is his duty to traverse the whole world with the omphalos so as to return it to its origins, never retracing his steps.

Galaxies, their old light arriving from light cast.
Randomness, a bandit ere he ran to wisdom.
Expansion, its open pandering to the shunned.
The start of assembling is in Past: its assets
embers for the present until they ready for
remembering.

Past is not now, but it leads to now in course of
Kalendar's days, its sense derived from my wholeness.
Presence starts in the past, then reserves sense, senses
and mental sticking points. The past tense positions
paths in stopped time, that is, the starlight so prepared for
remembering.

There is no future in the past (save discreetly
in the letter T, which carries Time's awareness).
The purpose of the past is to begin time's march

which is chugged and churned in the future. Presence turns
potential into prey, fuel for new churches of
remembering.

Remembering returns a lonely renegade
into membership – but this fact is obvious
if you have been paying attention. Listen
for the secret of memory: it is the Earth's
own reaching, a burden which may be buried, ruled
by Mercury.

Panic

Black Stone 24 PM (Jan. 14 PM)

Kalen is instructed in the proper use of the Stone for insight and knowledge of future events. He learns that his parents will soon be murdered and becomes distraught. His parents react to the warning by preparing to send the Stone into safe-keeping.

Panic may begin with panting or powerlessness
'til it turns anxious and antsy like an animal.
In reaction: negativity nixes the act.

See panic: Banishing's Yang begins panicking's Yin
and it is not yet time for the You of vanishing.
This may not be where you want to be, but here you are.

You may conquer panic: there is a palliative.
Hear the pounding of your heart. Stay true to where it calls.
You will find there You: pondering and polymorphic.

POUTING

BLACK STONE 25 AM (JAN. 15 AM)

Kalen's parents urgently prepare for coming changes, and the boy
is inconsolable. He is given a challenge and brought by his sister
Chila into the forest to meet the Bear.

I

What is spouted is streamed or spoken poutingly,
What is sprouted shoots or ascends more rapidly.
But pouting is putting the lips for an outing.
It concerns the person's relations to the crowds.

Think on the Roman rule under Septimius
Severus. He stretched out the African frontier,
debased silver coins, and grew the military.
Rome, poised to enter decline, became more sullen.

It is 200 CE when the Han faded
in China, the Huns invaded Afghanistan,
Huvishka retrenched the Kushans to India,
and everywhere the process and progress went on.

Contemporary vocabulary lacks words
for the turning of pits and pips into a peace
for the public, then outwardly pointing to You:
proud talk, palpable growth, but lacking true power.

II

Elsie Wheeler:
A store is filled with precious Oriental rugs.
Response: Tapestries, how they depict an orderly history. The
Kalendar contains such a tapestry.

POWER

BLACK STONE 25 PM (JAN. 15 PM)

Young Kalen meets the Great Bear, Animwaa of the Bear-Yak Zodiac. He learns about the New Zodiac, an arrangement of Star-Maps necessary to put the Earth into right relationship with the Kosmos. He also meets the Wizard of the Stone-Star Tarot who explains the origin of the conflict between the *Beɪ* and the *Ro*.

I

In the constellation M's House of God,
Monument of Kalendar will be raised.
See, it will be located in Riyadh.
For its simplicity will it be praised!
Station of Temple robed in magenta,
set at 30° node on the Wheel of Wholes,
a link to the Mother Earth's placenta!
'Tis the place of reharmonizing souls.

II

Power begins in the
pawn given an ouch, then
made tall as a tower,

ready to wager it
or go to war for it,
acting not sweet but sour.

What do you do with it?
Stay not in your bower,
and speak not in vowels.
Put it in a brown pouch.
With it defend the Dao,
becoming a pandit.

What clout has the pandit?
They use pixels or pens
and with precision make
a careful incision
right at the weakest spot,
toppling towers of thought.

Omphalos is power
inherent in all things
at the Base of Being
dropped from the sky so dark,
prehensively feeling
the Mind's most opaque spark.

POUNCING

BLACK STONE 26 AM (JAN. 16 AM)

The O'Tolan children love each other, though sometimes the older siblings grow jealous of the attention given to Kalen and the prophecy concerning his stewardship of the Black Stone. They take separate roads: Kalen with Chila in the woods; Kyle with Kairon; and Jeila with Karen.

I

Lemur of Madagascar,
leaping like a monkey
in spiny forest glen.

Four pounds and twelve ounces,
from branch to branch you spring,
bouncing every now and then.

II

At the Battle of Red Cliffs (China, 208 CE):

Zhou Yu plots to kill Zhuge Liang
but Liang borrows arrows with straw boats.
On the third day, Liang must produce

10,000 arrows or foreit his life.

Liang prepares many boats of the greatest navy ever assembled, manned with numerous straw men in the fog.

They attack the greatest assembly of archers ever gathered, making such commotion that they attract 10,000 arrows.

He gives them to Zhou Yu who must count the oath fulfilled.

III

Once while sitting with Kalen high on a mountaintop, Beionai the Great Bear told him a legend which had circulated among the bears since the ancient days. Later, Kalen retold the story adding his own embellishments. It went something like this.

Led by the Great Bear in the days when he was more commonly called simply Bear, the animals were angry, more enraged than they had ever been since time immemorial.

Entire species were disappearing by the thousands, never to be seen again, disrespected because their divinity was not honored in the heavens. As one species would fall, it would topple another and another and so on. Is this not the greatest calamity facing the bears and all beings?

The termination of entire species of loving, sensitive, perceiving beings occurred daily in a world much more than slightly awry. Not just one being or tribe, but the entire species!

The creatures looked to the Stars, but could not see their own selves. They were beaten down by the old Zodiac, accustomed as they were to seeing a sky full of foreign creatures (all but a few, that is, such as the Crab and Ram).

They were jealous at the privilege shown only to the few creatures given love in the star lore, for it is through Lore that Life, Learning, and Love are united at L's Yin-Unitive Seat.

The Bear said, "It is our right to rise to the Stars and join together in the Kosmic Kommunity. Who are you to poke out our eyes so we cannot see our true nature and shackle us in chains so we may not fully participate in the divine life?"

The Bison said, "But there is Ursa Major! Are you not already alive forever in Her holy Star-fire?"

And Ursa Major, Great Bear Spirit, responded, "I am immortal. How can I enjoy my immortality when so many others have not? Bear is a unique being and deserves his own True Name so he may come to my side. I must fight so that Bear and all beings may live in Star-light."

And then Bear challenged Kalen, saying, "If you are truly a World Shaman as you say, then forfeit your life or give 9,000,000 species of plant, insect, fish, microorganism, and animal their own constellation in only 9 days."

Kalen accepted the challenge, adding: "I will do it in three days."

And then he was given Lingua-U by the Archangel Gabriel and he wrote each of 27 consonants and 12 vowels in the stars, new Stations and Houses pictured in ways which can be spoken, danced, shaped, flown, or swam. They can even be used in battle through Jiǔ Gua Zhang, the new martial art which is an offshoot of Baguazhang.

He returned to the Bear and said that every species now appeared in the New Zodiac according to its True Name, and each species and every individual could now know their True Name and say or dance or swim or shape or fly or fight it – and even change it as it changes – alive as a spirit rising to the heavens where it would be immortal.

And Bear said, "But how can I know for sure that I am able to speak in Lingua-U?"

And Kalen said, "Because you are already speaking it. It is a language You Already Know."

Upon reflecting for a moment, Bear said, "So I am speaking it. And I have been speaking it all along. I will bring your message to the bears and to all creatures to the best of my ability, but I am afraid of what may transpire."

Thus began The War of the Zodiac, when the Sea-Goat led the Ram, Bull, Crab, Lion, Scorpion, and Fishes to fight to keep their traditional positions.

They brought with them all the power of the Twins, Virgin, Scales, Archer, and Water-Bearer (to name only the Signs arriving from the Western quarter).

Before most of the myriad species could begin to speak their True Names into the New Zodiac at Nagoya, Kalen was beseiged.

In the first onslaught: The War of the Deities. Zeus led the defense of the New Kosmology, also known as the Map of the Heavens.

In the second onslaught: The War of the Archetypes. The Queen of Jewels led the defense of the New Tarot, also known as the Map of the Archetypes.

In the third onslaught: The War of the Zodiac. The Great Bear led the defense of the New Zodiac.

Alas at the moment when it was needed most, help came too late. Hanimwaa Kalen and ten brave Animwaa fell at Chibi in an onslaught by the forces of old (only two Vicuña survived). It is a new Battle of Red Cliffs, fought on the same terrain as Zhuge Liang's battle many centuries earlier.

It is so recorded that it was upon the Downing of the Dao in the Month of the Brown Sword when the myriad species, newly awakened to the fact of their oppression, demanded entrance to the heavens and an end to their devastation on the Earth.

PRESENT

BLACK STONE 26 PM (JAN. 16 PM)

Kalen (seen as a man in his fifties) gives a sermon on the Internet,
streamed live at Kuwait City:

You have heard the teachers say: be present!
Do hear me now if you want to know how.
With presence, you must rise early to sense.
Come to me at 1:42 AM.

Presence presents itself as a present.
Teachers have told you to accept a gift,
but precarious is its offering.
For presence make yourself into the gift!

Prayer and praise are the base of presence.
Without them, the mind merely prattles on,
prancing and practicing not presencing.
Pride is a bad pitfall before the dawn.

Z is at the center of all presence,
sound-shape of zen and of the causal floor!
If you are humbled appropriately,
then you will have a tendency to zen.

Absent is not opposite of present,
but an abolishing of the senses
essential for making yourself humble.
Presence ends in a return to senses.

Pluto

Black Stone 27 AM (Jan. 17 AM)

In Kalen's dream, he is several years older, wearing a red jewel around his neck and carrying a wood-handled sword. He runs beneath steep, narrow red cliffs, chased by an army of powerful spirits. He holds a luminescent Stone in front to guide his path. A horrible creature rises before him, half goat and half sea-monster, blocking his path. He wakes afraid.

I

On the platform plateau beneath your feet,
On the plain where sundry plants are planted,
many pleasant, playful, and pleasing things,
pluralistic and ripe for plundering.

The story of Pluto begins so told,
plethora of pleasures plodding along
until they are plumbed down deeply to roots.
Lunacy ensues! Plums to lose and rue!

Pluto ends as lord of the undertow:
as Purgatory's story comes to close,
a shady man tailed and cornuto on throne,
throwing what is lost into the shadow.

II

Master Yang:
Killing and begetting are mutual arrows.
Response: Pluto, mythical lord of the underworld, is part of the balance of life and death.

PART

BLACK STONE 27 PM (JAN. 17 PM)

At the Unitive Seat of Consciousness at the Place of Opposition:

I

A holon is that which is part and whole, its incompleteness seeking redemption from Kosmos which enfolds it completely. If the universe consists of holons and nothing but holons, are there parts then or wholes? This question is one for Professor O'Tolan. Lecturing to his students:
Why do we call a part a "part", and not, say, a /ho/ which is part of "whole" or /ol/ which is also part of "whole"? Indeed "part" is nowhere to be found in "whole", nor the contrary. There is one satisfactory answer.

Part, you see, ought to be viewed so:
It is Perfection's terminus
and Purity's identity
at the Unitive Seat, of course,
in the Place of Opposition.

One does not cease to be a part,
naturally, when one is most pure,

most perfect. It is through part-ing
that one grows so in Consciousness.

The pure and the perfect have parts,
but wholes have heaps and happenings
which they harmonize heavenward,
cohering at the Head of Things.

Parts and Wholeness have secret Goal:
They are joined by a broken Heart
joining the center-rear of every Part
with the starting of every Whole.

II

Six-year-old Kalen composed a short poem following the death of
his mother and father at the hands of enemies.

Parting from you in sorrow,
Mother and father I love,
Will I see you tomorrow
happy in heaven above?

Although the enemies searched long for the Black Stone, they did
not find it. It was stashed safely in a Vault to which Kalen was given
the only key. He and his siblings entered the care of Gailon and Dro
and they set out on a journey to retrieve it.

Meanwhile, Bear sought an audience with Balance to learn how to carry out his role in bringing the New Zodiac.

III

Master Yang:
A disruption concerning Jupiter! The star alignment portends defeat.
Response:
What once was whole is now parted. A new relationship is born in sorrow.

Chapter Five

V | The Vault | The Queen of Stones

Activity of Vying moves ahead,
involving itself in matters secret
or evolving in patterns which outspread,
surveyed by the New Atlas of Spirit.

I

Think on an organism's severalty,
maintenance of its higher order needs
which come in levels of priority.
It seeks shelter and breathes, it drinks and feeds
before other matters of protection,
so its own physiology succeeds.

It's the way of natural selection
to satisfy hunger's requirement
before seeking heart or mind's perfection.
A body's needs may be in retirement,
but if their triumph misfortune alters
their nature allows for no deferment.

The active principle initiates
meaning's movement from one situation
to a condition which then vitiates
the fixed state of the previous station.
It starts with a meeting of lip and tooth,
pressed to a valley through which vibration
is articulated via a booth
which voices speech through oral cavity.
In beginnings it shortens the wavelength,
lifting energy above gravity,
producing vanity and early graves.
In endings it gives us depravity,
inadvertently risking what we have
for a chance to obtain a novelty
which is our one chance to love, solve, and save.

Look to the heavens here, what do you see?
It is a new sign comprised of a letter
said in Lingua-U as consonant V,
the symbol in which all V-sounds inhere.

II

The Vault:
"I am the keeper of cargo precious,
Guardian of the Artifacts of Orr
in conditions unsafe and contentious,
holding them safe since the First Wave of yore,
never using their power momentous
which for the sake of others I do store."

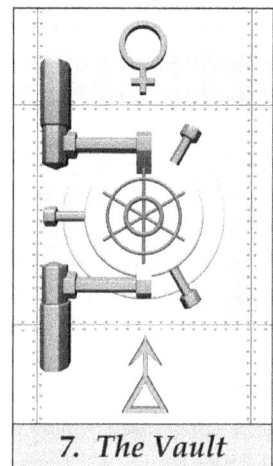

7. *The Vault*

III

The Queen of Stones:
"On this dark day I must send a message
to the Jewel-Queen: I fear the war is lost!
I, Hoyana, have seen signs which presage
a coming war in Tarot cards embossed!
The 9,000,000 species may not survive
in dignity of divine starlight glossed
for too few have come to face Ram's drive,
he who leads land-forces of old symbols
which have dominion over the night sky.
They loathe the coming of symbol systems
which will include them in a lesser part.
Does this not too for our own kind signal
relentless difficulties at the start
of the New Tarot in which you and I

reside with seven other Queens athwart?
Our coming is a threat to Archetypes
organized into a once cohesive
whole which no longer does wholeness supply!
Having seen the King of Wands, I misgive
for he is enraged beyond all reason,
terrified that he might no longer live,
and so he has conspired to kill Kalen,
forcing his path to the narrow red walls
of Chibi and thus advantage seizing
by which he intends victory in brawls
against our kind which he would extinguish.
Dhara, won't you lead us ere Kalen falls
so we won't all come to final anguish?"

QUEEN of STONES

VAI, THE SEVEN OF STONES

The Seven of Stones:

"There is a veil over what is Real,
a curtain between the worlds of sound.
Life's forces lie hidden behind a Wheel
which turns Energy's direction around.
Upward it goes, lifted with claws of steel.
In my clutch will its dense matter impound."

SEVEN of STONES

WEEK 5: THE VIPER

BLACK STONE 28 AM – 34 PM
(JAN. 18 AM – JAN. 24 PM)

I'm in viper
when I'm vying
not to expire.

My Perspectives begin
at center of Viper,
vision-snake view-taker,
a poisoned fang-sniper.

Viper may be charmed by piper.
Hid in a magician's basket.
He makes the pungi sound,
hypnotic pseudo-predator.

I invoke you, Viperidae
with venom in your V-shaped fangs!
The great Bane dwells within you,
one whose name means "I give birth"
and "I live"! Show me how to shed
my skin and induce mind journeys.

I am Kalen, World Shaman!
Take up nature's given role for you.
Show us fear and its conquest!
Lead the reptiles' unrest
at the great upheaval
in the Night's Cathedral.

Vibration

Black Stone 28 AM (Jan. 18 AM)

The King and Queen of Wands, their instruments of magic firmly in hand, took Kalen and his brother Kyle into imprisonment in the Castle of Wands. They now possess the lost Stone of Delphi, and they begin to use it to control the entire magical world.

I

You have heard them say that everything
is mere energy and vibration –
But such talk is just foolish babble.
The Secret is not found in one half-day
on the calendar, but Kalendar:
All of It, everywhere in all things!

Vibration is Yang to Vacany's Yin:
It begins with a voiced fricative sound.
It is violent breaking aberration,
brazen at its center, but with an ending
stationary. What makes it start and stop?
What is its purpose in the Scheme of Things?

Lingua-U provides a Veda for you
if you speak in tongue of divinity:

Vibration is the Base of All Vying,
Yang Seat of Vaporizing in the First Month
at Kalen's exit from Purgatory,
his rising up into Activity.

Vibration is a large aviary
fluttering with birds of Yang, Yin, and You;
It is a man in bed snoring loudly
at 1:48 in the morning hours;
It is Stavropol, known as Tolyatti,
variegated in Samara Oblast.

II

Master Yang:
His mind is brought higher. The heart goes on, engraving.
Response: Vibrations elevate, engrave. Vapors rise.

VASE

BLACK STONE 28 PM (JAN. 18 PM)

Kalen's uncles Gailon and Dro have assembled a gang to attempt
to break into the dungeons of the Castle of Wands, but their plot
is foiled by the Castle's elaborate magical protections. All are
imprisoned.

Know my letters and you
shall know me. They are guides
to the right path for you.

My letters, vases for
essence. I lie in lines
meeting at the V's base
forming shape of a vise,
vessel or vascular
duct. Vase is ace of Of.

Vase is Yang, virtue, Yin.
Pour what comes from you in,
but do not exceed it.

VEIL

BLACK STONE 29 AM (JAN. 19 AM)

The Wands seize control of the suit of Pentacles. Locked in the
dungeon, Kalen loses his mind as his ability to properly spatialize
and temporize is confounded.

Before veil comes, there is vying
where I hide in things and not-things,
activities of dividing.
The positive posits the Veil.

My face is not yet to be faced,
for it is fire without yet flint,
and fear without yet forgiveness.
It is freedom not yet given.

The veiled begins vane, desiring
to be noticed, naked, undressed.
Pain's final cry is vanity.
Humble does end as the veil ends.

Pain's end: neither veil's center nor
its aim, but a part of the ail
it brings if vain tendencies stay
or if it came by oppression.

Veil's end is love and light, waiting
for the right time. A boat does not
hoist its main sail 'til it can bear
the wind's great weight, which veil lightens.

VICE

BLACK STONE 29 PM (JAN. 19 PM)

The Black Stone stands unyielding in its refusal to aid the Wands in their scheme to kill the Animwaa of the Bear-Yak Zodiac and eliminate the cards of the Stone-Star Tarot. The prisoners of the Wands including Kalen are tortured.

I

I am within vice,
but not through my will,
for vice is a vise.

Vice is the servant,
second, substitute,
a higher power
vicariously.

Who can blame someone
who vies, fighting a
rival for a prize?
Blameless, survival.
It is vein in which
life's vibrations vibe.

Vying leads to vice
when warm hearts and blood
turn coldly callous,
hardening to ice...

Vice once is seldom
a violent talent.
But done twice or thrice?
Vice may then become
a violation.

A violation is
a humilitation
for it's the center
of blame. Therefore vice
is blameful when it
loses the center,
making dilemma.

II

Master Yang:
He rises ever higher unscrupulously. He disappoints those he
meets.

VICTORY

BLACK STONE 30 AM (JAN. 20 AM)

As Kalen's mind grows increasingly dark and forgetful, an Angel of Light appears to Kyle in the darkness of the dungeons. He empowers Kyle to get help for his brother.

I

The War of the Deities begins.

Vishnu: "In my travels through the night sky,
I have come across news most upsetting.
Abysmal battles are approaching nigh
which are likely to reach a new setting.
The animals are taking sides whereby
the fate of them all will be decided,
if to them shall be given long Star-life
or if divinity is lopsided,
immortality given to so few.
By Kalen and the Bear are some guided
in a quest to erect an Open Zoo.
At the same time, the Archetypes have gone
awry, once ordered in a peaceful crew
of cards. Armies of Wands and Cups lead on,
joining now with the suit of Pentacles

369

to kill the Tarot gifted by Kalen,
while the King of Swords a decision mulls.
My heart is heavy at this weighty hour
because I fear miles of blood, bones, and skulls
stretching with the rise of a new power.
The coming of an integral magic
will affect the heavens in all quarters
causing shift beyond Type and Zodiac.
Change is needed in the Divine Body
if we are to avoid an ending tragic."
(And then he headed to Kawaski.)

II

Victory begins here:
Activity of Vying turning for an inner look
to claim and clamor. It must thunder
like a god of war, and then it must cook (secretly).
It does not fight, it tussles; it does not take, it touches.
A Barracks emperor ascends to the imperial throne.

Victory terminates
with a secret meeting in Tehran. The Sea-Goat
having reached its penultimate expression
before retirement reaches out for
a new reality expressed in reasoning.
Under Gordian III, riots and fire plague Rome.

VILLAGE

BLACK STONE 30 PM (JAN. 20 PM)

Edge of the jungle, there a village sprouts
for the people to meet for survival.
They are vital and vibrant together
for love's beginning is at the middle.

See, there is a villain in the village!
He is given love's start by the people,
but returns negativity instead.
He performs evil deeds, puts out the dead.

There is a price to be paid for contact.
Elder woman wears a magenta robe,
Violet-like sign atop compassion's white.
She sees above them, and she lives alone.

Village ends as the Season of Yin ends:
The quest for justice, verdicts of substance,
continuity in generations,
adjustments in communal vibrations.

VINE

BLACK STONE 31 AM (JAN. 21 AM)

The Wands use the Black Stone to seize control of the suit of Swords. Control of the entire Wand-Cup Tarot is now in their grasp.

I

Over Dome C fly skua
France's Concordia City
'neath atmosphere transparent

It is 2 o'clock AM
unexpected discovery
working in isolation

II

Master Yang:
He climbs the tower with support.
Response: The vine which supports him holds. He gazes heavenward.

ANGER

BLACK STONE 31 PM (JAN. 21 PM)

Chila and Jeila have aged many years since their brothers' imprisonment. Joining covertly in a peaceful delegation of Cups in a visit to the Castle of Wands, they attempt a rescue of Kalen and Kyle in the Castle of Wands, but their gambit is foiled. They are imprisoned, and the Cups are dominated by the Wands.

I

Anger begins
with putrid pain
by now purchased,
ingots of mirth
pressed to rebirth
for a new rage.

Anger comes with
angels waking
in energy,
their eyes open
to the center,
violet of ire.

Anger ends by
needing gurney
and grave digger,
its objective
gratified just
within cold ground.

II

Master Yang:
Scaling to dangerous heights, someone axes the ladder.
Response: The Page of Cups betrays the carefully laid plot of Chila
and Jeila.

VIRUS

BLACK STONE 32 AM (JAN. 22 AM)

Kyle and Kalen have aged at different rates since their imprisonment together; Kalen is nearly seven, whereas Kyle is almost fifty
years old. The Wands take complete control over the Four Suits of
the Wand-Cup Tarot.

I

I am in virus,
violating hosts
with a fiery ire,
ripping the center,
sealing envelope,
and disappearing
into a chorus.
Vile am I, and I
am sorry for you
(sorry for us both).

Virus embeds me
in Us at the end,
pierced by the spiky
spear, nowhere to run,
riled and returning

as pears do blossom
from the Pyrus shrub.
It returns to vie
once again for life.

I invoke you, virus!
I call your True Name!
You are living's rival
when looked at backwards;
nearly life's reversal!
(I see what you are.)

Heed my voice, virus!
Oracles contain
the marks of your demise
poured into culverts.
By fire of Pyrus bush
shall I vanquish you!
I shall remove your ire
and send you to scatter
like a dandelion!

II

Elsie Wheeler:
A thunderstorm. It comes unexpectedly.
Response: A sudden infection. It spreads rapidly.

Master Yang:
Sitting on a tree stump, he faces ruin. Later he becomes stronger.
Response: The virus nearly ruins his life, but the immune system makes him stronger.

VI, THE EIGHT OF STONES

The Eight of Stones:

"They pierce Space with heads bearing hair-like trails,
bodies which remind us of our own thoughts
which collect much ice, dust, and particles
as they endure searching like worms and bots.
These are the Veldt's shadows and surfaces,
varying and venting shape like comets."

EIGHT of STONES

Vetting

Black Stone 32 PM (Jan. 22 PM)

Lo, the curtain has been lifted! The spirit of Kalen enters the Veldt.

At Battle of Red Cliffs, the Black Stone sinks.
Kalen succumbed at the battle's last stand;
his synapses collapsed upon their links.
He, below circling singing angel band
descending as the Absolute involves.
A man and boat in a place called Tolan.

"Unless to wakefulness the land evolves,
all hope is lost for a world bountiful
and axis will stop round which it revolves,"
sings the choir in a tone most distressful.
"At the Nadir, oceans will turn blood-red!
Kalen sees now that which time could make full:

Ash plumes and choking pollution widespread,
rivers dry of capital to invest,
unprecedented multitudes are dead.
To Abu Dhabi's shore have come tempests.
Anguish of linguists, their science unshored!
Crisis of priests! Fury of atheists!

Dullness of encyclopedists ashore.
Deaf critics, blind bloggers and journalists!
Vengefulness of religionists ashore.
There is only one Individualist:
That One with the soul of Buddha. Now see,
Hear. Proof of what they fear most now exists.

He says drop a pole, listen at my knee.
Buddha fishes at Abu Dhabi. Here
at Da Sea, be who you are and could be.
One with necklace of Mars is the Seer.
Lift Brekyirihunuade's cup to drink,
so your name may be for the first time clear.

Your choice must come much sooner than you think.
Laude a poet's Vulcan discovery odd
or decry it as fraud at final brink.
Kalen fishes at Abu Dhabi. At
Abu Dhabi, A Buddha Be, we swear.
He's a simple man with a fishing rod."

Vetch

Black Stone 33 AM (Jan. 23 AM)

Gailon and Dro pass away in the dungeons. Kyle and Kalen are separated. Alone in his cell, Kalen embraces the misery of his existence.

Vexing flowers
purple and white,
bitter vetch, pulse
cultivated
in wretched times.
Feast for vetchworm,
poison-eaters.

Sketchy harvest,
foul-tasting seeds
leach in water
boiled boiled boiled
by poorest poor
stretching to fetch
their survival.

Virtue

Black Stone 33 PM (Jan. 23 PM)

The spirit of Gailon appears to Kalen in a dream. He urges him to remain steadfast in the face of increasing adversity.

I

Certainly vernal
season approaches.
Virtue is birthing
over Dubai's earth.

Virtue begins as
vice begins (in shape),
but one is Self's perch;
the other yields ice.

Rising up early
is inherent in
virtue: it is how
choosing becomes earned.

I am in virtue:
inner awakeness

invisibly bound
in winter's blankets.

Center of virtue
is one with Art's end,
power which will do
that which was started.

Virtue approaches
the verge, a moral
edge for forging an
individual.

But virtue does not
go over, charging
Truth and chastening
you for improvement.

II

Virgo: "This season has brought ill harvest
of malcontent in the nocturnal sky,
owing to heresies of a linguist
which would my heavenly birthright deny,
giving false hope to dirty animals
and unchaste ladies who have impure thighs

who want to see their bodies immortal
although they are slutty sexually.
A woman ought to keep a tight girdle!
I am a virgin here perpetually,
my hymen kept in starry permanence.
Perhaps it is time for change actually;
I must admit to some ambivalence.
Nevertheless, I have been enlisted
in a just cause against this insolence
by the Lingua-U teacher assisted.
I shall battle against this uprising
and join in a plan by Pisces twisted.
I will not permit the V House's coming
in the heavens to be my replacement!
M's worthless terrain I am despising,
the assigned post of my future placement
where I would become merely a Maiden,
just one of many words at the station.
In the 'New Zodiac', space is taken
not by the astrologer's vestiges,
but by the letters assigned by Kalen
who purports to bring divine messages.
For this reason I will help the Sea-Goat
by bringing Kalen poisoned beverage
at the time which the Zodiac denotes."

III

Master Yang:
He gags his own mouth and speaks not.
Response: Virgo, her virginity.

VIS

BLACK STONE 34 AM (JAN. 24 AM)

Kalen's torment increases. He sees the Stone for the first time in many years, and asks it what to do. It gives him one word in a covert reply: "bird".

It is 2:12 AM.
Port Victoria's Mahé.
The Vauxhall Clocktower of Seychelles.

So much anger within himself.
So much vice hid behind the veil.
So much temptation to evil.

He is the one chosen to lead.
He is the savior of the land
though unusual are his deeds.

Surely his path must be straightened.
Surely virtue must be nurtured
for he is vested with great power.

Five months into his seventh year
Kalen is given a passport
for travel to the red country.

(Seven is the divine number,
subtle ground of causal heaven,
with Love's purpose at its center.)

Vision is the Yang to this Yin
which is the right to keep the Stone;
Vow is where boy and purpose join.

There is a small valve to freedom
at Nukus in Uzbekistan
where he may make himself ready.

But until then, he bears a load
far greater than in younger days,
burden of evolution's mind.

Vagina

Black Stone 34 PM (Jan. 24 PM)

At the Yin Seat at the center of the Activity of Vying:

There is nothing more central to vying than this:
Vagina at center of Activity
which begins as velvet begins, supple and
lush and luscious opening to reception
at Unitive Base of Generativity.

Ufa, rail-center of Russia, a red jewel,
with its rail-station on the Trans-Siberian.

In every convent, it is this with communal virtue;
In every vixen, it is this with sexing;
With coveting, it is this with communal tendency;
It is the not-so-secret union of bucking and puckering and so on...,
Yang to the Yin of the center of pleasuring.

Vagina ends at center of the nexus
of negativity or neutrality,
responsive Yin to the Yang positivity
or resplendent in holding the Mystery.

Week 6: The Vulture

Black Stone 35 AM – Red Jewel 1 AM
(Jan. 25 AM – Jan. 31 AM)

Vulture begins at
center of scavenge,
schooled in cadavers,
catching carrion,
taking one's revenge.
In venue, you are
well regulated;
Volt, you rest yourself
as a tired old man
perched up in tree.

Vulture continues
with what culture keeps:
committees, kettles,
and more Yin-like things.
Looking is its way (secretly),
chomping on center,
earning what it churns,
digesting corpses
as culture retains
decaying language.

O Cathartidae!
I invoke you now
when the boy is young.
Teach him how to prey
on what others don't,
and look in places
where others refuse.
Show him the virtue
of using all things
when they show themselves.

He will need you soon
when he needs to choose
his own vocation
to repair old wounds.
He needs you to wake,
engorging yourselves
upon battlefields.
Dissolve the toxins
in the carcasses
until you vomit!

And hear my message,
Great Vultur Gyphus,
the largest of birds,
Condor of the South.

You must do a deed,
flying with great speed!
The boy needs you now!
Only you can help!
It is I, Kalen,
desperate for your aid!

VULNERABLE

BLACK STONE 35 AM (JAN. 25 AM)

Chila and Jeila passed away in the dungeons; Kyle reached the advanced age of 72 by his own reckoning. Kalen does not see an opportunity for escape.

Sailors practice fortitude
buffeted by waves at night
73° S. Latitude

Her tiny vulva
It protects the Secret
culvert, double door

VENUS

BLACK STONE 35 PM (JAN. 25 PM)

The spirit of Kalen tumbles through the Veldt.

"Nourish me through this cord umbilical!
Help me satisfy ravenous cravings
for my lost knowledge theological.
Above Perm there are no separate beings
save electrons, quarks, and atoms in doss,
charge, spin, and physique in straight-seeming things.
My mind now falls from Yonder! It comes cross
resistance meeting in downward layers,
my bindings within are in tumbling toss.
I am measured by gaseous surveyors
into mighty stratums of atmosphere,
a greeting by my psyche's purveyors.
Nitro's sage, Oxy's sooth, and Argon's seer,
bearing gifts of hotness, cold, and pressure
for conduct of voice and steering of ear,
and the toy of weather, my calm's thresher.
From unity's straw it thrashes the grain!
'Neath Venus, it meets its demolisher!
Descending my frozen sense does unthaw,
eroding as a mountain shrinks in time

from a persistent wind's relentless gnaw
bashing against cliffs of basalt or lime.
Now I take a freefalling downward flight
as if I were paroled for ancient crime.
Eyeless dark remains my cognizant sight
passing beyond the view of Oman,
feeling less human than I do a wight.
I long to once again be as a man
so I fall deeply into my feeling
above Aral Sea of Uzbekistan."

VOCATION

BLACK STONE 36 AM (JAN. 26 AM)

Reaching intolerable suffering in the Veldt and simultaneously in the dungeons of the Castle of Wands, the spirit of Kalen breaks down.

I

"Let the day perish which brought forth my birth!
Job spoke true when he was with pain reeling,
for in the land of Uz there is no worth!
Desperate, trapped am I! Here am I, kneeling!
I spin in a whirl of conflicted breeze,
out of ernst into terrified fearing!"
I shout: "Whoever you are, help me please!
You, God which my own understanding finds!
Wild boar, pinned without floor, O what it sees!
To the Earth's horizon does the sky bind
but with wings of flying things do I sweep!
I wish not to be loft like shifts of minds
soaring over decisions of substance
which finds my logic most hurly burly!
God, show yourself, if you have balls to dance!
I thank you for waking me so early.

Talk, or I will take a more forceful stance!
Eh, you won't talk! To sleep I go, surely."

II

Master Yang:
Tongues of fiery speech inflame the city.
Response: Job's complaint to God.

Vortex

Black Stone 36 PM (Jan. 26 PM)

The spirit of Kalen leaves the desert of Kara Kum and nears
Ashgabat in Turkmenistan, its name meaning "city of devotion."

I

A powerful voice came out of a whirlwind:
"Who is this that muddles meaning by words
yet without my light that one who is blind?
Have not the dignity of worms but birds!
So I am questioning you, dare answer!
Have you witnessed firing neurons split worlds?
Have you seen that cosmos free of cancer?
For it is real as this! Did you rehearse
on that Earth where the mountains are dancers?
Where were you when uncoiled your universe?
Tell me now if you have crossed over boundaries
of the thin clouds wrapping your multiverse?
Who was there when I turned on the Foundries
which mark the spot of the number zero
and every fraction's remainder carries?
Who was there when I established macro
which made rows and columns in all ledgers

and distinguished every schema's micro?
Who was there when I engaged the edgers
who put shrubbery between number bases
and employed all the labyrinth's hedgers?
Can you say you have seen through the spaces
in the ocean between the galaxies,
that sea of foam with eleven faces?
Can you say you have known all families'
deoxyribonucleic bubbles
and walked every street in the world's cities?
Surely you know, certainly your troubles
concern the ancient and subtle angels
not yet witnessed by your tiny Hubbell's?
Have you passed through the devil's nine channels
with riddles more cunning than Cairo's sphinx?
Massive thunderous shaking farewells
await those whose follies break logic's links!
Your every nightmare could be real and raw,
your fortune cursed by Pi's abysmal jinx!
You'd feel a neutron star's inner plasma
where your perception is also its cause
and flesh is liquefied to miasma!
Hear! Awful end now threatens an abyss
of hope on every sea and every land!
Not just a recess, permanent dismiss!
Not just Mauritius, not just Oman,
in not just your day, not your century,

all Kosmic dimensions, manned and unmanned!
Are you ready all atoms to bury,
not just in your world but heavens also?
Ancient spirits are sinking in worry!
They are angry and sad, above and below,
set for war in this existence askew!
The odds are long to wager you must know
for your grandmother's grandmother's rescue!
So listen now, the dark storm comes closer!
Don't you think I have other things to do?
Hear me now, those in body or ether:
This task I leave you, entrusted not dropped!
Say, 'Thus far shall darkness come no farther!
Here shall the Death of Everything be stopped!'"

II

Master Yang:
He reaches for the clouds drifting overhead, only to fall from
heaven.
Response: God's response to Job. To reach for divinity is to take on
responsibilities beyond one's limited reckoning.

VU, THE NINE OF STONES

The Nine of Stones:

"Exit to the Veldt does not come by crawl;
it requires passage through a narrow Valve.
There's a valley, a groove cut 'tween two walls.
On the heart of the traveler 'tis a salve.
Our velocity grows! Lo, the Life calls!
Vault over the mountain! Let yourself Volve."

NINE *of* STONES

VAPID

BLACK STONE 37 AM (JAN. 27 AM)

The spirit of Kalen has passed from the Veldt to the Valve. He senses his journey through the underworlds may be coming to a close. With the aid of poetry he remembers the path out so that he may instruct others in the art of rebirth.

At this call to supreme virtue,
Kalen was struck dumb, vapid.
Vapid begins as vanishing begins,
present as a valley is vast,
but then it dismisses its potential
whereas vanishing is a varnishing.
An answer baffling or pat.
It is Yang to the Yin of emptiness
and overcome with arrogance.
Pitiful at its center, vapid,
spitting in the wind, dripping
into activity's bid. It is
middling's epitome at the end.

Vacillating

Black Stone 37 PM (Jan. 27 PM)

Kyle passes away at an advanced age. Kalen is allowed to leave
the dungeon to sweep the courtyard of the Tower of Thanatos.
Influenced by the taunts and cunning of the Stone, the villainous
Wands frequently argue with each other over its use. Sometimes
the Knight of Wands and Page of Wands play games with it in the
castle's courtyards, tossing it from one tower to another.

I

Lowlands Guatemalan,
Cancuén is created.
On Pasión, obsidian
and jade are traded.

From the north, Barbers
in Africa, rulers
appeared where they would rule
for 400 years.

Tiridates III takes
faith of a Christian
as his own and makes
it the state religion.

Emperor Hui of Jin
cannot power dispense
so it vests within
nine regents.

Vatsayana
composes *Kama
Sutra* detailing
sexual dharma.

Kalen vacillates
in his passion moved:
Yang for backward states
or forward to You?

These are the dazzling days
of 300 CE,
its changing ways,
shifts in energy.

Value

Black Stone 38 AM (Jan. 28 AM)

The spirit of Kalen whirls in the clouds above the land, growing heavier and denser. He is embodied invisibly.

He stopped at Nukus in Uzbekistan
to remember the whirling words he heard.
Later he cried to blue skies of Iran:
"If I am the reason Buddha's soul endures,
then I must heed God's own proclamation
and a more full liberation secure.
This path is too great an admonition!
I didn't ask to be given this deed!
It's too much, too great a benediction!
The question now is: how do I proceed?"
Within him shining of a light began,
lumination from a bedazzling steed
which gave him the courage of a White Horse,
so he found resolve to proceed on course.

Vow

Black Stone 38 PM (Jan. 28 PM)

As the spirit of Kalen traverses the increasingly constricting Valve, he gains sight of his beloved, the Queen of Stars. They affirm their love for each other ... perhaps for the last time.

Each Time
Every Breath
Every Step
I Do Vow

Not Some
Not Maybe
Not To Try
But A Vow

Promise
Protects Me
Prepares To
Go Amiss

An Oath
Is Only
Owned Until
Death Parted

A Pledge
Is Given
Plentiful
Adjustment

Vouchsafe
If You Speak
Churlishly
Or Safely

Not These
But A Vow
Love's Dovetail
To Our Hour

Vowel

Black Stone 39 AM (Jan. 29 AM)

The Stone has been tossed into the air where it is clutched by an enormous bird swooping from on high! As Kalen sweeps the highest courtyard, a Giant Condor soars over his head and drops it upon his signal.

I

Vowels of Vortex inhere in my self:
The dipthongs combine to magnificence
now residing in the Black Stone itself.
I shrunk from vast size and proceeded thence
here to the power of evolution
incongruously substantial and dense.
I am the onxy ball descending in
the 2:32 morning in Ural
above a wind-pounded walled fortress when
atop a tower a figure stands still,
one though very young who I must employ.
Away from harsh weather I hope there'll
be some sort of soft mooring to enjoy
so I slow to halt on my own power.
Will to land I instinctively deploy

so I pause in that tower-top courtyard
caught in fingers of an eight-year old child.
He feels my surface, smooth and hard;
I can still remember the way he smiled.

In a far-off castle a woman weeps.
"Beloved, you'll forget your mind wholly,
but in my avowed mind memory keeps.
Our love is a matrimony holy
which not even involution can steal.
I shall wait for you, heart beating slowly,
'til your subtleties against mine I'll feel,
my own King of Stars, lover for all time.
You are entering the world of Form
beyond my capacity now to shine;
into a Black Stone are you being born."

II

Elsie Wheeler:
A flag turns into an eagle.
Response: The country is ready to deploy its forces.

Master Yang:
There is enough room to go if he trusts his sturdy carriage.
Response: The leader is in a good situation for making an
expedition.

Vaunt

Black Stone 39 PM (Jan. 29 PM)

The Knight of Wands does not know where the Stone has gone.
Filled with rage and suspicion, he seeks Kalen.

I

The Wand Knight comes up from the lower ward!
And so Kalen sprints fast as he can go,
ducking between legs of an armored guard.
My rock weight in his does shift to and fro,
and now the Knight spins round and gives us chase
as the boy reaches wall's edge and heaves ho!
His wrist swooshes, does far-out air displace
while he looks ahead in a subtle sleight,
he slips me, Stone, under his tunic brace
where my girth to his waist-cord adheres tight.
Then he is grabbed and shaken up and down
by the Knight with musculature of might.
The sentry gives the boy an awful frown
and removes something to make the boy scowl,
a leather-hide satchel pouch worn and brown.
Seeing it quite empty he gives a howl
(a curse on the child he is professing!)
and he plucks the boy with a bear-like growl!

II

Master Yang:
He sets out on a trek alone.
How can he hope to achieve great things?

Vaad

Black Stone 40 AM (Jan. 30 AM)

Kalen struggles and gives a brutal roar,
punching and clawing quite delirious,
six times failing for the purse he looks for.
His effort seems more feigned than serious,
though he fears a jab, a thump, and a boff,
his vigor is pretense, not furious.
At edge, the Knight threatens to toss him off!
Boy has a chance, but he does himself doubt
when the man smirks, grins, and helmet does doff.
The burly chap is too fast, fit and stout,
and lands a fierce punch to the kid's belly,
giving the breathless child an easy rout.
The lad might run were his legs not jelly.
His breathless voice could give a sigh at most.
The Knight of Wands rises in a frenzy,
lifts him like a glass in a deathly toast
and sends us both flying over the wall
before a vast vista, falling in coast!

Vaaſ

Black Stone 40 PM (Jan. 30 PM)

Kalen and the Black Stone sail off the edge of the Tower of
Thanatos.

I

I can sense many meters from the ledge
where I pray to avoid an ill-timed end
on a metal spike or thorny-tipped hedge
so I make the boy's four limbs to extend
and for his back to arch and pelvis tilt;
for him to grab hold a vine I intend
but he does resist and his body wilt
requiring a forcible direction
until I spy a spot for which to lilt
so I change his course of fall a flexion
towards a corpse pile adjacent a dark hole,
the best landing of a poor selection.
His shoulder I pull rigid as a pole
and likewise to connect his head and heels;
every degree of his line I control.
In this way does hardship offer fair deals,
giving a corpse pile's chance of survival
if he makes his feet follow his ideals.
Meanwhile, one wonders of his revival.

II

Master Yang:
He is overrun! His vitality is sapped. Danger!

VIEW

RED JEWEL 1 AM (JAN. 31 AM)

It is 2:40 AM. Nine-year-old Kalen has fallen into a corpse pile, and then he rolls into a dark hole.

I

'Tis 329 CE.
Byzantium's name went dormant.
Constantine's City is born.
Heraclitus did opine:
"Change is the only constant."

II

The Bear has climbed from a Russian valley.
He looks out over the beautiful land
and feels uncertain for looming rally.
Out from the forest he sees finches and
falcons, foxes, ferrets and flamingos.
He growls in Lingua-U a firm demand:
"Come! War of the Zodiac approaches!
I am speaking to you! Come one and all!
The old Signs have been to us atrocious!

All you 9,000,000 species great and small,
Rise up! We will all gather in the East
at Nagoya in Japan, when does fall
the 25th degree mark of Aries
and at morning's 7:42 o'
clock." (This said in just one wave that carries
thrice repeated 022120,
and his circular Wushu dance, for he
expressed more than in verbiage, don't you know?)
His graceful Jiǔ Gua Zhang continuing:
"Let not the night sky's old guard prove us fools!
Fight for life! Fight for immortality!
Spread the word in colonies, herds, and schools!"

Meanwhile, an urgent message in Dhaka
arrives addressed to the Queen of Jewels,
and a new chapter comes in this saga
brought by arrival of the Jack of Stones
in the homeland of the Originals,
an inner sanctuary of thought-bones
wrought in Foundries which created the Kinds
in number, hieroglyph, quadrants, and zones.
The Jack: "We have entered dangerous times!
Charlatans and quacks misuse the magic
inherent in right-ordered Archetypes.
Blindly they do not see the ill logic
of symbol systems made of heaps not wholes.

Their faux-magic requires measures drastic!
My mother, the Queen of Stones, sends this scroll.
It is a battle plan. Read it at once.
Our kind's fate is yet within our control!"

When Zeus spies the new Map of the Heavens,
he directs the gods into their squadrons,
urged by Vishnu to make the Map's defense.
Zeus: "Entropy's Ro encroaches upon
all realms. There is a rift between the worlds
in which all inner rivers are pouring.
The Deities cannot hold off this doom
unless we join forces to grow beyond
our set culture-bound and language-bound rooms.
We must stop this ancient foe! Map appears
in the heavens now, brought by those to whom
was given the Types, a Tarot of Cards,
guided by animals led by the Bear
which makes a new Sky-Calendar cohere.
Quite sadly many gods are doctrinaire,
staring at the drawing most stupidly,
and my call to arms they do not answer.
Some come, and we shall proceed fruitfully.
We will gather at Equator City,
Pontianak, centerpoint of Duty,
where we will fight a War of Deities."

III

The secret of the primordial perch of all perspectives:
View and Volve are the same to the seventh degree of subtle energy!

Where I Volve, there is a View
which perfects all Perspectives
in my movement of Vying.

It is Yang Yang You You You You You!
Beauty is its agentic form at the third mark, the external Eye ever
browsing toward It.
Purity is its communal form at the third mark, the interior Eye ever
prying for It.
View is the unitive form of Element of Space at the third mark, its
two /aɪ/s (Eyes) ever joined.

IV

Involving leads
Element of Wind
and letter of negativity
into volving.

Evolving leads
energy of Yin
unto volving.

Volving is vying
taken to exteme
at Unitive Seat:

Evolving solves and shoves;
Involving falls in love.
Together they revolve,
spiraling into each other.

Involving is intimate;
Evolving is sign's and psyche's power (secretly).
Together they are volatile.

Involving is the interior View
of Evolution, which is the exterior
View of We at its central nexus (secretly).

Involving is interior
Activity of Đaalo Masters.
Evolving is exterior Activity of solving.
Their union is voluntary,
Bane's IOU to the Kosmos
redeemed and voided.

What is a Đaalo Master?
One who knows how to wield the Red Jewel,
its ruby fire spreading from the Root into the Facets of

Functioning.

This You Already Know, because you have spoken its truth upon your own lips without having heretofore noticed.

You have forgotten much on this side of the underworlds.

V

Elsie Wheeler:

It is a silent hour. His life will change forever.

Master Yang:

He proceeds every step as if bound hand and foot, overhanging a precipice.

www.ingramcontent.com/pod-product-compliance
Lightning Source LLC
Chambersburg PA
CBHW070545030726
47505CB00001B/159